WASHOE COUNTY LIBRARY
3 1235 0372
P9-DVY-348

The Lodger

The Lodger

Louisa Treger

Thomas Dunne Books
ST. MARTIN'S PRESS NEW YORK

THOMAS DUNNE BOOKS.
An imprint of St. Martin's Press.

www.thomasdunnebooks.com
www.stmartins.com

Designed by Anna Gorovoy

Library of Congress Cataloging-in-Publication Data

Treger, Louisa.
The lodger: a novel / Louisa Treger.—First edition.
pages cm
ISBN 978-1-250-05193-6 (hardcover)
ISBN 978-1-4668-5265-5 (e-book)
1. Women—England—London—Fiction. 2. Boardinghouses—England—London—Fiction. 3. Triangles (Interpersonal relations)—Fiction. 4. Self-realization in women—Fiction. 5. Wells, H. G. (Herbert George), 1866–1946—Fiction. 6. London (England)—History—19th century—Fiction. I. Title.

PR6120.R44L63 2014
823'.92—dc23

2014022422

St. Martin's Press books may be purchased for educational, business, or promotional use. For information on bulk purchases, please contact Macmillan Corporate and Premium Sales Department at 1-800-221-7945, extension 5442, or write specialmarkets@macmillan.com.

First Edition: October 2014

10 9 8 7 6 5 4 3 2 1

For my late mother, Hazel, and my father, Gerald,
for my children, Adam, Imogen, and Alexandra,
and especially for Julian, with love

1906

One

DOROTHY STEPPED OFF THE TRAIN. SHE COULD feel the clammy sinking sensation beginning to creep round her, as though she was a ghost drifting through the world of the living. Taking a deep breath to anchor herself, she looked around. It was a small clean station, brightened by hanging baskets of ruffled mauve and white sweet peas, the sharp green of their leaves almost translucent in the May sunlight. She told herself there was nothing sinister; no one was going to find her guilty. It was just a visit to an old school friend, recently married.

A short, tiny-footed man was hurrying toward her, already talking and flailing his arms in the air. He stopped in front of her; he wasn't much taller than she was. He had sandy hair and a scraggy mustache; he could easily pass for an undernourished shop assistant. Yet as this thought flickered through her mind, she noticed his grey-blue dark-ringed eyes, vivid and edgy, taking her in approvingly. Instantly, hot color stained her cheeks and she willed it away fiercely, impotently.

He either didn't notice, or he chose to ignore her confusion: perhaps, she had misinterpreted his look? He held out his hand; his grip was warm and confident. "Miss Richardson, how nice to meet you. I'm Herbert Wells, but my friends call me Bertie. I'm delighted you've come for the weekend; Jane has spoken of you so often."

"Jane . . . ?" She faltered, disoriented.

He grinned. "My wife, your old school chum. The rest of the world knows her as Amy Catherine, but I've shoved the name Jane on her, and she has graciously taken it for everyday use."

She returned his smile hesitantly; she was unmoored by him. Jane? The name didn't fit her friend. It was practical and plain; a touch governessy, even.

Bertie carried on talking. His voice was high and reedy, almost atonal. But the words he spoke soon dissolved any taint of weakness or mediocrity. He asked questions by making statements: "You haven't much luggage. We can take it ourselves, without help from the porter. You found us brilliantly. The house isn't far from here." Words seemed to stream off the ends of his mustache and tumble down his waistcoat.

They approached the house from behind. As Bertie explained on their walk, it was built to open onto a view of the Kentish sea. He had designed it himself, he added, and Dorothy could feel his pride in creating such a home for his new wife and the family they would one day have.

It was an imposing and attractively proportioned house,

crowning the cliffs ninety feet above the ocean, with lawns and arbors reaching down to the beach. Dorothy saw a tennis court, a croquet lawn, and several alcoves sprinkled with chairs for reading, thinking, or writing. The walls of the house were thick, and gave a sense of great stability and continuance.

As soon as they stepped through the Gothic front door, Amy Catherine—or Jane—came hurrying to greet them; she hugged Dorothy with a little cry of excitement. "Dora! I'm so glad you're here, after all this time!"

The contact with someone from Dorothy's old life—perhaps it was the pressure of Amy Catherine's warm and pliant body against hers—brought a flood of feeling: a blend of relief and pain so potent, Dorothy feared it would crack her open.

Dorothy broke away and looked at her. Slender and fine-featured, Amy Catherine had thick fair hair and large limpid brown eyes. She was simply dressed in a white muslin blouse and navy skirt, with no ornaments.

Amy Catherine was studying Dorothy's face carefully.

"You're as pretty as ever," she pronounced, in her soft clear voice. "Your hair has turned slightly darker blonde, but it suits you, and you've still got your lovely complexion. You're looking a bit tired and thin, though. A weekend of sea air and home cooking will do you no end of good. Let's go straight upstairs; I'll show you to your room before dinner."

She led Dorothy up a wide green staircase to an airy high-ceilinged room that had an unobstructed view of the sea. A stream of golden light blazed through the open lattice windows, and shone in patches on the ceiling and walls. The room was dominated by a canopied four-poster bed, its counterpane embellished with brick-red flowers. A Primus stove stood inside the fireplace with a polished brass kettle on it. A little table nearby, covered with a brightly patterned cloth, held a teapot, a lemon, and a glass. Amy Catherine opened another door to reveal an adjoining bathroom. "See, you can live as though you're in your own home," she said gleefully. "Everything's bang up to date. You're one of our first visitors."

"It's perfectly lovely, Catherine; I'm dumb with admiration. Just look at you, a married woman, running a grown-up house." As she said it, she remembered how even in their school days, Amy Catherine seemed to possess a cryptic knowledge of how things worked, and exactly what needed to be done to get on in the world. Dorothy had half envied her without really wanting to be like her, because even the contemplation of such efficiency stripped the world of its beauty and mystery.

"You dear old thing!" Amy Catherine walked over and hugged her. "I heard about your mother, Dora . . . I'm so sorry."

Dorothy broke free and sank onto the bed. She couldn't reply; this was what she had dreaded. How much had Catherine been told? Was she thinking what everyone else thought, but no one had dared say to her: *If you hadn't left her alone, she would still be alive . . .*

"My father . . ." Amy Catherine hesitated. "He went the same way."

Dorothy managed to find her voice. "Yes, I heard."

Amy Catherine sat down beside her. For a time, neither of them moved nor spoke. But there was relief in having faced the same horror: each knew the brush of its dank webbed fingers. For once, Dorothy didn't feel blighted, removed from humanity.

"I'm glad to see you," Amy Catherine said at last. "We've heaps of time to talk and catch up."

"I'm glad to see you, too, Cath."

She was taken aback to find the name sitting awkwardly on her tongue. The thoroughness with which Bertie had transformed her old friend into Jane was astonishing.

DINNER WAS PRESIDED over by two cheerful women servants. As they carved and opened bottles, Bertie turned to Dorothy. "So, you were at school with Jane."

She nodded.

"What was Jane like at school?"

"Well," she began, "she's still the same. People are themselves; they don't change much, do they?"

For a few moments, there was nothing but the sound of the fire flickering in the mild air. He was confounded by her banality. The maids began to hand around plates piled high with rich-smelling meat and vegetables.

"Did you see the sunset?" Bertie asked, at last. "It was extraordinary this evening; a pink effulgence basted all over the sky . . . God evidently ate raspberry custard for supper."

"Don't be provocative," Jane said mildly. "I sold my soul to the devil a long time ago, but for all you know, Dora's a believer."

"What does selling your soul feel like?" Dorothy asked, trying for light-heartedness.

"Quite exhilarating, really."

Bertie drained his glass of wine. "I hope you aren't offended by our lack of piety, Miss Richardson?"

She shook her head.

"Good," he said. "You see, personally, I think God was invented by man. Primitive man looked at the cosmos and couldn't bear the idea of being alone; it was too isolating, too downright depressing. So he created 'Mr. G' as I like to call him, out of his fear of natural phenomena and his unquenchable need for reassurance." He paused for breath, making little grunts in the back of his nose, as if he was trying to stave off rejoinders or interruptions before he'd had a chance to marshal his thoughts. "Most people don't want to admit that there's nothing but man, or—dreadful thought—that we're descended from the ape . . . but the picture's not entirely bleak. We've made some marvelous discoveries as we've evolved, like science. We should all be looking to science for salvation, not religion. Religion has had its day."

His way of seeing things made life unbearable. No God. No creation. Everyone fighting for existence, like animals . . . the strong clawing their way over the weak. Dorothy could feel astonishment and belligerence spilling out of her and—despite herself—admiration. She tried to rein in all her tangled emotions behind a relaxed enthusiastic smile, but they streamed from the pores of her skin and obstructed her limbs, making her ham-fisted with her cutlery. What made him so infuriatingly sure of everything? He was like a volcano, continually bubbling over with urgent thoughts and incandescent ideas.

He was still going on about scientific imagination, scientific invention. "It's our mission . . . imposing scientific method on primordial mayhem; we are winning against mayhem . . .

nothing that came before science was worth contemplating . . ."

"I don't care a button for science," Dorothy burst out, unable to restrain herself. "It's just speculation; tittle-tattle about the cosmos."

"My word! What an extraordinary view!"

"It's true. Darwin chattered about apes and when he got old he exactly resembled one, and felt sorry that he hadn't given more time to other interests, like art and music. One day, someone will find out that his conclusions were mistaken, that he omitted or miscalculated some vital piece of the puzzle, and his hypothesis, which has given thousands of people sleepless nights, will be discredited."

"Darwin was a great man. His theories aren't a matter of speculation, they are fundamental truths; the cornerstone of biology . . . I can't see your difficulty with him, not even with the strongest of magnifying glasses."

Bertie proclaimed facts, not opinions. Dorothy disagreed with nearly everything he said, and was beginning to resent the way he monopolized the conversation.

She wanted to talk to Jane. "What do you remember about Miss Sandell's school?" she wanted to ask. "Do you remember our English teacher, who was Browning's pupil? What about Fräulein Schneider—she was so hot tempered, her lessons were a series of emotional scenes. Do you realize how lucky we were to be given classes in logic and psychology instead of household skills, to be taught to think for ourselves and form opinions? I didn't then, though I'm starting to now . . ."

But Bertie's lively monologue prevented her from finding out what Jane thought or felt.

As the meal progressed, Dorothy sensed uneasiness in Jane. She seemed to be chronically fearful lest a misunderstanding, an argument, a failure of good humor should occur. She was a jumble of anxiety and confidence. Her manner was bright, yet her voice was soft and unprepossessing. Her conversation consisted mainly of introducing subjects for the others to take up and develop, trying to keep things going. During pauses in the talk, she looked uneasy, almost scared. Once dessert was served, however, she seemed to relax visibly, as though a great weight had rolled off her.

"Tell us about your life, Dora," she said at this stage. "It's so long since I've seen you properly." The reflections from the many candles on the table illuminated Jane's pretty bare arms and glowed in her eyes.

Dorothy hesitated, searching for words to describe how far she had come. This was why she'd reached out to Jane after all this time: she wanted a long-standing friend to help reconcile her past self with the strange adventure of the present. And Jane had responded to her letter at once, with an invitation to stay for the weekend, so perhaps she felt the same need.

Dorothy took a sip of the delicate amber wine, feeling the warmth of it sliding through her veins, giving her courage. "After my mother died, I longed to escape from the world of women," she said, slowly. "So I moved to London; I live in a boardinghouse in Bloomsbury. I'm a secretary to a Harley Street dentist at a pound a week. The hours are long, and I don't have much leisure. But the reward is a kind of freedom—I'm able to attend lectures and a range of political meetings. London is a melting pot of societies and ideas, and I can dip in and out of them as I please."

She stopped, realizing that in order to hold the Wells's attention, she would have to be clever and amusing. She probed her mind for a suitable anecdote, yet without knowing quite how it happened, found herself pouring out her heart about work. She told them about the grueling hours, the cold which turned her fingernails blue, the cleaning solution used for dental instruments that dried and cracked her skin . . .

She broke off, worried she'd lost them. But Bertie was nodding sympathetically.

"Years ago, I worked as a draper's apprentice," he said. "I knew the grind of it all: the endless hours, the suffocating tedium, the many petty tyrannies. The feeling that I was trapped forever in a mindless, soulless machine from which there was no way out . . . but I can suggest a way of freeing yourself at one blow."

"How?"

"Do what I did. Write a novel."

She raised her eyebrows. "Just like that?"

"Of course not. It takes more work than goes into many a doctoral thesis, and countless arid days and fruitless attempts."

Dorothy found herself watching the curious mouthing of his lips as they formed the words, half hidden by the thin mustache, and saved from weakness only by his ironic smile.

"*The Time Machine* was born after years of poverty and disappointments and cutting my teeth with journalism," he went on. "I wrote it on holiday in Sevenoaks. Do you remember, Jane?"

"Indeed I do, my dear."

"I couldn't have done it without Jane," Bertie admitted. "Her unwavering belief in me kept me going, even long after

I'd ceased to believe in myself." He turned to Jane. "Remember how we used to feel: it was you and me against the world?"

"Yes, I remember." Jane was looking at him fondly.

For a moment, Bertie laid his hand on the back of Jane's neck, beneath her hair. It was an astonishingly private gesture, so intimate and tender, Dorothy could hardly bear to watch. A pang of envy and longing shot through her.

"I wrote at an open window on hot August nights, with the moths hurling themselves against the lamp," he said. "I could hear the landlady in the garden below complaining loudly over the fence to her neighbor about my immoderate use of her lamp. So I wrote faster than ever, but she was still unhappy with me. She'd discovered, by snooping in our luggage and finding divorce papers from my first wife, that Jane and I weren't yet married. She was scandalized by our morals and by the shameless way we'd foisted ourselves on her and taken advantage of her innocence . . ."

As they were about to get up from the table, Bertie said "Hasn't she got roses in her cheeks now, eh Jane? You must come and see us more often, Miss Richardson. Being here evidently agrees with you. And we like having you around, don't we Jane?"

A sense of belonging was being offered. For a moment she hesitated, not quite sure how to respond. "Thank you, I like being here," she said shyly.

Meeting Jane's eyes, she was surprised by their suddenly tense and watchful expression.

DOROTHY GOT READY for bed in the comfortable high-ceilinged guest room. When she turned out the gas, the windows shone faintly with moonlight. The air around her was still warm from the gas. She climbed into the four-poster bed, feeling drained. Perhaps, she'd be able to sleep properly here.

She closed her eyes. Almost at once, the well-known flashbacks started arriving, playing themselves out vividly behind her sealed eyelids, transporting her back to the event that had torn her life apart.

She sat upright, trying to erase the image of her mother's body sprawled on the floor, runnels of blood forming viscous pools on the tattered linoleum. So much blood; Dorothy never knew a person's frame contained that much.

She pressed her knuckles hard into her eyes; pinpricks of brilliant white light danced in front of them. But it was useless; the memory was indelibly seared into her mind. Life had turned her inside out in seconds; everything disintegrated, and nothing was ever the same. All that was familiar vanished in a few instants, and the grief and guilt were like swallowing splinters of broken glass.

AFTER BREAKFAST THE next morning, Dorothy went for a walk in the garden. Jane was busy with household chores, and Bertie was nowhere to be seen. She was relieved to be alone. The night had left her raw and disunited; she needed space to gather up the scattered pieces of herself and glue them back into a semblance of normality.

The garden was large and well kept, and it took time to explore. At the bottom of the lawn was a rose garden filled with lush bushes, the roses still in bud. A covered walk made of growing plants trained over a trellis ran down the middle of it. Pansies and foxgloves bloomed thickly in wide flower beds. She wandered arbitrarily across a walled vegetable garden that held cherry and apple trees, and through a door into a terraced square.

Bertie was sitting at a stone table, pen in hand and sheets of paper spread in front of him. Jane had warned Dorothy not to disturb him, but when he looked up and saw her, a pleased smile lit his face. He patted the empty space on the stone bench next to him and said, "Come and sit with me for a while."

"Are you sure? I don't want to disturb you."

"It's only a book review. Something I'm scribbling for *The Saturday Review*."

She did as she was told, feeling suddenly awkward and shy. She glanced down at her hands twined in her lap. They looked large and raw, like inert cuts of meat—repulsive. Why did no one else's hands look like that? Bertie's hands were strong and blunt-fingered; his rolled-up shirtsleeves revealed forearms covered with golden hairs. She looked up and saw him following her gaze. His eyes were densely blue; the dark bands circling the irises looked like they had been dipped in ink. His expression was hard to read.

For a long moment they sat in silence, the sunshine pouring down on them like melted butter. The air was cool and refreshing; Dorothy could feel it soothing away the ravages of the night, making a delicious contrast to the warmth of the sun on her face. A light breeze moved Bertie's sandy hair.

"May I look?" she asked.

"Not yet. It's still in its infancy." He stacked up the pages with care and placed them face down on the table.

"Is it easier than writing novels?"

"In some ways, but it's a great responsibility. The reviewer must take care not to destroy early attempts, especially ones by writers who are just honing their skills. Authors are like tender young seedlings, they need a great deal of nursing. Sadly, not all critics realize that."

Bertie paused, his face alight with humor. "We reviewers tread a fine line; it's not easy to get right. Some of us behave like careless gardeners, soaking the plants in the water of compliments and drowning them, while others refuse sustenance entirely until the plants shrivel up and die. There are a handful of wise and long-sighted caretakers, but they're a rare breed."

Dorothy smiled, half closing her eyes. His views seemed less objectionable than they had last night. In fact, he had a vivid way of looking at things that lifted them out of the commonplace.

She opened her eyes. The sunlight cut into the trees in front of her, producing a mass of glittering spires. Two blackbirds, singing a duet in contrary rhythm, stopped at the same moment. In their silence, she could faintly hear Jane, out of sight behind the red walls of the vegetable garden, humming and enjoying herself as she worked. Dorothy could picture her in her old faded bonnet, a basket at her feet and her beloved red-handled gardening shears in her gloved hands.

Two

IT WOULD BE BETTER NOT TO SEE THE WELLSES again. There was something all wrong about being with them . . . back in London, it seemed wrong. Heavy-limbed with fatigue, Dorothy got off the train and dragged herself up the long platform. She could feel the weight of her Gladstone bag thumping against her leg. Inside was her signed copy of *The Time Machine*.

The station was shrouded by clouds of billowing grey smoke. The platform lights, battling to cut through it, served only to thicken and reflect the murk. The air smelled of smoke and metal; a dry bitter tang that scorched Dorothy's nostrils and lingered unpleasantly in the back of her throat. The dark figures and spectral faces of fellow passengers loomed out at her as they approached, then vanished again, as though gulped down by the besieging shadows. A train shrieked suddenly, a harsh blast that startled her.

Her family and the Harley Street dentists would certainly think spending time with the Wellses was wrong if they knew Bertie had divorced his first wife for Jane. They had heard of his work, they knew he was standing on the brink of fame . . . that people were starting to talk about him. But if they saw how he had looked at Dorothy, they would be shocked. They would never understand his extraordinary ideas, his way of seeing the world. He was rather like Lucifer; a fallen angel. It would be impossible to describe the visit to anyone she knew.

The sense of lit streets waiting for her under the night sky, of a rich interesting London life, revived her for the walk home.

Emerging from the station, the quiet dark buildings and the blackness between the lamps seemed to expand around her. The moon was almost full; a hard, cold plate in the sky. She savored the clipped sound her footfalls made on the irregular flags of the pavement, the traffic rumbling past, the sudden blaze of yellow shop light. People walked by, looking pallid under the streetlamps; their faces caught up in invisible thoughts. A young woman in a silver cloak and a matching floating scarf, walking rapidly, her head bent. A bald man with a terrier in a tartan coat. It was a relief to feel part of the familiar London atmosphere, to be absorbed by it.

She followed Endsleigh Gardens as it opened out of Gower Place, bordered by the gloom of the dimly lit Euston Road and the mysterious bulk of St. Pancras Church. The roadway was lined with majestic plane trees, their shadows clear on the narrow pavement; dense with secret perspectives.

The dusky figures of prostitutes stood at intervals against the lamplit green. They looked like sentinels, warning her.

She knew they would be there, yet the sight of them never failed to send a jolt through her.

A strident voice rang out as Dorothy turned off into her own road . . . "I said to him, I'll bloody stab you if you come any closer . . ." The words ricocheted around Dorothy; she fought a rising desire to break into a run. The street was full of anger and violence. The woman's grating voice seemed very near; Dorothy could picture her truculent expression . . . Jack the Ripper had carried out his grisly murders not so very long ago, not far from here . . . he had left his horribly mutilated victims in plain sight, for anyone to stumble on. Dorothy could almost hear the pad of footfalls behind her, she half braced herself for the cold bite of the knife in her neck . . . Fear quickened her steps to an urgent trot.

She reached her front door with relief. The house had always seemed to belong to her. The first time she'd seen it, after answering the advertisement for boarders, she had the sense it had been waiting for her through all the years of turmoil. It was a refuge, despite its air of genteel decrepitude—or perhaps, because of it. She loved the sleepy grey street, the high stately houses with their rows of gracious balconies, the green squares at either end like oases, sweetening the air with their breath.

She fished in her bag for her proud latchkey and opened the door. The hall was hushed and deserted. Gaslight streamed down onto the smudged marble top of the hall table and glared against the dining-room door. The interior had a rich comfortable brownness. It was one dark even tone throughout, like living in brown soup. Dorothy walked up the dimly lit stairs, past dark landings and closed doors whose polished wood gleamed dully. The tall windows were concealed by soot-stained lace curtains. Dust lay in the cracks between the floorboards and coated the skirting. There was a strong smell of dust in the air.

She reached the short winding flight of uncarpeted stairs that led to her attic room and ran up it thankfully, anticipating the peaceful evening that lay ahead of her. She would be able to mull over her weekend with the Wellses; to straighten it out in her head. In the train, she had been battered by a gale of thoughts. They had swept over her tumultuously, each exchange with Bertie and Jane rising up and clamoring to be analyzed. An interval of solitary reflection was necessary; she could picture the gaslight under the sloping roof, making a winter coziness in springtime.

The brass doorknob wobbled in her hand; the hinges creaked as she pushed open the door.

She gasped; peace draining out of her. Standing on the hearthrug was Benjamin.

Dorothy looked at the frock-coated Russian student in dismayed silence. She was stricken with guilt for not once having thought about him during the weekend. At the same time, she had the strange sense that their not-quite-ended entanglement had already shifted into the past.

Her mind flew back to the early days with him. She had been cajoled into giving him English lessons by the landlady, who was anxious to retain her hold on a well-to-do foreign boarder. They had quickly discovered a shared love of books and ideas. Yet it was as though their joyful establishing of common bonds across different languages and cultures had happened to two entirely different people, who now seemed slightly out of focus, like a fading photograph.

He was walking toward her; he grasped both her hands;

his sonorous voice rang out: "Ah, I am glad to see you. How was your weekend?"

Disengaging herself, Dorothy said it had been good. She was stirred, despite herself, by his gentle resolute features: the wide forehead, the kind dark eyes, the lustrous black hair, and neatly pointed beard. She crushed her feelings with urgent resolve. After all her attempts to extricate herself, tenderness would not do.

"What was your friend like?" he asked eagerly. "Still *sympathique*, as she was at school?"

While she described Jane, she wondered if he could sense the change in her. This was the man who knew her thoughts. But her connection with him seemed hollow and treacherous now. "What did you do all weekend?" she asked guiltily.

"I have been resting . . . the whole day until about an hour ago," Benjamin said. "I am a little sleepy, but there are many things I want to tell you . . ."

The thought of having to bend her mind around his thickly accented sentences was exhausting. "It's late. Can't we talk tomorrow?"

"But I want to talk to you now. I have been waiting all weekend to see you."

A fitful night breeze touched the window, making it rattle gently in its frame. Dorothy sighed. "Go on then," she said.

"With you, I have been perfectly happy. Happier than I've ever felt in my life. I don't want to let go of that; I can't." His white eyelids were downcast; the black lashes skimmed his cheek. He raised his eyes again, searching and earnest. "I know now what real love is . . . I would even give up my Judaism for it . . ."

"I'd never let you do that. You must keep your religion."

"You must marry me." His voice broke pitifully, in expectation of a rebuff . . . He was falling again into his determined hope. Her heart ached for him. He seemed unable to relinquish the hope of her changing.

She said, "You know I can't. I'm sorry. Our worlds are too different; the gap is unbridgeable. We've been through it countless times and, deep down, you agree."

"Look, Dorothy, instead of refusing me, why don't you tell me what you want from marriage? Perhaps we can reach an understanding. I am neither obstinate nor intolerant. I am just trying to grasp what you want—"

"It would never work. As a husband, you'd slide into the role of Jewish patriarch, complete with prayer shawl and traditional views; utterly secure in your store of ordered knowledge and never questioning its value. You have admitted as much yourself. We'd be a disaster together, because I could never be the compliant mate you really want. Anyway, I am quite sure now that I don't want to marry anyone."

She walked to the window and stood with her back to him, gazing unseeingly out of it.

He put both hands on her shoulders and turned her around gently to face him. "You think you will never marry, ever? What makes you so certain?"

"It would mean giving up this life . . ."

"Your independence is precious, yes. But at what cost? A few years from now, you might look back and regret."

There was silence, except for the traffic rumbling along Euston Road. Benjamin moved away from her and stood in front of the empty fireplace. His lightless eyes scanned the distance unseeingly, as though he was remembering some faraway thing. He radiated European culture and polish. What was he thinking? Was he musing about the distant beauty of Russia; about the expansive life of foreign universities, the study of Continental philosophy and literature, to which he belonged?

He cleared his throat and spat; there was a flabby thwack as his saliva struck the grate. Dorothy stared at him in icy disbelief. His foreignness had at first seemed so rich and compellingly strange, but in the end, it was the thing that drove them apart.

Invigorated by disgust, she found the courage to speak. "There's no point in carrying on. It will only get more painful."

"You are right, it will hurt us both." He exhaled noisily. "Perhaps I should leave this house."

The pit of her stomach was dropping away. "Do you want to?"

"No, of course not. But it might be easier if we are not under the same roof . . . Next week, I shall look for new lodgings."

There was nothing to say. She had never realized how sad it was when love turned to dust. Though she no longer wanted him, she shrank from the thought of letting him go. It was confusing and contradictory. His departure would leave a yawning void; this corner of Bloomsbury would be haunted forever by his gestures and his warm deep voice . . . Unthinkable that the kind booming voice would no longer be part of daily life. She felt herself recoiling from the loneliness that would sweep in to fill the vacuum.

I shall miss him in so many ways, she mused. His sensitivity; the things he understands without being told. And his absolute sweetness; there is not an ounce of malice in him . . .

the things he does for me. Small tender things, like doing up the buttons of my coat when it's cold.

She imagined him walking away from her toward a new life, new attachments. Jealousy ripped through her: she would rather see him dead than in love with another woman. Remorse immediately followed: she was self-centred, a monster. I am unworthy of him, she reflected sadly. He would be better off with someone who adores him unconditionally; it's what he deserves.

It was her fault their attachment had curdled. In the end, she spoilt everything, for reasons only half-understood. It was something in her nature that flailed out and wreaked destruction . . . I have nothing left now but my pugnacious and agonized self, having violently charged at things and smashed them up, she thought miserably.

Stealing a look at him, she saw an ashen somber face. He was contemplating life without her and resigning himself to it. He had one hand on the doorknob. "Good night, I will let you rest now."

There was a terrible weariness in his voice. He went out, shutting the door softly behind him.

DOROTHY HURRIED DOWNSTAIRS the next morning on her way to work. Her eyes were salty and prickly and her chest was tight. It had been a restless night; she felt ill equipped to deal with the week that lay ahead.

Mrs. Baker, the landlady, was standing in the hall. She looked more dingy and decayed than ever, Dorothy thought, taking in the badly dyed hair, half blonde, half grey; the ill-fitting false teeth. Yet Mrs. Baker's youthful figure and smile managed to transcend everything.

She put a small firm hand on Dorothy's arm. "Here you are, young lady. Had a good weekend?"

"Yes, thank you. I went to stay with a school friend I hadn't seen in years and her husband. It was . . . interesting."

Mrs. Baker fixed her with a look that seemed to seek out her invisible thoughts. Dorothy colored, wondering what the landlady guessed.

"I see you're rushing out. Will you at least have a cup of tea before you go?"

"I can't," Dorothy said. "I'm late for work as it is."

Through the half open door of the dining room, she could see the boarders gathered at breakfast. Mrs. Baker's oldest daughter, Carrie, presided over the tea tray; the younger girl was passing around a plate of bread and butter. The dead fern rested in its usual place at the center of the table. Mr. Cundy was helping himself to jam. The young Canadian doctor sat with his back to the door: a lean dark-grey upright form, long necked and fair haired.

Sunlight was falling onto Mrs. Baker's faded skirt; she brushed some specks of dust from it impatiently. She seemed to hold the mysteries of the running of the large house in the palm of her hand: the unknown dark caverns of the kitchen and basement, the apathetic smudgy cleaning sessions in the endless rooms, the punctual appearance of daily breakfasts and dinners, the enigma of guests arriving and disappearing at different times. The entire world of the house resided in Mrs. Baker's radiant, encouraging smile, which was given to every one of her boarders, as if she liked them all equally.

Carrie came out of the dining room. Offering Dorothy a shy good morning, she turned to whisper something in her mother's ear. Dorothy watched Mrs. Baker's face darken. There was trouble in the house.

"Is everything all right?" Dorothy asked, anxiously.

For a moment, Mrs. Baker seemed to want to tell her something. Dorothy watched her expression harden and close up; she sighed. "People! You'd have a poor view of human nature, if you had this place to run. It opens your eyes, with one thing and another."

Dorothy wondered if another boarder had left without paying rent. Her old sense of the house as a refuge disintegrated slightly. To Mrs. Baker, it wasn't a refuge at all: it was ceaseless demands and anxiety, problems she had to keep to herself, and a sprinkling of decent folk thrown in amongst the riffraff. She would never manage to make it profitable. The house was full of people living on the edge of catastrophe, who didn't pay their bills. One or two hadn't paid anything for months; Mrs Baker had even lent them money . . . Dorothy wondered where they would all go if the boardinghouse failed.

"Off to work with you, young lady. Don't worry about us, you have enough on your shoulders. It's not as warm as it looks this morning, so mind you don't catch a chill."

"Oh well, I'll try not to. See you later."

Dorothy opened the front door and stepped out into the shock of the bright morning.

DURING THE DAYS that followed, the weather turned unseasonably warm. Dorothy's attic room was sweltering. When she came home from work, its dense oppressive smell of dust nauseated her.

She shut the door behind her and took off her hat. Pulling a chair as near as she could to the open window, she sat watching low sunlight blazing off the leads sloping down to her parapet. Traffic thundered along Euston Road. The skylight above her head was a brilliant glare. She let her thoughts drift . . . There had been no word from Jane or Bertie; no invitation to visit them again. By the look of things, they had given up on her already.

In part, it was a relief. She couldn't banish the uneasy feeling there was something wrong about seeing them, something irregular about the whole setup. It was preferable to keep her distance; their continuing silence was for the best.

She felt curiously flat, dulled and exhausted by the fatigue of a day's work in the heat. Her heart beat sluggishly, her head throbbed, and her eyes were dry. She should get something to eat, but she was too tired to go out and she couldn't afford one of Mrs. Baker's shilling dinners; there was barely enough money for next week's food. As minutes crept by, hunger and loneliness gripped her. There seemed nothing in her life but bitterness. It was a heatwave in spring and life was passing her by, in a stifling dusty attic.

A sleepless night lay ahead of her; the top floor was a heat trap that refused to cool down, even in the hours before dawn. She crossed the room and washed her hands with the sliver of soap in the dish; it was cracked and darkly veined with grime. The washstand swayed precariously as she splashed her face with lukewarm water. She dried herself with the threadbare face towel and surveyed her room. Everything in it was grubby and decrepit; it was a seedy room in a cheap boardinghouse. Her eyes burned with tears and she sank onto the hot floor.

As she lay there, curled in on herself, a picture came into her mind of the Wells's sitting room, far from the noise and grime of London: it would be blazing with open-windowed spring sunshine. She imagined the life of the house going on without her . . . everything revolving around Bertie's writing, Jane and the servants tiptoeing about so he wouldn't be disturbed, the nourishing meals, the bright comfortable rooms, the flourishing sea-facing garden.

She thought about the sense of belonging she'd felt in their company, about listening to Bertie's ideas, torn between infuriation and reluctant admiration. Helplessly, she let her mind flit back to their conversations: "You must come and see us more often, Miss Richardson. Being here evidently agrees with you. And we like having you around, don't we Jane? We like having you around . . . like having you around . . ."

A flicker of feeling tugged at her belly, like electricity.

Later, she dragged herself downstairs to get a bread roll and a bit of cheese for supper. There was a letter for her on the hall stand; she recognized Jane's hurried yet elegant writing instantly.

She tore it open and devoured the words, fatigue forgotten: "You must come and see us as soon as possible . . . We have been frightfully dull without you . . . This weekend? Let me know as soon as you can . . . sooner . . ."

Three

ON THE FIRST EVENING OF HER VISIT, DOROTHY came shyly down to dinner to find Bertie and Jane sitting side by side in front of the drawing room fireplace.

"Look at you!" Jane exclaimed, rising to her feet and holding out both hands to Dorothy. "You've spent the week toiling in city heat, yet you look as fresh as you did when we were at school."

Dorothy took her outstretched hands. Bertie stood up, his eyes on Dorothy, taking in the way her hair fell, the creamy lace tie that transformed the old black silkette evening dress she hadn't the money to have altered. Her clothes had made her sick with their shabbiness when she dressed for dinner, but his eyes and the candlelight seemed to draw them together into a pleasing whole.

"You ought always to go about in a tie; they suit you," he remarked.

"You wear ties better than anyone I know," Jane said, adding "I wish I could hang things around my neck and look as nice."

"Dorothy can hang anything around her neck and look nice."

"An old shoe lace or a—a—a string of sausages!" he finished triumphantly.

"Idiot!" chided Jane.

Bertie was still looking.

He gave her his arm as they walked into dinner, saying confidentially: "Well, you must tell me everything you've been doing. Taking London by storm, I'll be bound." The little creak in his voice meant he knew he was about to be entertained.

"Did you have a good week?" Dorothy asked when they sat down.

"It was better than average, thank you," Bertie said. "After days of sweating blood, my book is finally turning a corner. It's getting a new lease on life. I managed to get to that elusive state of deep concentration from whence my best work comes."

"Can you tell me about it? It sounds fascinating."

"I'll try, though it's hard to put into words . . . It's a strange, unpredictable mode of being—so profound and revitalizing, it's almost a trance." He paused, making the little grunting sounds in the back of his nose. "You mustn't hesitate, nor worry about which words to choose. When you are in the right mood, they appear faster than speech or even thought; your pen follows them as quickly as your hand can move it across the page, and sometimes, the most exquisite phrases spill out. It's hard to explain what a wonderful feeling it is; it smooths out all the creases in your mind, and completely revives you. And you see life with such clarity . . .

"The English language is marvelous raw material; you can do whatever you want with it . . . You can make it strut or flow or dance; it can be as hard as marble, or as intangible as gossamer or froth. I don't think there's another tongue with as much flexibility."

Dorothy sat watching the singular mouthing of his lips beneath the thin mustache, arrested by his ability to illuminate and color and enhance a topic, making her see in a new way. She was too caught up in the distraction of listening to the way he put things to articulate her growing sense there was something wrong in it. Were authors consciously aware they were producing "effects"? If so, it meant writing was a clever trick, a sell. Bertie's approach was too knowing: his presence intruded into the story, showing the reader how clever he was, yet unwittingly draining the life from his work in the process. Style was nothing but a trick that ruined books.

She emptied her glass of claret and felt its tingling warmth running through her blood, dissolving her opposition. A mellow glow began to fill the room, turning everything in it into a warm blur. The only chill was Jane, who looked paler than usual and said very little.

Bertie carried on talking, his grey-blue eyes returning to Dorothy's face. His eyes were intense, hooded, holding secret depths. Dorothy could feel herself flushing all over her body.

She glanced at Jane uneasily, and saw that Jane was watching her, with a coolly appraising gaze that held both dismay and recognition.

WHEN THE MEAL was finished, Jane announced she had a headache and went to her room to lie down.

Bertie took Dorothy into his study. They sat side by side, in matching deep and worn leather armchairs. The clear blaze of a coal fire cast a soft light on the books and papers scattered on his desk.

He said quietly, "Jane tells me you've had a bad time at home."

Dorothy nodded; the room pulsated curiously.

"Do you want to talk about it?"

"I'm not sure . . . It's not easy to talk about."

"If you feel able . . . if you think it would help at all, I'd love to listen."

She fell silent, looking at the patterns on the deep red Turkish carpet, feeling the familiar dragging anxiety in the pit of her stomach. She inhaled deeply. "When I was seventeen, my father went bankrupt."

She paused again, wondering how much to tell Bertie about their troubles. An image of her father appeared in her head: Charles Richardson was a tall man with long white hands, golden-haired, and charismatic . . . He used to call Dorothy his "son" sometimes, because she was a disappointing third daughter, not the longed-for heir. He came from a family of tradesmen, but he wanted more than anything to be a gentleman of leisure and cultivation. He was a passionate amateur of the arts, and a keen follower of the latest developments in science.

His money came from selling the family business in wines

and provisions. He invested most of it speculatively. He wasn't interested in secure investments: he needed more money than he had to support his lifestyle. He knew he was living beyond his means, but he was stubbornly optimistic that things would work themselves out. He never talked to his family about financial matters, but an atmosphere of tension filled the house nevertheless. Dorothy and her sisters became increasingly uncertain and anxious, and their mother's innate softly smiling vivacity turned into a taut watchfulness. She laughed less often than she used to; her face, in repose, looked haunted, glimmering with exhaustion. She began to suffer from headaches.

Charles seemed not to notice the change in her. He insisted that appearances be kept up at all times. They entertained lavishly, putting on a good show. He prided himself on his cellar. There were supper parties, musical evenings, tennis and boating afternoons, huge picnic parties and dances in the drawing room. Charles hired a governess for his daughters. He kept up membership of his club, and of the British Association for the Advancement of Science. He never missed a gathering of the latter, at home or abroad.

After years spent struggling to cling to solvency, a crisis struck. Charles's investments tumbled. He told his family they must rein in their spending and entertain less. There was no cause for alarm, he reassured them. But some of the servants were dismissed, and the girls had to refresh last season's dresses with new ribbon and lace, and wear them again. The situation continued to deteriorate; after a while there were no dinner parties at all, and Dorothy and her sisters were expected to help with the housework.

He was still unrealistically optimistic when he was forced to tell them that the worst had happened and they were bankrupt. But they understood only too well the gravity of their situation. After all the years of masquerading, of pretending to be like other people, their disgrace was sealed. Bankruptcy was a stain they couldn't escape from.

"What are you thinking?" Bertie asked, wrenching Dorothy away from her musings. "You have a habit of leaving your thoughts lying in your face, you know. I want that one; the one that crossed your features a moment ago."

"I was thinking . . . my father's bankruptcy wasn't the worst of it," Dorothy said slowly. "Not long afterward, my mother became ill. A lifetime of being obedient to him, and the strain of pretending to other people that our financial problems didn't exist were too much for her. She began behaving strangely . . ."

She stopped, unable to check her rising tears. After a moment's hesitation, Bertie took her hand and captured it gently between both of his. She caught her breath. In spite of her grief, her hand floated and tingled in his warm grasp. And yet it also perturbed her greatly, so she withdrew her hand, and forced herself to keep talking.

"The doctors suggested a change of air. Clearly, something had to be done. With money given by my brother-in-law, Philip, I took her away for a few days to Hastings. My mother was very attached to me . . ." Mother was tiny, smaller than any of her girls; she had dark eyes and delicate features. "You should have been a man, Dottie," she was fond of saying, in a tone that was half flirtatious admiration, half reproof. "You are the only one who understands me." "My family pinned its last hope of recovery on my being with her . . ."

"You were very young to be given that responsibility. It would have been a heavy burden, even for someone far older."

Dorothy did not reply. She was remembering sleepless nights in the small lodging house room they shared, listening to her mother's tormented voice cleave through the darkness: blotted words and high-pitched laughter and silence. Dorothy had lain frozen in bed, stupefied by anger and anguish. Refusing to believe those sounds were coming from her, the kindest gentlest creature she knew. But they were, and there was no one to help. "It's clear now," said a shrill voice. "I have seen the truth . . . I have no illusions." Mumbling and cackling . . . Dorothy was more frightened and helpless than she'd ever been.

With effort, she carried on talking.

"As a last resort, I took my mother to see an old homeopathist who lived at the other end of town. When the consultation was over, he took me into another room and explained urgently that I must summon help immediately, a trained nurse. My mother ought to have professional help twenty-four-hours a day. He seemed to understand the strain I was under, and spoke about my youth. 'It's a grave mistake for you to be alone with her,' he added. My face flamed with shame as I explained we couldn't afford help. He listened sympathetically, and repeated that it was essential.

"By the next day, I felt I was going mad myself. I went out for a short walk . . . when I returned she had taken a knife, and . . ."

Tears were raining down her face.

"My poor girl." Bertie placed his hand on hers, then removed it. He offered his handkerchief; she waved it away.

"It's . . . my fault . . . if I hadn't left her . . ."

"She was beyond your help—or anybody else's. You must try not to blame yourself."

There was another long pause. Dorothy's sobs were turning to hiccups. She couldn't help thinking what a sight she must look, her eyes and nose red from crying. She could feel her hair escaping from its pins.

"You have come through it exceptionally well," he said, at last.

"Do you think so?"

"Yes, there's a natural poise that shines through you, and no outward sign of scarring. You're open, straightforward; there's not a trace of hysteria or bitterness. I admire that."

"Really? I'm not sure; I've never spoken about it to anyone before," she stammered. "I don't know why I find it easy to talk to you."

He swiveled around to look into her eyes. "Oh Dorothy, I hope that's true . . ."

For a long moment, they stared at each other. The fire was nearly out; it was getting cold. Outside the room, the hall clock softly struck eleven. Rising to her feet, Dorothy stumbled toward the door, and he did not try to stop her.

IN HER BEDROOM, she undressed and unrolled her knot of hair, feeling it heavy and warm about her shoulders, like a stole. She thought about the focused light in Bertie's eyes when he looked at her, heard the creak in his voice that meant he was anticipating pleasure. Her hand tingled as she remembered how it felt imprisoned gently within both of his.

Feelings surged inside her, sweeter than anything else, yet

more shameful. How had her initial irritation with Bertie turned into this? Her face was hot; sleep was going to be impossible. He was a married man, the husband of her oldest friend.

Married, yet seeming nearer than other men. More alive, more understanding than anyone she'd ever met.

She pulled herself up short. She must be wicked or insane—perhaps she was both—even to entertain such thoughts. She couldn't permit them. She must force herself to stamp them out.

When she was in her nightgown, she turned off the gas and got into bed. As soon as she closed her eyes, the flashbacks started.

She was walking; she had to escape for an hour. The town was quiet, the summer visitors long gone. She wandered through streets hemmed in by tall grey-stone houses, their windows blank and unrevealing, like unseeing eyes. The sky was low, the air humid and tasting of sea salt. Her pulse pounded in her head so loudly that once or twice she thought it was footsteps following, and turned around to scan the empty pavement behind her.

She was desperately trying to forget the self-loathing that consumed her mother's soul. Mother couldn't sleep, couldn't eat, couldn't sit still, or stop talking. Dorothy, woken night after night to read the Bible and tend to her, was nearly as exhausted as she was. If she didn't manage to think about something else, something ordinary and pleasant, she would go mad herself.

Think about . . . boating on the river in summer: sunlight on the trees, the sound of water slapping gently against bobbing sculls. For a moment, she managed to hold it in her mind's eye; she could feel the sun on her skin, could hear the river, and even smell its dankness. But it was quickly replaced by the image of her mother's pain-filled, accusing eyes.

After about an hour of walking—she'd lost track of the exact time—she returned to their miserable, genteel lodging house. She hated the house, and its landlady. Appearances were everything, and not so much as a ripple could be allowed to disturb its refined facade.

She climbed the stairs slowly and opened the door to their room. The grimy white lace curtains were drawn against the daylight; it was dim and hushed, and smelt faintly of dust. From above came the soft creak of a door swinging gently in the wind. Her mother was nowhere to be seen. With a sick knot of foreboding in the pit of her stomach, Dorothy realized she shouldn't have left her alone. Not even for a minute; much less an entire hour.

There was a stain spreading across the threadbare linoleum; sticky and rust colored. It was flowing toward Dorothy's shoes. She tried to draw her legs back, but she found herself fixed to the spot.

Then she saw her mother lying on the floor: her skin waxy grey, her eyes open and staring dully. She seemed to be looking right through Dorothy.

A sound escaped from Dorothy's open mouth; an animal-like expression of shock and pain. She took in the wide glistening gash at her mother's throat, the soiled bread knife lying by her outstretched hand . . .

DOROTHY CAME DOWNSTAIRS the next morning to find Bertie sitting at the breakfast table, an untouched cup of tea in front of him. He did not return her smile.

"Is something wrong?" she asked, uncertainly.

"Such a weight of despair has fallen on me from nowhere," he confided, "like a meteor from outer space."

"Can I do anything?"

He shook his head. "Whenever I'm at home for too long, I get fed up and depressed. It's what I call my fugitive impulse. The only thing that helps is getting away, going out into the world . . . I need a change of surroundings, new life." He looked past Dorothy with unseeing eyes that were fixed on escape. Evidently, he had built this handsome and comfortable house for his pretty wife, only to feel trapped by his domesticity.

As Dorothy helped herself to toast and coffee, he said "Last night, life seemed perfectly sweet. I don't understand why I've fallen, suddenly, into a pit of sadness."

"Oh?"

"I mean, nothing in my circumstances has changed. Yet I feel so . . . unsettled and estranged. My life seems nebulous and ephemeral; everything is sliding away from me as I try to grasp hold of it. I'm plagued by dark thoughts, which skitter all over the place in the most disturbing way and won't be controlled." He rested his head in his hands, as though its weight had become too much for his neck to bear.

They sat in uneasy silence. The strong succulent smells of coffee and frying rashers seemed an affront to his mood. Dorothy buttered her toast and took a bite, laboring to chew as softly as possible. She set it down on her plate again. Her heavy knot of hair was pulling at the back of her neck; her fringe prickled her forehead disagreeably.

There was a completely different side to him, she realized. The sparkling charm had vanished. Underneath his success and his intellect and marriage to Jane, he was unhappy and lost and needing solace. Dorothy experienced a keen urge to comfort him. She had woken up full of resolve to be sensible, yet his pain and complexity only drew her to him more strongly.

Jane walked into the room, looking fresh and pretty in a dark green gown with white lace at the collar and cuffs. "I feel so much better for a good night's rest," she said, as she sat down. "Did you sleep well?"

"Like a baby," Dorothy told her.

"I had an awful night," Bertie said, irritably.

Jane's face fell, but her voice was even as she said, "I'm sorry to hear it, my love. What happened?"

"I had the most horrifying dream."

"Would it help to tell us about it?"

Jane poured a fresh cup of tea and passed it to him; he waved it away. He was making the small grunts in the back of his nose: *hnc hnc*. They seemed to say: Don't bother me; can't you see I am trying to think?

"I was wandering in some godforsaken and noxious slum," he said at last, "completely displaced and confused. It was grotesque, and yet horribly familiar. I couldn't find my way out of the cramped, twisting streets that went endlessly on and on, framed by small and squalid houses. Nauseating smells rose from open sewers. Hungry, grimy, insufficiently clothed children came to the doors and stared. I passed an emaciated girl with a grey face, who peered at me dimly, her cloudy eyes struggling to focus. She had no front teeth, nothing but rotten stumps. She caught my arm in a grip that was surprisingly powerful for one so slight, and refused to let go. 'Not unless you take me with you . . .'"

"What happened then?" Dorothy asked softly.

"In trying to shake her off, I woke myself up. With the horror of my dream still fresh I got up and made a cup of strong, sweet tea. Going back to sleep was out of the question. I passed the time til morning trying to write. I like working in the middle of the night. It's so peaceful, so focused."

"You always work well in the still hours," Jane said.

"I didn't last night. It's maddening, really, when it's all been going so smoothly . . . I became locked in a battle with my own style. The words and phrases seemed to develop unruly minds of their own; each one marched an independent association and inference onto the page, and choked off what I wanted to use it for . . ."

"When one has a great deal to say, style is a constant problem." Jane spoke with quiet authority, as though she was used to soothing his doubts.

"I feel as though I'm always on the brink of producing clear and eloquent prose. Yet what I set down on paper is insufficient; it fails miserably to live up to the purity of my intentions."

"You're a wonderful writer," Dorothy said. "Nobody else sees life so clearly; you're like a pathfinder in a new world. Your voice is fresh and vivid, your presence leaps out from every page."

Bertie shook his head. "My work is poor and unsatisfactory in every way. When I started this novel, I could see the plot with utter clarity. But on rereading it, I was horrified. It was thin and pathetic; completely lacking in sparkle or profundity. Bits of it didn't even sound like me; it appears I've been plagiarizing, half consciously, from Henry James."

No amount of reassurance from Jane or Dorothy could convince him otherwise.

AFTER BREAKFAST, BERTIE shut himself into his study, and Dorothy did not see him again until it was almost time for her to go home. He emerged as she was dragging her Gladstone bag down the stairs.

"There you are," he said, smiling at her; he was his old self. Evidently, his moods lifted as suddenly and inexplicably as they arrived.

"Yes, here I am." She set down her bag and straightened up.

"Are you leaving us so soon?"

"I'm afraid I must."

"Come and talk to me before you go."

"I can't. I'll be late for my train."

"Just for a few minutes."

There was no refusing him. He led her into his study, a high-ceilinged room with book-lined walls. The French doors leading to the garden were wide open, and a fresh breeze from the sea sauntered in, stirring the curtains and the heap of papers on his desk. The room looked across the bay to the distant French coast, and everything blazed in the light he cast.

"Well, what have you been doing with yourself?" he asked.

"Jane and I went for a stroll along the beach. It was a chance to catch up with what's happened since we last saw each other. Actually, when I'm with her, it feels like no time has passed since we were schoolgirls walking to Miss Sandell's Academy together, along the Upper Richmond Road. We used to chatter about everything under the sun . . ."

"Oh, I wish I could have heard you," he said, wistfully. "I'd have been fascinated by the to and fro of your budding minds. Tell me more about being at school with Jane."

"Well, we often wondered what we were going to do with our lives."

"What did you envisage for yourselves?"

"I thought I might become a musician or an actress. Jane was going to take a degree in mathematics. I was rather in awe of her scientific cleverness and confidence; she seemed destined for a brilliant future. Though it seems neither of us ended up exactly where we imagined . . ." She broke off, mortified by her tactlessness in implying that Jane hadn't fulfilled her potential.

But Bertie didn't appear offended. "I'm glad she had you for company," he said. "Sometimes, I worry she finds it lonely when I'm shut away writing for hours on end."

There was a pause. He was sitting close enough that she could see he had different colored irises: one pure blue, the other with a small patch of grey that dispersed into minute flecks around the edges and merged with the surrounding blue.

"I've been thinking about you," he said.

"Oh?"

"Yes, when I should have been working. It was most inconvenient."

There was an extraordinarily focused gleam in his eyes as they met hers again. She felt an answering pulse deep within her belly, electric in its intensity. "What . . . what were you thinking?"

"That you're not like other women."

"Really? In what way?"

"There's nothing catty about you; not a single drop of poison or pretense. One feels that at once. I also like it that you're not afraid to speak your mind, and you have a mind worth listening to."

He was the only person, apart from her family, who saw her difference as a positive attribute, a mark of character. It made everything seem better.

"I feel sure you'd never disappoint a chap," he went on. "You aren't like those women who appear intriguing when you first meet them, but grow tiresome once you get to know them. It's no end of a letdown."

She opened her mouth to reply. Presently, he would find out she was something of a misfit, and not as interesting as he believed. Before she had a chance to form the words, she heard Jane's voice: "Dora! Dora, where are you?"

Dorothy looked at Bertie. Something passed between them; that crackle of electricity again. She shivered.

Jane was getting closer. "It's late! You're going to miss your train."

She appeared at the door. She seemed faintly agitated; her cheeks were flushed and she was a little out of breath, as though she had been running. "There you are!" she exclaimed. "I've been looking for you everywhere."

"I was down here the whole time."

"Really? You might have told me." A fleeting look of irritation crossed her features. "Are you ready? I'll walk with you to the station, but we'd better hurry."

Bertie held out his hand, suddenly formal. "Well, it was nice to have you down for the weekend."

Dorothy took his hand. "Thank you. I enjoyed it, too . . ."

She hesitated; it was surprisingly hard to leave him. A tide of shame and remorse welled up inside her: what was she doing harboring these feelings? Having to conceal them from Jane immediately tipped their friendship onto a false footing. She wondered what on earth they would talk about on their way to the station.

Her hand slid from Bertie's warm grasp and she forced her legs to move across the deep red Turkish carpet, one step at a time.

Four

IT WAS AN EXTRAORDINARY MOMENT WHEN YOU felt the bicycle sailing forward. Dorothy was lifted off the ground, skimming through the moving air. I've got the hang of it, she thought . . . I am cycling! She was no longer merely struggling along, trying to forget how wobbly she felt. She could actually control the bicycle's instability. She could steer with confidence, not worrying about crashing into people.

She pedaled tirelessly, delighted by her unexpected reservoir of energy, looking around her at Regents Park as it swung past. The wide stretch of succulent grass was studded with daisies. The broad pathway was lined with people sitting on benches; behind them, flower beds flared with color. The translucent fuzz of new leaves blurred the stark lines of the trees, reminding her of an adolescent boy's first growth of soft facial hair. Globes of cherry blossom were in their full glory, brilliant pink against the cobalt sky, and seeming far too heavy for the frail branches that sustained them. On the other side of the road stood gracefully proportioned Nash houses, their cream stucco gleaming in the sunlight. There were feathery white clouds in the sky . . . The heavy London air had turned into a fresh breeze flowing around her.

She could hear the squeak of her gear case, the slurring of firm tires turning on the smooth pathway, the trill of her bell as she approached a turning . . . How funny I must look with my knees bobbing up and down, all bunched up in my skirt, she thought.

The feeling of freedom was exhilarating. She couldn't remember ever feeling quite as free. Friends and work—even Bertie—were nothing compared to this. To be able to ride a bicycle transformed life; she felt like a different person. She pictured herself cycling around London in knickers and a short skirt the whole summer long . . .

AT DINNER AT the boardinghouse that evening, she told Miss Boyd about her joyful afternoon. Miss Boyd had wings of dark hair coming down from a skillfully twisted bun, and clear dark eyes that shone through gold-rimmed spectacles. It was her last evening at the house; she was leaving the next morning to take up a teaching post in the north of England. "I know exactly how free of constraints you felt in the park," she said to Dorothy. "Isn't cycling glorious?"

Gaslight streamed over the white tablecloth and was reflected in the heavy wooden chairs and huge tarnished mirror hanging above the mantelpiece. A handful of boarders sat around the table, looking haggard and washed-out in the light. There was a new couple: a lady with soft pinkish cheeks wearing a lace cap, and a grey-haired old gentleman with a patriarch beard. They were making jerky remarks, one after the other, about the fine weather.

"Where is Mr. Benjamin?" Carrie asked Dorothy.

Dorothy shrugged; she didn't know where Benjamin was. In the three or four weeks since he'd announced his intention to look for other lodgings, she had hardly seen him. She supposed he had already found new companions. She had pushed him away with such hasty exasperated resolve, yet the reality of him disappearing into another world was strangely painful. Was he with kindhearted people, she wondered; was he already part of their lives . . . estranged from her; altered?

She turned to the Canadian doctor on her other side: a tall grey-clad form. He was an up-and-coming young surgeon; one of Mrs. Baker's favorite boarders. ("A *very* nice dependable gentleman; he always settles his account on time. I wish I had more like him.") He had fair hair and blunt, even features.

"Wasn't it a marvelous day?" Dorothy asked him. "Did you see the late afternoon light?"

"Well, no; I was trapped inside the hospital all day," Dr. Weber said regretfully.

Did you see the sunset? It was extraordinary this evening . . . God evidently ate raspberry custard for supper. Dorothy's breath caught in her throat.

Dr. Weber was saying, "But on my walk home, I did think it the finest sample of London weather I've seen. Generally speaking, the weather is the worst part of living in London." His low steady voice held a curious rounded intonation.

"I don't know what you've got against London weather. It's peerless; you won't find a better climate anywhere."

Dr. Weber's laugh rang out, lively and deep-chested. "I can't say I totally agree. Before the current fine spell, it rained for a week without stopping."

"I suppose only a handful of people think English weather marvelous. But it has its own character and charm. I love the misty atmosphere of dull days; it makes everything mysterious and exciting."

"Well, there we part company, I'm afraid. I can't see any merit in your grey days."

He smiled at her, showing strong even teeth. His manner was easy and genuine, without being complacent. Dorothy could see why Mrs. Baker was so happy to have him. He was completely oblivious to the shifts and secrets of the bankrupt house, yet he brought an influence into it that was wholesome and distinguished.

Mrs. Baker was carving the chicken. Carrie handed around two heaped dishes of vegetables. Mrs. Baker put a generous helping of chicken and gravy in front of Dorothy. She took it to pass it on.

"That's for you, my dear," Mrs. Baker said. Dorothy thanked her and was rewarded with the smile that she loved. It smoothed every line from Mrs. Baker's worn face and made it luminous . . . her eyes were perfectly kind; her whole being exuded kindness.

"I don't know if I should tell you . . ." Miss Boyd began, looking down at her hands.

Dorothy turned her attention back to her. "Tell me what?"

"I went out late last night and cycled around Bloomsbury—in nothing but a petticoat."

"Really? How brave you are! It must have been blissful."

"It was. I could have wept with frustration, afterward, at not being able to shed my deadly layers of clothing once and for all. It would transform life."

"That magnificent feeling of freedom."

"Yes, and not only that; think of never having to clean the mud off your skirt again."

"I know. It would be heaven."

A smile irradiated Miss Boyd's face, making it nearly beautiful. She hadn't exchanged more than a few words with Dorothy until now, but their spontaneous last-minute affinity, cemented by a shared love of bicycles, seemed very sweet. It was like one of those sudden mysterious friendships that flower between schoolgirls.

"I spend hours trying to keep my skirts clean," Miss Boyd said. "It makes me furious to think of all the other things I could be doing with the time. Life is unfair, for women."

"Don't tell me you'd rather be a man, Miss Boyd."

"Oh, sometimes I would." She sighed gustily. "The world belongs to men. They hold everything in their hands."

"*I* wouldn't, ever. I'd simply hate to have a man's mind."

"Why?"

There was a pause, while Dorothy struggled to explain herself. The mind of a woman was deeper, more instinctive and less articulate than that of a man. Women were able to see many things simultaneously; they were more profoundly, richly alive . . . Men saw life in terms of externals, and only one thing at a time. Their sense of superiority was born of being free to be out in the world, but they did not understand what went on below the surface with people.

Miss Boyd gave up waiting for an answer. "Aren't you glad

you are alive today, with all these things going on?" she asked.

"What things?"

"Well, cycling and things. Aren't you going to have any pudding?"

There was a loud hammering on the front door; a peremptory noise, not in the least sociable. Mrs. Baker looked up sharply. Carrie was already on her way out of the room to answer it.

"That was a fine dinner, Mrs. Baker. Thank you," Dr. Weber said.

"Well, you wouldn't have me starve my boarders."

"I certainly wouldn't. Fortunately, the reverse is true."

"Another helping of pudding, Mr. Cundy?"

Mr. Cundy was sitting at Mrs. Baker's right hand, looking about for the dish of apple pie. His black hair was brilliant with grease.

"I don't mind if I do. It seems a crime to let it go to waste." He smiled sideways down the table, his eyes not quite meeting anyone's full-on. "Your dinners are miniature masterpieces, Mrs. B, a bright spot at the end of a hard day's work. Something a chap looks forward to . . ." He helped himself to pie as he carried on; his obsequious mouth feeling clumsily for compliments.

Carrie hurried in. Something in her face caused a hush to fall over the assembled group.

"What's wrong?" her mother asked.

"A dreadful thing," she said, in low stunned tones. "It's Mary-Lou Jones—"

"Who?" the new gentleman asked, cupping one hand against his ear.

"Mary-Lou Jones. A typist; she rents a room down the road . . ." Carrie seemed unable to go on.

"What happened?" Dr. Weber prompted gently.

Carrie turned her large watery blue eyes on him. "She threw herself out the bedroom window because she owes her landlady thirty shillings, and the landlady asked her for it outright."

A buzz of consternation rose from the shocked table. Something had entered the room—a naked despair—and many were only too familiar with it.

"That is *terrible*," Dr. Weber exclaimed. "Is she still alive?"

"I don't know; I don't think so. She fell from the top floor. There's a policeman with her and a crowd of people . . . I saw grey stuff coming out of her head. Oh, it was horrible."

"I'll go and see if I can help." Dr. Weber picked up his hat and went out hurriedly.

Dorothy couldn't face the roomful of people and their excited revulsion. Asking Mrs. Baker to excuse her as well, she went upstairs to her bedroom. She sat down on the greyish-white counterpane and hugged her knees, feeling rattled and queasy.

She tried to imagine Mary-Lou Jones opening her bedroom window and clambering onto the sill; she would have been hampered by her skirt. She saw her balancing precariously on the edge like a voluminous bird; looking vertiginously down at the ground.

What did the moment of unalterably pushing herself off feel like; had her skirt billowed out around her as she plummeted through the unresisting air, like a sail or a parachute? What could have been in her mind? Did she, even then, wish it undone; did she wish herself safely back in her room, with the window fastened? Or was life so bad, she couldn't wait to die and put an end to her pain. Had she welcomed the hard pavement as it rushed up to meet her?

Dorothy shivered as she contemplated the richness of a consciousness being snuffed out in an instant on a grimy London street, to the uncaring accompaniment of cab whistles and hansom cabs rattling and jingling past.

St. Pancras clock struck ten. Mary-Lou was part of a growing army of outwardly confident young female office workers in the city. But their independence came at a price. Dorothy understood very well the precipice edge the girl had walked, the constant pressure of keeping everything going.

At least I've got my freedom—I'm managing—I'm not dependent on anyone, Dorothy thought, gazing into the empty grate, torn between fear and exhilaration.

Five

DOROTHY BEGAN TO STORE UP HER IMPRESSIONS of London for Bertie: little sketches and anecdotes that she hoped would ignite his interested attention and bring that precious creak of appreciation into his voice. "You're a good raconteur, Dorothy," he would say, with a glint of amusement in his eyes. "You have a certain style, you really do. You're coming on no end."

She described her life to him, making him laugh with her descriptions of the endless procession of boarders and their eccentricities.

"There's an alcoholic Portuguese waiter sharing my top floor at the moment. Has the room next door to mine. He comes bumbling up the stairs in the early hours."

"Watch yourself, Dorothy. I hope you lock your door at night."

"Actually, I don't. He staggers about and swears a bit. He

has difficulty getting into his room, and sometimes, poor thing, he is sick on the landing."

"It appears to be a most colorful establishment. But I do think you should lock your door. You've no idea how desirable a girl like you is to an old reprobate. You're a golden girl. You're like . . . like a ripe juicy peach."

"Am I? . . . Funnily enough, I feel perfectly safe with Mr. Abella. Mind you, he owes weeks of rent . . ."

"Another one of your disreputables, Dorothy. Your Mrs. Baker houses an extraordinary gallery of them. Seems to attract 'em."

"I suppose she does . . . the exception, of course, being Dr. Weber. They don't come any more respectable than him. Did I tell you he's been rather attentive to me lately?"

Bertie's eyes darkened. "No, you didn't."

"He's taken to intercepting me in the hall in the mornings, on my way to work. Helps me on with my coat, tries to keep me talking until I'm almost late. He says his day hasn't started well unless he sees me first thing."

She wanted Bertie to know what it felt like being inside her skin. Waking up to the clear bright chiming of St. Pancras bells, in her first room of her own. Resting in bed, watching the grey morning light lying in pools on the faded carpet, falling onto the dark yellow grainy wallpaper, the battered yellow chest of drawers and tiny wardrobe. She knew this room intimately, better than any place she had known in her wanderings.

She wanted him to live her excitement as she left work, the long monotonous day scrolling shut behind her. Stepping out into the dusky light and the clamor and spectacle of

London hurtling past. Feeling the pavement under her feet, the lamplit evening expanding around her. Watching the endless file of hansoms and horse omnibuses rattling along, bearing hordes of unknown people to unknown destinations. Being shoved and elbowed by home-going workers, as she took in the profusion of colorfully decorated shop fronts and posters that seemed to promise immeasurable delights. The thickening darkness mingled with the gold of city lights. The sound of a barrel organ was all but drowned out by evening-paper boys shouting their headlines stridently, reminding her that the great capital was but the foreground of a worldwide drama . . .

She wanted him to experience with her the adventure of simply taking a bus across town without being accountable to anyone. The sense of being easefully carried along, drawn by the momentum of the traffic. Watching the city unfurl from the bus windows, the glory of the silhouettes of buildings outlined against the sky. Joyously in love with life and with her freedom, giddy with the feeling. Thinking, *Until you've been alone in London, you aren't entirely alive.*

BERTIE SAID, "I see London has taken hold of you, as it took hold of me." His eyes gleamed as he looked at Dorothy standing in front of the mantelpiece. Summer light poured through the wide open windows of the drawing room. They were waiting for Jane to come downstairs for lunch.

He began to pace up and down. "You should write up your impressions. You have a gift for words. You've had enough experience to provide material; you've won your independence in the face of staggering difficulties. You ought to set it all down." He stopped walking. "Hang on a minute, perhaps *I* should write a book about *you* . . ."

Dorothy laughed.

Bertie sat down in an armchair, motioning her to join him. "Seriously though, it's only by drawing on his or her own life and emotions that a writer animates fiction. In a small way it's like being God: you create characters in your own image, and you breathe energy and warmth into them as best you can."

His words reverberated inside Dorothy, reinforcing something in herself; scarcely articulated, but there. She had always wanted to write; probably, everyone secretly wanted to write.

"A few years ago, I went to a garden party where they had a palmist telling fortunes," she said. "An extraordinary dark wrinkled creature, like an elderly monkey in a head scarf and earrings. She looked at my hands and asked if I'd done any writing. I said no. She said, 'Start straight away, you were born to write. Don't let anything put you off. Start writing, and make sure you keep going' . . . She also told me I'd marry late in life . . ."

"So, have you written anything?"

"I can't. I wouldn't know where to begin."

"Sit down with an empty sheet of paper and a pen. I find that if you take almost any idea as an opener and let your mind run with it, there comes out of blankness, in a way I find impossible to explain, some small embryo of a story. If I could turn myself into a writer, you can, too . . . Why don't you write something and send it to me."

SHE NEVER TOLD Bertie that London held a dark side, too. At times, she was afraid that the strain of keeping everything together on her meager salary would break her. By the time the rent was paid, there was hardly enough for food, and no chance of saving for old age. She was chronically hungry and cold during the winter months as well (by no means the least attraction of staying with the Wellses was their well-stocked pantry). Work was increasingly monotonous and the hours were gruelingly long. She was plagued by terrible tiredness, which seemed to gather force inside her, like a malignant and threatening tumor. She was losing weight. The cheap black dresses she wore for work were hanging off her, making her look like a shabby malnourished crow. What if she fell ill and was unable to earn a living? She couldn't be a dentist's secretary for ever.

Sometimes, there seemed nothing ahead but a bleakness that would deepen as the years crawled by. A future utterly lacking in prospects . . . thinking about it was so frightening, it made her want to curl up and cease to exist. At least that way, there would be no more struggle. It was easy to see how the young typist down the street had lost her reason and thrown herself from the top floor . . .

In this mood, the city seemed uncaring, indifferent. Bertie was right when he said London had got her. London was taking her health and devouring her youth. It was London that killed you, in the end.

There was a particular narrow and gaslit lane off Regent Street. Dorothy always seemed to drift into it unknowingly . . .

the rusted sign hanging above the cramped shop for Browns Teas reminded her of a visit with her mother, just before she became ill. She'd sat opposite Dorothy, not saying much, small hard lines of tension about her mouth. Refusing to eat, despite Dorothy's best efforts to persuade her . . .

Dorothy couldn't stay the flood of memory and guilt. Why did she keep forgetting the tea shop was here? What drew her so irresistibly to it? . . . Some malevolent force brought her here . . . it would tear her mind apart . . . it was nudging her into madness because she was herself and nothing could change the shattering event that had wrenched her world in two and plunged her into a darkness that still threatened to destroy sanity and life.

"I LIKE HAVING you around," Bertie admitted.

Lunch was finished, and Jane had gone outside to speak to the gardener. Dorothy and Bertie were alone in his study; the rest of the house suddenly seemed far away.

"I like the way you use your hands when you talk," he continued, "it's very musical. And the way your hair falls in pale gold curtains, your laugh . . . you don't know how attractive you are."

His words brought pleasure, yet a jagged fork of alarm pushed through Dorothy's stomach, like lightning. For some time, Bertie had been hovering near an invisible line—now, he had crossed it irrevocably. The boundaries had shifted: perhaps, they no longer existed.

She stammered, "Most of the time, I feel like a hopeless misfit. I'm so awkward with people . . ."

"You're not awkward with me. But you never build me up or flatter me. You only argue with me."

"You want flattery? Listen to this then—ever since I met you, you've blotted out everyone else. Other people are colorless in comparison; no one quite matches up . . . it's most annoying and uncomfortable."

He turned sharply to look at her. "Is that true . . . ?"

Dorothy flushed deeply. "Yes, it is. From the first moment I saw you coming toward me on the station platform. Though I can't stand your ideas . . ."

"Forget my ideas, Dorothy, I shan't have any more of 'em. Take back anything I ever said. Let's spend as much time together as we can. We'll talk, voraciously. I don't want there to be any inhibitions between us."

For a long moment, his blue eyes held hers. He put his hand on her knee. She could feel the warmth of it tingling through her thin summer dress. When she was with him, her body spoke a language of its own—or rather, it sang.

The feeling rising inside her was the sweetest thing she'd known, yet it made her a terrible person. It was so strong, it swept everything else away: all the anchoring principles, like honesty and loyalty and not hurting other people. The principles underpinning her idea of herself as a fundamentally decent person.

It was nearly impossible to draw back, yet she had to. Gathering her strength, she dropped her eyes and moved her leg away from his hand.

"What's wrong?" he asked.

She looked at him steadily. "Amy Catherine . . . she's practically my oldest friend."

Bertie sighed. "I knew this was coming. I have something to tell you about Jane and I, and I'm not sure how to explain it to you." He hesitated, looking out toward the garden. "My whole adult life, I've been searching for something in a relationship with a woman, something rare and beautiful, not fully understood . . . something that would satisfy all my needs, from the most cerebral and artistic to the purely physical, and give my life meaning. You see, my heart craves a perfection of mental understanding and bodily response. I want tenderness and intellect and passion all wrapped up in one dear mate for life. And I want to return those gifts in abundance.

"When I met Jane, I thought I had found my ideal. Sadly, it became clear early on in our marriage that this was not the case. Jane more than satisfied my need for companionship, but there were certain physical incompatibilities. How shall I put this? She and I have completely different temperaments, and . . . well, different bodily demands. Jane has never been a particularly sensual person . . . she doesn't see our relationship as being preeminently sexual. She regards my, uh . . . my *appetites* as a sort of sickness. In this respect, we are vastly mismatched." He paused again, glancing at Dorothy. "I don't want to shock you."

Dorothy kept her face carefully expressionless. "I've never been shocked in my life. Go on."

"The realization of our incompatibilities was dreadfully painful. Perhaps I expect too much from one person but—oh God!—I could not reconcile myself to what I had. I was riven by intolerable longing; I couldn't rid myself of its raw ache. At the same time, I didn't want to betray Jane. She was so dear and good; she'd never given me any reasonable cause for discontent. I was torn between my desire not to hurt her and my desire for completion. I couldn't sleep, couldn't work. I was divided against myself." He stopped and raked his hands through his hair, visibly upset.

"What happened?"

"Well, with time, we reached a recognition of our differences. Jane's the most loyal and understanding wife I could ask for, but it hasn't been easy for either of us . . . We've come to an agreement, whereby each of us has the freedom to satisfy our physical desires with other people."

"You mean you have that freedom," Dorothy pointed out, drily.

"In theory, both of us have it. In practice, yes, I am the one who makes use of it," Bertie acknowledged. "But without it, our marriage would surely have collapsed, and neither of us wants that . . . We're allies now, rather than lovers. Such passion as there was between us expired a long time ago, leaving a great deal of affection and mutual support. Jane's only conditions are that I don't keep my friendships secret from her, and I don't have them with women she dislikes. She and I continue to love and respect each other, and everything goes on as before."

"Surely it's not that simple," Dorothy protested. She was disturbed, despite her efforts not to be, by their arrangement. The thought flashed in her mind that she wasn't the first, and she probably wouldn't be the last. She remembered that Bertie had left his first wife for Jane, which caused something of a scandal at the time.

"You make it sound so . . . so clear-cut," she went on, struggling to find the right words. "What if the other person wants more? Love naturally brings jealousy and possessiveness. You can't go putting limits on it . . ."

He picked up a tendril of her hair that had escaped from its heavy bun, and smoothed it lightly between his thumb and fingers, spreading sensations through her body that were like pinpricks of colored light. She half closed her eyes.

"I think you could be the incarnation of all my dreams and desires," Bertie murmured. "I'm greedy for you . . . for all of you—flesh and bones, innermost thoughts and secret fantasies . . ."

Through the open French windows, they could hear Jane approaching with the gardener. "And those evergreens need a good pruning . . . oh yes, and next summer, I'd like an absolutely enormous bed of azaleas along that wall, a great blaze of color . . ."

Dorothy pulled away from Bertie. His skin was flushed; his eyes densely blue. Sighing, he got to his feet and walked over to his desk.

Six

THE MORNING STRETCHED BLISSFULLY AHEAD OF Dorothy. The room was very warm with sunlight and a blazing fire. Jane was wearing a delicate gauzy little dress; she glanced up affectionately as Dorothy came in.

"How are you, my sweet?" she asked. "I hope you were comfortable in your room. Did you sleep well?"

"Yes, thank you. Like a top."

Jane motioned her toward the wide chintz sofa and Dorothy sank into it gratefully, enjoying the maternal fussing.

"Tell me, really, how you are. You look much rosier this morning. You were utterly washed out when you got here."

"I was tired to death," Dorothy said, from the depths of the sofa. "I'm nearly always tired to death nowadays."

"You shall do absolutely nothing while you're here; I insist on it. You'll lounge around in your room, and only come out to eat and play when you feel like it."

"Yes, please. It sounds utterly blissful."

A maid entered the room briskly and hovered just inside the door. Dorothy let the quiet murmur of their conversation flow over her "—and open all the windows once you've finished washing up the breakfast things, and put flowers in the bedrooms. Oh, and don't forget to leave the letters in the box when the postman comes . . ."

"How are your sisters?" Jane asked, when the servant had gone.

"Oh—doing splendidly, I think. I haven't been to visit them for a while."

Dorothy glanced down at her hands. Jane had changed since their school days; she'd been swallowed up into the life of household women, losing the intellectual daring that Dorothy used to admire. They were not entirely at ease with one another; it was a struggle to find things to talk about. She was sure Jane felt the strain, too. What if all they had left in common were their feelings for Bertie?

"How is your mother?" she asked.

Jane rolled her eyes. "She was devastated when I went off with Bertie, you know, because he was still married. In fact, she swore she'd kill herself. I ignored all her pleas and threats, so she sent a posse of uncles and cousins round to our lodgings to make us see sense, but that didn't have the desired effect either." Jane hesitated and laid her hand on Dorothy's arm. "Oh Dora, I wish you'd been around to confide in. I loved Bertie and believed in him utterly, but at times I felt so isolated and demoralized. I was defying not only my family, but the whole world."

"It must have been difficult," Dorothy murmured, heavy with secret growing shame.

"Yes, it was for a long while, though things improved once Bertie's divorce came through and he married me. Mother began to accept him grudgingly. She comes to stay fairly regularly, and she and Bertie are almost civil to one another these days . . ."

The door opened and Bertie came in. "Here you are," he said impatiently. "The fire in my study has gone out. I can't get it started again; the wood must be damp. There's smoke billowing everywhere . . ."

"I'll see to it," Jane said, rising swiftly to her feet. "Back in two ticks, Dora."

They both went out.

Dorothy stayed on the sofa, listening to the sounds of the maids going about their daily chores in other parts of the house. She was thinking how skillfully Jane managed Bertie's house and his moods. Jane provided a perfectly stable background for his writing and responded tactfully to his every whim. She was there when wanted by him, never underfoot when not. Bertie admitted to Dorothy, with rueful humor, that every writer should have a Jane.

Yet Dorothy noticed a trace of fear in Jane's dealings with him, an almost desperate wish to assuage his irritability. Beneath the cheerful surface of life in their house, there was tension. Bertie was frequently away. There was an artificiality about Jane; a careful watchfulness. This was present in everything from the eagerness of her smile to her concern with current affairs; she was utterly devoid of spontaneity.

Dorothy was dimly beginning to realize that Jane protected herself by freezing many of her own emotions and needs. "Jane" was a persona created jointly by her and Bertie, someone who was able to cope with the demands of their joint life. Amy Catherine was more real; real and vulnerable. But she was all but buried beneath the construct that was Jane.

Jane came back and sat down next to Dorothy on the sofa. She took Dorothy's hand. "I'm glad you're here, old thing," she said, giving it a squeeze.

A panicked sense of her own treachery swept through Dorothy. She fought down a sudden overwhelming urge to confess everything. Why couldn't Jane see the attraction that burned like fire between her and Bertie? She wanted to tell Jane to send her away before it was too late; never to invite her again.

She glanced remorsefully across at Jane and saw, with a sharp pang of pity, that Jane was losing her looks. Her skin seemed drier and less dewy. The fine lines which had begun to appear around her eyes had deepened. To save trouble, she did her hair in a tight bun on the top of her head, which didn't suit her.

"You know your old hairstyle?" Dorothy asked, suddenly. "You wore most of it down, and it flowed around your shoulders."

"Yes, what about it?"

"Well, I preferred it. It flattered you better."

Jane responded with a swift hurt look. There was an unmistakable flash of dislike in her large brown eyes, which vanished almost immediately. It made Dorothy wonder how much Jane guessed.

BERTIE OPENED HIS study door as Dorothy was walking down the passage. "Come and talk to me."

"Shouldn't you be working?"

"I can't work," Bertie admitted. "My mind and my thoughts—are just swirling about . . . I'm distracted by wanting you. It's like someone murmuring continuously in a room while I try to write."

He saw the doubt in Dorothy's eyes, and he answered her gently, without her having to put anything into words. "Jane is the anchor of my existence. You are the zest."

Dorothy stepped into the room and he shut the door behind her. There was silence.

"Damn you!" he burst out. "Not having you is interfering with my work, my mission . . ." He flung a hand at the untidy heap of pages on his desk.

"May I look?" she asked cautiously.

He nodded moodily. "It's in its infancy still. It's an essay called 'The Contemporary Novel.'"

Filled with curiosity, Dorothy picked up sheets covered with small, densely written prose. He had never let her see his work in progress before.

We are going to write about it all. We are going to write about business and finance, and politics and precedence, and decorum and indecorum, until a thousand pretenses and a thousand impostures shrivel in the cold, clean air of our elucidations. We are going to write of waste of opportunities and latent beauties until a thousand new ways of living open to man and woman. We are going to appeal to the young and the hopeful and the curious against the established, the dignified and defensive. Before we have done, we will have all life within the novel.

When she'd finished, there was silence.

"Don't you like it?" Bertie asked, at last.

"I more than like it . . . it's brilliant. You are almost the only writer who can cut loose from the old ways of thinking, and you aren't afraid to tell the truth. You're going to change lives and make a real difference to the world."

He smiled broadly; Dorothy could feel his enormous pride in his mental agility. He was like a ringmaster entering the circus tent with a spring in his step, knowing he was going to tame wild animals and bend them to his will.

"I want to describe the contemporary social and political system in England," he said. "With all its flaws and corruption and its terrible disregard for the poor . . . through writing about it, I want to raise the status of the novel to the level of political debate . . . I'm fired by a vision of a world still decades in front of us. I can see its truth and urgency, yet I can't seem to bring it into being. It's my work and duty, my set of rules for life and the only religion I have—"

"You know the huge difference between you and me?"

He shook his head, smiling. "Tell me."

"To me, literature is an end in itself, a thing of beauty and wonder. To you, it's a vehicle, a tool. It has a purpose."

"Of course it does. A book without a purpose is simply the writer's impertinence."

He got to his feet and moved closer to Dorothy. The exasperation in his voice belied the warmth in his eyes. "But it's absurd to think that having a purpose rids a work of beauty . . ."

They were standing very close now, eye to eye. Dorothy started to say something, but Bertie placed one finger lightly on her lips. He took her hot face between his unsteady hands and kissed her half-open mouth. When he kissed her, she trembled and he held her closer, wanting to kiss her again. But she pulled away and left the room, overwhelmed by the softness of his mouth beneath the scrape of his mustache and the web of tangled emotion it produced.

BEFORE SHE WENT down for dinner, Dorothy examined herself in the long bedroom mirror. She was revitalized; no longer the ground-down Londoner who had arrived on the Wellses' doorstep. The removal of tension and fatigue made her face look fresher, emphasizing the softness of its lines. A brisk walk along the beach in the afternoon had brought a healthy flush to her cheeks. The gaslight showed up the gold tints in the coiled mass of her hair and the warm brown depths of her eyes.

She made her way unhurriedly down the wide green staircase. There were raised voices coming from the drawing room. Faintly shocked, she hesitated on the landing, which was lined with bookshelves and decorated by stuffed birds. She didn't know whether to interrupt or to tiptoe back upstairs.

She could clearly hear Jane saying, "You seek each other's gaze. You meet her eye, she looks away. You make her feel . . . *desirable*."

Dorothy's breath caught in her throat.

Bertie sounded strident, cross. "This is beneath you, Jane. You know that while you stand over my life, no dalliance of this sort will ever wreck what we share. You are my fastness, my safe place. You are wedded to me—beyond jealousy."

Jane answered in a low voice. As hard as Dorothy strained, she couldn't make out her words.

There was silence. Then the sound of muffled sobbing.

When Bertie spoke again, his tone had changed. There was a tenderness in the high voice that made it almost husky. Dorothy was intruding on something so intimate she could hardly bear it. But she couldn't tear herself away.

"I know I've been restless and peevish for the past few months," he admitted. "When I'm at home for more than a few days at a time, I get into an impatient and claustrophobic state, I can't help myself. I know how ugly this sounds, forgive me . . . the crude fact is that I have bodily appetites you are too fragile to meet. I truly love you, but I have this basic need for the thing itself. I must have it when the craving takes me, to release tension and leave my mind clear for work. You and my work are my true obsessions. The sex thing is merely refreshment. Believe me, I have no satisfaction in being enslaved to its tiresome insatiability." He paused. "I have loved you profoundly from the first moment I met you, and I always shall. You're my little helper and my dearest mate. You are part of me and you've been the making of me. Hush, my dearest love, hush. I can't bear it when you cry like this."

There was silence. The stuffed pheasant next to Dorothy stared at her with glassy, accusing eyes. She imagined Bertie had taken Jane into his arms . . . perhaps he was kissing Jane, as he'd kissed Dorothy two short hours ago—she couldn't stand it. She was simply "the sex thing," a passing "refreshment." He was using her to slake a simple hunger and facilitate his work.

Dorothy's face was flaming. Nausea and bile rose in her

chest so powerfully, she was afraid she might be sick. She crept tremulously upstairs.

She sent a message through the housemaid that she had a headache, and wouldn't be joining them for dinner. Then she slipped on a coat and quietly left the house.

It was a cool evening. A fine rain was falling, and the rich scent of damp earth rose from the ground. As Dorothy crossed the lawn, she lifted her burning face to receive the rain. Waves of anguish and shame were pouring out of her body, like a smell; the air was thick with it. This pain could not be endured. It would fade with time; it had to. She wished she could wind time forward, or go to sleep and wake up when it had stopped hurting.

She could hear the roar of the sea below her, and wet trees sighing and rustling in the wind. It was almost dark, and the tips of their silhouettes were visible against the sky, but only just. Heavy clouds covered the moon, swallowing everything down into shadow.

She made her way through the rose garden. The red roses were like dark shadows; the white ones resembled pale faces in the dimness, watching her. She passed the vegetable garden and the terraced square, and took the uneven track that led down to the sea. It was getting darker; she had to strain to see where she was going. The path was treacherous, and once or twice she stumbled. The rain soaked through her clothes and hair. She was starting to feel cold and afraid, but she didn't want to return to the house.

Her foot caught on a twisted root lying across the path. She lost her balance and the ground came rushing up to meet her . . .

Dorothy lay convulsed against the cold slimy stone. There was searing pain in her left knee. A sticky ooze of blood was spreading beneath her stockings.

She was freezing, but she didn't want to move. She was maddened by shame and pain; tormented by the hurt she'd caused Jane. Without Bertie's interest illuminating her life, she was nothing.

She couldn't stand being alone with the stabbing needles of her thoughts. There was no reprieve from them, except in madness; a swiftly enfolding, redeeming madness that would obliterate awareness. She welcomed the idea. The line between sanity and madness seemed pitifully puny: both states harboring the same impulses; the difference lying merely in the mind's power to exert a restraining signal . . . She couldn't struggle any longer. If she could only see her mother again, if she could spend a few minutes with her, she would willingly sacrifice the rest of her life . . .

Tears came. She wept for a long time, silently, there on the path.

After she'd cried herself out completely, she felt calmer. A strange, icy numbness descended on her, as though she was on another planet and the air was lighter. She stumbled to her feet. Her clothes were wet and muddy, with sodden bits of grass and leaves sticking to them. Clumsily, she brushed herself down. Her knee was still bleeding. She shambled slowly back toward the house.

Seven

HER TASTE OF BLISS WAS OVER BEFORE SHE'D EVEN had a chance to grow accustomed to it. An annihilating torpor threatened to engulf Dorothy; a strange, frightening state. She lay on her bed, rigid. All the good things, all the hope seemed to have drained from the world. It was terrifying to feel the meaning seeping out of everything, leaving only blankness in its wake. It was like dying; like being buried alive.

Her face was contorted with the effort of holding back tears. She raised her throbbing head from the pillow and glanced around her attic room. It had lost its charm; become nothing but a confined space in which she waited for the next visit to the Wellses. And now there would be no more visits.

A bout of weeping seized her then: hard, dry sobs. She was surprised by how much crying hurt. She wondered wretchedly who she could talk to, whose company might ease this withering pain.

Benjamin had finally found other lodgings and moved out, leaving her relieved, but with a gaping sense of loss. She thought about the other boarders and her various London friends. No one was quite right.

Mrs. Baker. She pictured the landlady's kind weary face; she seemed at that moment very like Dorothy's mother. I'll go and find her, Dorothy thought. I couldn't possibly confide in her. Bertie is a married man; she would be shocked to the core; her good opinion of me smashed. But she is real; just being in her presence is a comfort. She knows that everyone is alone, and the hustle and noise people make is just a front to try to hide their loneliness and fear.

DOROTHY OPENED THE drawing room door. At first sight, the room seemed deserted; the gas was turned frugally low. But in the dimness, she could just make out two figures: a man balanced on the arm of the sofa, and someone sitting close beside him. They remained silent and motionless as she approached; they must be newly arrived boarders, shy of introducing themselves, perhaps. She walked over to the table next to the fireplace and poured a glass of water from the jug standing on it. The jug was almost empty; a thin trickle leaked into her glass, petering out before it was an inch full.

"Would you like a drink, Miss Richardson?"

It was Mr. Cundy.

"Oh yes, I would," she answered awkwardly, glancing at the woman on the sofa. She found herself gazing into the eyes of Mrs. Baker. Mrs. Baker wearing a low cut silk blouse and a blue velvet choker around her neck!

Mrs. Baker was neither annoyed nor pleased to see her. She seemed caught up in some private reverie and Mr. Cundy carried on the conversation, telling Dorothy about the benefits of keeping well hydrated. Dorothy thanked him absentmindedly, still focused on Mrs. Baker's uncharacteristic indifference to her surroundings; her strange air of being utterly absorbed by some internal preoccupation.

Mr. Cundy fell silent. Dorothy studied them both, surprised by how similar their expressions were as they gazed back at her. They looked benevolent, tolerant, almost patronizing. Flickering behind their eyes was some kind of shared joke, from which she was excluded.

She had been a bumbling idiot, crashing in, oblivious. They had probably been discussing Mrs. Baker's struggles with the house. Mrs. Baker had confided in him, and he was advising her on how to make it more profitable. Dorothy had rushed in interrupting them; entirely wrapped up in her own problems. Mrs. Baker had been right not to welcome her. Yet without Mr. Cundy there, Dorothy was sure she would have been her usual warm receptive self.

Goaded by her thwarted desire for comfort, she hurled herself against the barrier of their unstated alliance. "I see I've barged in on a private conversation."

"Not at all, young lady," said Mrs. Baker tartly, sitting very upright on the sofa. "We weren't talking about anything in particular."

"It looks to me like you're in the middle of something," insisted Dorothy mulishly.

Mr. Cundy regarded her with calm satisfaction. There was something different about him, a quiet assurance. "Not at all," he said mildly. "I was only explaining to Mrs. Baker the theory of natural selection."

They wanted her to go away. They wanted to be left alone to continue their discussion without interruption. She lingered for a short while, making graceless small talk. When she couldn't think of anything else to say, she excused herself and left the room.

AFTER THE FIRST shock passed, Dorothy found she couldn't stand being alone with the shameful echoes of her aborted love affair. As a result, she worked late at the dental practice whenever she could. She welcomed busy days: long sittings, where appointments overran and she had to stay in Mr. Badcock's room, clearing and cleansing instruments with the patient in the chair, knowing that her other duties were piling up elsewhere.

She liked the brief moments of forgetfulness that came with throwing herself into her work. She did her best to assist Mr. Badcock as quietly and as expertly as possible, trying to make the patient forget there was a third person in the room.

It was tedious and slightly repugnant work. She cleared away the soiled instruments and scoured them with a solution so harsh it wrinkled her fingertips and split her skin. Afterward, the instruments had to be polished and repolished, a precise, fiddly, attention-consuming task. Yet the grind of being continually on her feet for the endless clearances and cleansings brought a strange relief. Her sense of her usefulness to Mr. Badcock was balm. She helped him with a new deftness and ease. Even the most difficult of his patients seemed manageable: the lady who vomited if an instrument touched the back of her throat, the retired doctor who went berserk under anaesthetic and sometimes tore Mr. Badcock's clothes.

She admired Mr. Badcock for his skill and his gentleness. Unlike other dentists, he was utterly sensitive to the needs of his patients. He never forgot there was a person in the chair before him, rather than a disembodied set of teeth and gums, as he went on endlessly performing root dressings and repairing crowns and tapping in fillings. He inspired trust; patients submitted willingly to being treated by him. But none of them knew that it was slowly wearing him down . . .

"I don't think that will bother you any longer," he would say, with a final sweep of his spatula, removing the absorbents and handing them to Dorothy. "Why don't you have a rinse? We'll make an appointment for next week." And the patient was himself again, getting up eagerly from the chair, free of pain and fear and the chilling knowledge that however strong the spirit, the body falls apart sooner or later.

Mr. Badcock, tall and thin, smiled his gentle grey-eyed smile behind the wire-framed glasses. His pallor and the lines around his eyes seemed deeper every day . . . his patients did not know how they sucked him dry.

One rainy evening at twenty past six, Mr. Badcock switched off the lights around the chair. The room looked cold and clinical in the dimness.

"Haven't you finished yet?"

"No," said Dorothy, without looking up from her pile of correspondence. "I must get these letters off and update the patients' charts and the appointment book." There were also the bottles of chloroform and carbolic in the cupboards to tidy and replenish; the boxes of gold and tin fillings to sort through; serviettes and clamps and saliva tubes to prepare for tomorrow's appointments . . . anything to avoid being alone within the four lifeless walls of her room.

"Why don't you leave the rest until tomorrow?"

"It's not late."

"All right then, as you wish. I'll say good night."

"Good night," murmured Dorothy. "See you in the morning."

The front door clicked softly shut on Mr. Badcock.

The rain had stopped and the building was eerily quiet. The fire was nearly out; the room was growing chilly. Dorothy paused from her letter writing and took a deep breath of iodoform-laced air. *Assume a contented air and eventually you will feel contented in spite of yourself*, she intoned under her breath. *If you can't have what you like, you must like what you have*. Perhaps if she said it enough times, it would come true. Her gaze slid away from the broken dentures lying on her heavy oak desk and fell onto the small aspidistra in the corner . . . its dusty lackluster leaves depressed her unutterably.

Without warning, tears came. She brushed them away furiously. Why hadn't Bertie written? Why had he left her alone to grieve and weep; to get through the rest of her life without him?

She picked up an unanswered letter, but found she couldn't read it through tear-blurred eyes. She dropped it back onto the pile. Nothing was as good as the elation she'd felt in his company, the sense of aliveness. She would probably never have that again. The only consolation was that she wasn't harming Jane; Dorothy was the only one who suffered. Probably, he had decided to draw back because of Jane.

Certain moments with Bertie would live inside her forever. Nothing could take them away. *What are you thinking?*

You have a habit of leaving your thoughts lying in your face, you know. I want that one, the one that crossed your features a moment ago. The two of them eternally sitting in front of the fire in his study, very close, not quite touching.

She was still talking to him in her head all the time, telling him things that had happened during the day, how she was feeling. Painting word-pictures of her life that presented it in an idealized light—how she wanted him to see her, rather than how it really was.

It was a bit like this when her mother died. Dorothy—guilty and shattered, but alive—had carried on speaking to her, the words dropping into a void.

WHEN DOROTHY GOT back to the boardinghouse, she decided to go to dinner, though she knew she couldn't afford it. She talked with great animation throughout the meal and was the last one to leave the table.

She lingered until the supper things were cleared, and sat down by the fire with a book. The room was hushed and peaceful. Carrie and Mrs. Baker took out a tumbled workbasket and began to sew at the table. Dorothy gazed into the dying fire. It seemed unbearably dismal. She tried to think about something else, but all that came to mind was the returning loneliness waiting for her upstairs.

The door opened softly. Mrs. Baker and Carrie looked up at once, but did not say anything. "Here's Miss Richardson," Dr. Weber said. "Evening Mrs. Baker, Carrie. Do you mind if I join you?"

"Of course not. Come in."

Dorothy carried on reading as Dr. Weber sat down opposite

her, opened a bulky journal, and began to look through it. "I'm taking the London medical exam in July," he explained, "and I've a load of cramming to do before then."

She nodded, trying to cover her surprise and also her sense that she had been thrust into a role. It was like a scene from a novel or play for Dr. Weber to bring his work into the room in order to be near her. To him, she seemed tranquil and assiduous; he felt he could study better in her presence.

As she read, she tried to assume the qualities he believed she possessed. If only what he thought he saw was true! She remembered the vaulting fever in her blood when Bertie's mouth touched hers, and nearly laughed aloud at how shocked Dr. Weber would be if he knew.

But perhaps if he remained a constantly admiring presence in her life, she might turn into the girl he thought she was. Perhaps if she were treated with homage, she would grow into the role of womanly woman; an exemplary doctor's wife and mother of his children. Surely it was not that difficult? It would mean involving herself in the running of his practice, managing his life seamlessly, training the servants with tact and discretion, never growing flustered or angry, creating a haven of replenishment and peace for him to come home to . . . She felt herself begin to exude these qualities; they altered her demeanor as she leant over her book. She could leave her messy shameful feelings for Bertie behind.

After a while, she roused herself and looked across at him, as though she had only just realized he was there. His body looked neat and hard in the well-cut Canadian suit; his skin was ruddy with health; his fair hair short and glossy, like the pelt of a young animal. He raised his head and his gaze met hers. She was touched by the look of appreciation in his eyes.

"It's a perfect evening," he said quietly (he pronounced it *purrfect*), pulling at a thread on his jacket sleeve. "Would you like to go for a walk?"

"It's late . . ."

He consulted his wristwatch. "Nine o'clock. You call that late?"

"I'd rather sit here . . ."

There was silence, except for the sounds of Mrs. Baker and Carrie packing up their mending things. They left the room quietly.

"I want you to know . . ." he cleared his throat, "How . . . how very much I enjoy our little talks . . . As I've said to you before, my day isn't a good one unless it starts with a few words with you. In fact, you're in my mind a good deal."

"It's nice of you to say so. I . . . like talking to you, too."

"I'm glad. I'd be happy to feel I was in your thoughts, even sometimes. It's a lovely place to be . . ."

If you think my thoughts are lovely, you don't know me very well, Dorothy felt like saying to him. My thoughts are full of anger and torment, putrid with unholy longing.

Their eyes met, and Dr. Weber gave her his white even smile. She felt enfolded by his smile: it welcomed her and drew her in, holding her up like a trailing plant supported by a fence . . . secretly wanting to guide and shape her. She dropped her gaze. There was a pause.

Dr. Weber abruptly began speaking about the historical interest of the neighborhood. He had been to look at the Old Curiosity Shop on his way home from work. He described the precarious overhanging upper storey, the uneven creaky floorboards, the sloping roof, and wooden beams.

"That shop wasn't the one that inspired Dickens," Dorothy

said. "It's been demolished; it's only the site. But there's a better local story I heard from one of my dentists."

She told him about the passage in Little Gower Place, and how body snatchers would take freshly buried corpses through it, under the cover of darkness, from St. Pancras churchyard to the hospital.

"Well I never! I'm surprised your dentists think it right to bother your pretty head with tales of the dead being disturbed."

He would have preferred no response from her; only an air of radiant listening. There was no true meeting of minds; he didn't really see her as Bertie saw her . . . being in his company was isolation far deadlier than staying single. No matter how much time they spent together, they would always be strangers. What was worse, he would not even realize. He would be satisfied with very little—serene attentive demeanor, banal conversation, and a limited sphere of activity. Perhaps he was the sort of man who wouldn't be fully happy with a woman unless he could patronize her and secretly despise her a little.

He was telling her that she shouldn't be troubled by the ugly things in life; she should be protected from them. But she hardly heard him; she was torn between a desire to lean against his respectability and a desire to shun it, in exactly equal measures.

Her mind began to race ahead of itself. Dr. Weber was a good man and far from stupid; he seemed to be growing truly fond of her. Marrying him would mean living the kind of existence her parents had led, before their troubles began. It might be her only chance for a gracious leisured life; no more worries or fatigue. But she couldn't get married just to stop being tired. And being with him would mean daily contact with sheltered women; busy well-dressed automatons, whose only horizons were family and home, and who were fearful and rejecting of all that lay beyond. It would mean enduring the company of self-satisfied condescending men, who were present a fraction of the time, but were more often away on their own business, which gave them an unwarranted superiority and the power that came with having money. She could never be part of that world; she simply couldn't conform to its terms. The cost of security was too high . . . she would rather die than smother, even on a pedestal with incense always burning.

Dorothy was starting to feel dizzy. In spite of the open window, the air was hot and oppressive. It hampered her breathing and made her feel like she had indigestion.

I'm as much a man as a woman. That's what gives me this awful clarity of vision, she thought despairingly. I am an oddity standing halfway between the sexes, looking at both sides . . . Most men will come to hate me—because I can't pretend for long.

She was torn by contrary forces that would never allow her to drop anchor and settle. Then her life would be full of conflict; driven this way and that, a ceaseless swinging to and fro. No wonder people thought she was inexplicable.

Dr. Weber was looking at her expectantly; he evidently wanted a reply. She gazed back at him in dismay; she had no idea what he'd been saying. Dorothy felt she must get into the open and walk for a long way, unbound. She rose abruptly and announced she had to go out. The look of hurt surprise on Dr. Weber's face shamed her.

She let herself out the front door, and was immediately

pierced by the beauty of London at night. There was a new moon rising, peering out between clouds, its frail radiance mingling with the misty darkness along the quiet roads, the haloes of lamplight at intervals on the pavement

At last, she was anonymous and free in London. Who could want anything more from life . . . ? She would return to her peaceful center, with only herself to please; no one else wanting to mold her into something she couldn't be . . . If she walked far enough and fast enough, she might manage to shed herself. She would no longer be a woman, tormented by longings and dissatisfactions . . . she would be a Londoner.

There was a familiar figure standing on the corner. She checked herself; she was used to seeing men who looked like Bertie. In fact, she couldn't stop searching for him on the street, scouring the features of others for a resemblance. Whenever she saw a short, sandy-haired man, she would hurry helplessly toward him, only to pull back in crushing disappointment and embarrassment when she realized her mistake.

He turned toward her and the light from a streetlamp fell on his face.

Her heart was singing. It was Bertie.

Eight

THE FIRE IN HIS STUDY CAST ITS SOFT LIGHT over the prone forms of Bertie and Dorothy. Her head was on his chest, his arms protectively around her. His body smelt of honey.

There was silence, except for the dry hiss and spit of the flames. Dorothy gazed into the landscape of fissures and molten expanses at their center, feeling the warmth on her face. A log tumbled, sending a shower of amber sparks skyward, like a cluster of fireflies. They floated down gently, expiring one by one before they reached the ground.

She found her mind full of pictures and thoughts: Bertie coming after her with renewed urgency; the way her stomach had fallen away at the sight of him standing there on the pavement. She had run into his arms, pressing herself against him like an abandoned creature, not caring who saw them.

She had fallen; she was living in sin; betraying Jane . . .

The hunger she felt for Bertie was all-consuming; it obliterated everything else, even her guilt. And he wanted her as badly . . . She was sure that if she weren't in his arms, it was only a matter of time before someone else would be. At least they both cared for Jane and wanted to protect her.

Bertie was uncannily alert to her slightest feeling. "I know how much I owe Jane," he said suddenly. "I acknowledge it and I resent it, too, because I know deep down that we're mismatched, and our marriage is in many ways a sham . . . I can't remember how or when the early romantic love I felt for her died. I still love her, though, in a different way, but I feel confused and resentful about the tie that binds us . . .

"I'm torn by conflicting feelings. On the one hand, nothing matters more than my work and not hurting Jane. And yet you have become the vital center of my life . . . I am caught between everything Jane and my work mean, and my uncontrollable desire to be in your arms . . ."

Dorothy stopped his words by boldly gluing her lips to his, and all else was forgotten in the heat of their bodies.

After a while, she drew back; this intimacy was too potent. She craved it, yet it made her feel overwhelmed, almost panic-stricken. Perhaps she needed time to get accustomed to their new situation.

Bertie sighed, propped himself up on one elbow, looked down on her tenderly. He brushed an escaped lock of hair away from her face.

"Lately, I've been in such a fatigued, restless, depressed state," he said, in a low voice that was full of emotion. "My life seemed a decayed old thing of jealousy and disillusion, and second-rate writing, and constant socializing with people I didn't want to see. I was numb and dulled. Then you came to stay, with your wild-rose coloring and your fresh mind . . . you've swept the staleness from my heart and brain."

She smiled up at him, suffused with warmth. His words seemed to close a door on all the wretchedness that had gone before; they carried her forward into a new transforming life.

"You've changed my mood, given me freshness and energy, a blast of intellectual curiosity and strength," he went on. "I can try to make Jane happier . . . I can write powerful and meaningful things because of the way I feel about you. It's as though you've made me anew." He brushed his lips lightly against hers. "You're what I've been searching for all my life. Perfect beauty and sensuality combined with perfect mental companionship."

Some time later, Bertie said "I wish there was a safer way of being together. It's too risky here . . ."

"London?"

He nodded.

"We can't go to my room," Dorothy told him. "My landlady would throw me out instantly."

"I know. We must be careful, I can't afford a scandal. I'll take a room somewhere, discreetly." He held her close and whispered, "I want to be as close to you as it's possible to get."

BEING IN LOVE lit the world. Her fatigue had vanished; she was brimming with vitality from head to foot. She felt capable of taking on any challenge. She was in control of her destiny; time was on her side. Every opportunity was open to her.

At work, she handled patients and dentists with an easy charm that had eluded her until now. She rose to every challenge, tackling letters and accounts with a swiftness and accuracy that surprised her. She thought up small improvements that made the practice run more efficiently. She dashed off letters to friends in her spare time, the words spilling effortlessly from her pen.

From time to time, she caught Mrs. Baker looking at her thoughtfully. The landlady seemed to know, without being told, that something momentous was happening to Dorothy.

Dr. Weber avoided her as much as he could. When they both happened to be at dinner at the same time, he made sure he sat as far away from her as possible. She felt his reaction was extreme, and was a little hurt by it.

BERTIE FOUND A room in a quiet boardinghouse near Russell Square, let by a sympathetic landlady. Dorothy visited him there for long half days and evenings, every week or ten days.

She'd knock on his door, her entire body humming with expectation. He opened it so quickly, he must surely have been standing next to it; his whole face lighting up as he wrapped his arms around her and said, "I missed you. I want to hear everything you've been doing and thinking since I last saw you."

They would take long walks through London and have dinner afterward at a restaurant. Or Dorothy might buy cold meat and salad and they'd picnic in their room; alone in infinite time, full of a sense of their liberating difference in relation to a convention-bound world. She experienced a keen pure happiness that was surely absolution? They talked about everything and nothing, their conversation made luminous by a bottle of wine. Bertie said his imagination was in a fertile state, and new ideas were blooming in his mind. He felt he was developing a new creative life.

"You have an astonishing capacity for happiness," he told her one evening.

"Well, if I do, it's your fault. You make me astonishingly happy."

"You make me happy, too. You keep me alive and vigorous and save me from stagnation."

After dinner, she lay shyly beside him on the narrow single bed, wearing nothing but her underclothes, with her hair loose about her shoulders.

"What are you thinking?" he asked.

"I don't know. Nothing, really."

"A shadow just crossed your features. All your thoughts show on your face, you know."

He said the sight of her made him wish he could paint. At the very least, he'd like to record every detail of her in poetry. He compared the curves of her torso to the stem of a plant, or to a cresting wave in the ocean. In the whorls of her ears he saw shapes like seashells. Her hips, unclothed, had the rolling outlines of hills. He told her that her skin was the softest he'd known. She felt remodeled by him; no longer a misfit, large boned and awkward. To him she was a poem, as enchanting as any heroine in literature.

Under his gaze, her body felt different: alert, vibrant, eager; coming alive beneath his touch as if from a long sleep. She felt glorified by him, realizing for the first time that her body could be a source of pleasure to another person.

Still, she hadn't given herself to him completely; she was stumbling at this final step. It was partly about betraying Jane, but also about her own fears. She was petrified of surrendering wholly to another person, especially someone as powerful and certain of everything as Bertie. She would be consumed by him. At times, lying in Bertie's arms, she couldn't tell where he ended and she began; her edges blurred into his. It was blissful, but terrifying.

She also knew that to bring an unwanted child into the world—with all the scandal that would ensue, not to mention the physical danger of childbirth—would be the end of her.

She and Benjamin hadn't done more than hold hands and kiss. After some initial attempts at persuasion, he had accepted her reluctance to go further. But Bertie was less respectful of her hesitation. "It would be good for you to make love," he said. He could drop from poetic heights to crassness with startling speed. "Few of us are mentally or physically healthy and whole without it."

WHEN BERTIE WENT home to Jane, it was a relief in part. Dorothy needed time alone to absorb every word that had passed between them; every expression and gesture, and every caress.

She also needed to return to herself, a process of restoration that could only be achieved in solitude and silence. In Bertie's company, she felt dislocated from a deep, essential layer of her personality. His need for constant stimulation and entertainment created pressure to provide answering signals. It shut off her inner life. She couldn't simply *be*; she found herself in a loud confusion, acting a role. She suspected she would feel like this with any man, but the strain was undoubtedly magnified by Bertie's force of personality, and by his desire to possess her completely.

After seeing him, she needed to spend time alone in her room. She lay on her bed in her old striped flannelette dressing gown, the dusty smell of the counterpane in her nostrils. She sometimes thought that this small room was the only place she truly belonged.

There was no sound inside the house; its substantial walls kept the boarders separate and sheltered. She could hear the familiar dull roar of traffic from Euston Road; the chiming of St. Pancras clock. Outside her window, sunlight gleamed along the leads sloping down to her parapet. The room was half in shadow, half in brilliant light. The battered chest of drawers and the tiny wardrobe in the corner stood in gloom. Streams of light fell through the long low window, settling in lakes on the warm grainy yellow wallpaper and the shabby carpet.

Hovering in empty space, she could feel her untouched inmost self unfurl and expand, free and strong, full of a marvelous quiet sense of life at firsthand. It was a blissful state for which she had no words; something that was always there waiting, if she could but reach it. It was anathema to all Bertie stood for. His mantra: work for progress rendered him oblivious to the reality that existed, all the time, in the deep silence at the heart of things.

Dorothy was beginning to realize that one's inmost self was lost and not found through close relationships.

Whenever she was alone, she found herself traveling backward in time, toward the beginning of memory.

She was standing immobile in bright sunlight, on a narrow gravel pathway between two banks of massed sweet williams. She looked at the dense clusters of flowers, very large and permanent amongst the tapered leaves: hot pink and crimson-centered, or scarlet and white-centered. She didn't know how old she was, but the blazing heads of the flowers were almost level with her face. She could feel the sun warming her hair. Everything was still and silent, except for a couple of large bees swaying heavily and drunkenly across the path in front of her, going from bank to bank. Their bodies seemed bulky and cumbersome; they hummed loudly as they went. A confusion of heady smells reached her from the flowers; deepest amongst them an odd but not unpleasant smell, pungent and spicy, like warmed cloves.

It was her first moment of intense awareness; seeing sublime things all around her. She had no memory of entering or leaving the garden; only flowers and bees in the sunlight . . . It was an unending summer's day, in a garden she would never return to. She couldn't remember the house, or any of the other details of the landscape. But what had lasted through the years was the sense of how extraordinary it was that anything at all existed; the continuing wonder of there being such a thing as life.

THERE WAS A letter from Bertie on the hall table. She ran to pick it up, cupping the envelope in both hands as she carried it up to her room, as though she was nursing a live creature that might escape.

She sat on her pillow to read it. Bertie's writing was an

exuberant scrawl, full of loops, dashes, and exclamation marks that looked as though they were about to fly off the page.

In some ways, a letter from him was even better than being with him because it could be savored at her own pace, yet she could feel his presence in the room with her while she read it, making things shine. It was like a sudden sharpening of all her senses, until everything reached a blinding pitch and she felt she must explode if it grew any more acute.

His letters were wonderful, terrible, searing. They were illustrated by sketches of two puppies, Dora and Little Bertie, in a basket or on a rug, in a variety of loving poses: eating, playing, cuddling, sleeping. Bertie called them his "picshuas."

My *darling girl,*

I've only been home a few hours and I keep turning round to tell you things, but you're not there! My love . . . what a shock it is! I feel empty without you, it's as though part of myself has been cut away. I can't get by without you because there is no one as loving, as sweet, as beautiful, as pillowy, and delectable as my Dora.

You are the woman of my life. I love you like I've never loved before; I surrender myself to you. I'm bored and cross when you aren't with me . . . I want to be able to talk to you, to hear your voice, to know your innermost thoughts.

I keep thinking how you looked in your slip on the bed next to me; how tender and creamy your warm skin is. I can't get the sight, nor the smell, nor the texture of you out of my mind. There's a quality about you that turns my head like champagne, and makes me want you quite desperately.

You've got under my skin and entangled with my imagination. No, it's more than that. You are . . . how shall I put it? . . . You're the embodiment of a vision of loveliness and reciprocating womanliness that's haunted me my entire adult life. How do you do it? I suspect you're some kind of enchantress.

I wish more than anything on earth that you were next to me now. I want to kiss your toes; I want to kiss the softness of your belly. I'm greedy for your thighs and your stomach and the base of your throat. I don't know how I'll manage until I can get to London; I want to feel you in my arms again . . .

Write back to me as soon as you can. I'm lost without you.

Your very loving Bertie.

JANE INVITED DOROTHY to stay for the weekend, welcoming her at the door in her old cheery manner: "Hello, Dora dear. It's such ages since we saw you, I hardly recognize you anymore."

Dorothy had tried not to run from the station with her heavy bag. She realized that in the moments before knocking on their front door, she had forgotten to breathe. She was so short of air, it was hard to speak. She felt giddy, audacious, slightly disembodied.

Jane held her by both shoulders, examining her face carefully. "You've put on some flesh, and it suits you," she said quietly. "I can't see a trace of your old pallor and fatigue. You're positively blooming."

Dorothy's grey hat suddenly felt hot on her head. Jane's words were like an accusation. Her stomach was churning; she could hardly meet Jane's gaze as she mumbled thank you. She was aware of the change in her looks. Her hair shone, her skin glowed, and her eyes sparkled. It made her feel odd, as though her new attractiveness was borrowed from someone else; she did not own it. It brought an attention she was unused to. People on the street stared—the women with curiosity and suspicion, the men with open approval.

Bertie was in the drawing room. There was a brief silence as his eyes met Dorothy's, like a sharply indrawn breath. They said hello carefully, their eyes skidding away from each other.

"Come and sit down," Jane said, piloting her to a chair by the window. "Let's tuck in; you must be hungry after your journey. I baked a cake this morning, but there are sandwiches if you'd prefer."

Dorothy looked at her with increasing unease. In London, Jane had seemed a great distance away. It was as though she'd receded or become two-dimensional; a figure viewed through a frosted screen. To see her in person, fresh and graceful and simply dressed, was almost shocking. To realize anew that she was real and substantial; that blood and feelings thrummed through her. She was capable of hurting Dorothy, and being hurt by her.

There was an expression behind Jane's eyes that didn't match her polished manner. She seemed to be acting the whole time; as though she feared if the chatter stopped even briefly, the ground would shudder and crack at their feet, catapulting them into an open abyss. Yet she behaved as she always had toward Dorothy. If she suspected that Dorothy was the cause of Bertie's frequent absences from home, she was a consummate actress, giving no indication. She poured tea and passed it around. She cut sturdy wedges of Dundee cake and offered the plate to Dorothy. The familiarity of the afternoon tea ritual only heightened the surrounding awkwardness, as Jane kept up a steady stream of questions about her family and work.

Jane was wearing a pair of long tortoiseshell earrings that Dorothy hadn't seen before. They accentuated the fairness of her soft mass of hair, and the slenderness of her neck.

"Those are frightfully pretty earrings," Dorothy said.

Jane's face lit up; she raised a hand to touch one of them. "Do you think so? I'm glad you like them; Bertie brought them in London for me."

Jealous anger ripped through Dorothy, sour and corrosive. She looked at Bertie, but he was busily brushing a cake crumb from his knee and wouldn't meet her eyes.

She sipped her tea and struggled to eat her cake, which clung stubbornly to the roof of her mouth. She was almost incapable of making the required bright small talk; it was too difficult to articulate the clever sayings that were part of an unspoken contract between the Wellses and their guests. She hadn't seen Bertie for over a week, and she had missed him fiercely. It was bittersweet to be near him, but unable to touch him, or allow her feelings for him to show. Forced into constraint and polite distance, achingly conscious of being a disappointing guest, Dorothy watched him and Jane together. Bertie was alternately very kind and very irritable with Jane.

THERE WERE GUESTS for dinner: a retired colonel and his wife, who lived nearby. The table, set with Venetian glasses, fine silver and cutlery, and great bowls of pink and saffron azaleas, looked festive beneath a gently shaded light.

Dorothy listened to Bertie holding forth, much as he had on her first evening with the Wellses. That evening seemed a great distance away, as though it had happened to another person.

"I'm worried about the international situation," he said. He was wearing a soft collared shirt, a blue-grey bow tie, and a flannel blazer of the same shade. Its color made his eyes intensely blue and bright. "I'm convinced we are closer than ever to conflict with Germany. What's more, India is in a state of flux. It's only a matter of time before something blows up there, with desperate consequences for our empire." His eyes roved from person to person, capturing and holding theirs as he kept command of the conversation.

The colonel nodded gravely, sucking at his mustache. "The fact is, half the government are asleep."

"Exactly! Snoring comfortably in their beds beside their pampered wives . . ."

Dorothy tried in vain to fasten her attention to the problems of the outside world. Her body felt like a weighted sack on the chair, too warm, jittery with desire. She shifted her weight, recoiling from the lamb cutlet on her plate. She wasn't hungry for food.

She thought, *I know what he looks like when he wakes up in the morning; I know the texture and smell of his skin and the firm muscles of his back, the touch of his lips on mine.* She hoped none of her thoughts or feelings were visible to the others.

Glancing across the condemned dinner table, she met the watchful eyes of Jane.

Afterward, Dorothy found herself briefly alone with Bertie

in the sitting room. The delicate scent of Jane's bunches of flowers mingled with the pungent odor of the large wood fire burning in the hearth. It was heady, intoxicating.

Bertie took her in his arms at once. "God, I missed you," he muttered into her hair. "You look absurdly pretty tonight. I shan't sleep knowing you're only down the passage. Shall I creep into your room when Jane's asleep?"

He kissed her hard.

She pushed him away, glancing nervously at the door. "Don't be stupid. We can't, not under Jane's nose."

Bertie's face was flushed; his eyes gleamed in the dimness. Dorothy wondered if she looked as heedlessly lascivious.

"Do you think she suspects anything?" she asked in a low voice.

He shook his head. "She's given no sign of anything being wrong, but don't withdraw from her, it would only hurt and confuse her. Go and find her in her study tomorrow, spend time with her."

"I feel horribly uncomfortable. What would we talk about?"

He caught her hand, stroking her palm softly with his thumb. He was breathing rapidly. "What do women talk about when we're not around? I've often wondered . . ."

AFTER BREAKFAST THE next morning, Dorothy knocked on the door of Jane's study. Hearing no reply, she tentatively pushed it open. The room was empty.

It was a pretty, feminine space, decorated with softly tied bunches of flowers and a prodigious collection of cut and colored cut glass ornaments. Dorothy sat down at her friend's desk, taking in the large brass inkstand, the blotting pad and solid-looking brass clock. She picked up the red-handled fountain pen and set it down again. She ran her hands over a tidy pile of household accounts. *So this was what it felt like to be in Jane's shoes.*

Her eye fell on the wastepaper basket, which held a single crumpled piece of paper. Overcome with curiosity, she fished it out, opening and smoothing it on the desk's well-worn surface. It was closely written, in Jane's small, neat hand.

She hesitated. What right had she to invade her friend's inmost thoughts? What if Jane came in and found her? Jumpy and guilty, soaked through and sick with it, yet unable to stop herself, Dorothy began to read.

I feel tonight, so tired of playing wiv' making the place comfy, and as if there was only one dear rest place in the world, and that were in the arms of you.

There is the only place I shall ever find in this world where one has sometimes peace from the silly wasteful muddle of one's life. Think! I am thinking continually of the disappointing news of it. The high bright ambitions one begins with, the dismal concessions, the growth, like a clogging hard crust over one of home and furniture and a lot of clothes and books and gardens, a load dragging me down. If I set out to make a comfortable home for you to live in and do work in, I merely succeed in continuing a place where you are bored to death. I make love to you and have you as my friend to the exclusion of plenty of people who would be infinitely more satisfying to you. Well, dear, I don't think

I ought to send such a letter. It's only a mood you know . . . I have been letting myself go in a foolish fashion. It's alright you know, really, only I've had so much of my own society now, I am naturally sick of such a person as I am. How you can ever stand it.

Dorothy could not go on. She crunched the letter up in her hands, sickened by her own culpability. If she gave Bertie up right now, an entire lifetime of devoutness and self-control would not atone for the injury she had inflicted on her oldest friend. Beneath the buoyancy and competence, Jane carried a toxic weight of self-doubt and bitterness and secret pain. And whether she knew it or not, Dorothy was adding to her suffering. (And how could she not know, in the deepest fibers of her being?)

What agonies Jane must have endured when she realized that the luminous mercurial man, who had wanted her enough to abandon his first wife, was falling out of love with her. That his heart no longer belonged to hers, that she had failed to capture and keep it . . .

Dorothy had a sudden vivid vision of Jane walking alone in her garden, unable to stop listening for the sound of Bertie's footsteps, yet knowing it would not come.

She let the ball of crushed paper fall back into the wastepaper basket.

Nine

BENJAMIN REACHED THE END OF HIS STORY AND buried his face in his hands. He had a particular way of inhabiting a chair: his head sinking toward his chest, his legs stretched out across the shabby carpet and crossed at the ankles, his half-empty cup of tea on the floor next to him. The sight was so familiar, yet it was as though he belonged to another world. Her life with him seemed flimsy and indistinct; perhaps it was a dream she'd woken from? Only her time with Bertie was real—real and vibrant.

When he moved out, Dorothy had told Benjamin he must call on her if he needed help: she had a foreboding he would get entangled in something of this sort. She'd heard him out in silence. As he talked, she watched the muscles of his face contracting to form the painful words. She listened to the rise and fall of his voice—so well-known and so alien—a curious meshing of argument and melody, as if he was holding a negotiation with himself. And she was able to see the images he conjured with perfect clarity, as vividly as if she'd been an actual witness to the wrecked romance.

"She was pretty," he said wistfully. "She had the most extraordinary hair; it glowed with red-gold lights, like fire . . . and the softest skin I've ever seen or touched. And she was full of life; everything else seemed colorless and dull next to her. She flattered me, made me feel capable of amazing feats. Fool that I was, I believed every word . . . I was gripped by desire, completely taken over by it. The only place in the world I wanted to be was in her arms." He paused, gazing at Dorothy, as though seeing her for the first time. "Have you ever wanted someone like that?"

"Yes, I have," she answered truthfully. For a fleeting moment, the shared experience made her feel closer to him.

"I think it was a type of madness, from which I am thankfully recovering . . . oh God, how is it possible to be so stupid?"

"Don't blame yourself. She showed you only what she wanted you to see. Nearly all men would have been taken in."

Dorothy understood only too well Benjamin's utter helplessness when confronted with this devastating combination of charm and looks. The girl sounded like the epitome of ambitious artificial femininity, playing to his vanity; he hadn't stood a chance. After Dorothy, the blatant flattery must have been sweet balm.

"There's another thing . . ." Benjamin cleared his throat, looking sheepish. "We thought she was with child."

Dorothy stared at him in horror. "Benjamin, no!"

"A false alarm, thank God." Shielding his eyes with his

hands, Benjamin described the ugly insults and reproaches, the broken engagement.

Dorothy squirmed with guilt: she had failed him by sending him out into the world, innocent and defenseless. She had as good as pushed him into the arms of a monster. She looked at the green silk tie showing beneath his beard; the gold watch chain decorating his waistcoat; the gleam of his ring, pale old gold clasping a circlet of seed pearls. With his fine opulent looks and the generous allowance sent by his father from St. Petersburg, he was a catch for anyone. Any adventuress. He was like a child, open and trusting, oblivious to the guile of women. Swift anger blazed in her because of his naivety; it mingled uncomfortably with her guilt, making her feel physically sick. In the end, she harmed all the people she loved best.

He sat upright, flexing his hands until the joints cracked. The profound melancholy in his eyes reminded her of a puppy who needs to be picked up and stroked. Yet his beard and his formal manners and serious expression might have belonged to a far older man. What a strange combination of childishness and middle age he was. As he stared into space, he seemed to be confronting the barren stretches of his future, alone . . . Dorothy wavered, tugged by the knot of feelings that still bound her to him. Poor needy Benjamin; how isolated and heartsick he was, stranded in this cold damp country he would never belong to.

He sighed noisily. "What shall I do?"

"Find new lodgings at once. Make a clean break, get as far away from her as you can."

"Again? I am always moving."

"I know. I'm sorry . . . I don't know what else to say. Look, how about another cup of tea? It might make you feel better."

As she poured, he stopped her forgetfully putting milk in his tea. Taking a glistening lump of sugar from the bowl, he popped it between his lips and proceeded to suck his tea through it with quiet practiced sips. When all the sugar had dissolved, he took another lump and carried on drinking in the same way.

Dorothy watched this ritual, filled with an achingly familiar disgust. Certainly, the girl wouldn't have cared how Benjamin drank his tea. She wouldn't have been repulsed by his habits, like Dorothy was. Dorothy cursed her own fastidiousness.

She tore her gaze away from his mouth and looked instead at the pallid black-fringed eyelids shuttering his face when he blinked; the earnestness of his gaze as he raised his eyes to hers. His eyes held an enduring fascination. He would always be dear to her. She looked at him fondly.

He caught the look and plucked a fold of her skirt, putting it to his lips "I know now why men kneel to women."

"Benjamin. Don't."

"I miss reading with you. Do you remember *Anna Karenina?*"

Dorothy nodded. *Anna Karenina* was the first book he had introduced her to, on a visit to the British Library. She remembered her opening encounter with Tolstoy beneath the gorgeously domed ceiling, accompanied by Benjamin's penetratingly whispered commentary and the angry glances of the readers around them. *Anna Karenina* had seemed alive in a way English novels were not. She could hear the characters' voices, feel the currents and shifts in the gaps between their conversations. The aliveness wove a strange beauty that was stronger than the anguish . . . Dorothy missed her shared reading with Benjamin, too: the dark-haired form sitting near her, contentedly absorbed.

"Is it even now too late for us?" he asked. "Nothing has been right, before or since."

Briefly, she cupped his cheek with the palm of her hand. He closed his eyes. She wondered if he could sense the heat that Bertie had aroused in her. She crushed a sudden shocking urge to kiss him full on the lips.

"Sweet boy," she said. "You don't give up, do you?"

As Dorothy walked Benjamin to the front door, Mrs. Baker was crossing the hall with Mr. Cundy. Mrs. Baker looked more dingy and depleted than ever. Beside her, Mr. Cundy gleamed with youth.

The landlady greeted Benjamin warmly, but with barely held-in curiosity. Mr. Cundy shook his hand heartily, not quite meeting his eyes.

When they had disappeared into the drawing room, Benjamin said, "I am surprised that man is still here."

"He's very much here. He seems to be perpetually closeted with Mrs. Baker these days. I think he's helping her straighten out her affairs."

"There is something evasive about him . . . nothing I can put my finger on, nothing evil, but I do not like him."

"I know what you mean. I hope he doesn't try to take advantage of her in some mean way, like the others. She's had an awful time, you know."

"I do not know anything about it."

"She was left penniless when her husband died, with two infant girls to bring up. His family behaved terribly. They disowned her, cutting her off without a farthing. She scraped and saved for years to get this house, but she'll never make it profitable. She doesn't have the first idea about running it; she thinks her failure is just inexplicable bad luck. Half the boarders don't pay their bills."

"That is terrible."

"I know. I worry about what will happen to the Bakers."

DOROTHY'S CONVERSATION WITH Benjamin crystallized her unease about Mr. Cundy. He was secretive and sly. He had ingratiated himself with Mrs. Baker, winning her confidence, making himself indispensible to her.

Dorothy wondered how she might broach her anxieties to Mrs. Baker without causing offense. She went down to dinner that evening, hoping there would be a chance to talk to her alone.

The room was nearly full; the other diners were already at their places. Mr. Cundy was sitting—at the head of the table! Mrs. Baker had given him her chair! He sat surveying the room with quiet assurance.

"Here you are, young lady," Mrs. Baker said, with the sweetly serene smile Dorothy loved. "Come and sit over here."

Mrs. Baker was wearing a new blue ribbon in her hair, incongruous against the badly dyed blonde and grey. She steered Dorothy to a chair beside a girl Dorothy had never seen before.

"Miss Leslie-Jones," Mrs. Baker murmured, as Dorothy sat down.

Dorothy saw a beautifully molded oval face, shining dark eyes framed by a mass of tumbling curls, and a satiny peacock-blue dress that gleamed in the dimness. Beside Miss Leslie-Jones, the other boarders looked dowdy and insipid. She had charm, a slightly unnerving poise and charm. Dorothy's appreciation of these qualities battled against the alarm that jolted through her suddenly . . .

The girl held out her hand with studied grace. "You must call me Veronica. It's a pleasure to meet you."

Dorothy took the offered hand. "I am happy to meet you, too. I'm Dorothy Richardson."

"Yes, I have seen you around the house. You always look as though your thoughts are far away, so I hesitated to introduce myself." Veronica paused; she leaned toward Dorothy, dramatically conspiratorial. "But I wanted to talk to you from the moment I laid eyes on you."

Dorothy was silent, trying to cope with the sense of invasion. Veronica's elegant poses were irritating, yet Dorothy was attracted, despite herself, by her warmth. Veronica was pouring glasses of water for both of them.

"Are you staying here for long?" Dorothy asked. "Or just passing through?"

"I don't know if I will stay. I came from Paris—I made my family send me there to study art. There are so many things I prefer about living in France."

"Such as?"

"Oh, I could give hundreds of examples. Mainly it's the food and the way of living, the little everyday things the French do so much more elegantly and comfortably. Then there's the way the English dress . . ."

She raised her eyebrows and drew her shawl more closely around her shoulders, as though trying not to become infected by the English lack of style. "But I do like this house. The atmosphere of faded gentility appeals to me very much. And Mrs. Baker is a perfect darling."

"I agree with you," Dorothy said warmly, glancing at the landlady, who was on her feet handing round plates of soup. By the look of it, there would be no chance of a private conversation tonight.

They began their meal. The usual talk started up among the boarders about the weather (more rain was prophesied). Things were passed around the table with a great deal of efficient politeness. Veronica began telling Dorothy about her family, ignoring everyone else.

Her oldest brother was in Simla: she made Dorothy see the unimaginable landscape of the Indian hill station—think Surrey, with slightly more dramatic scenery, she said. Dorothy could picture the brother standing in the clean bracing air: tall and aristocratic looking, benevolent and wealthy, coming to the rescue of his adored younger sister when their parents refused to pay for the art course. Veronica spoke of her younger brothers in the services, and her titled relatives and their country estate. She had broken away from them because she couldn't stand the suffocating life. There was a brief engagement to a curate. She seemed to have difficulty describing him, abandoning the attempt to explain instead the puzzling way he shrank and shrank in her mind, until he scarcely seemed real. She left for Paris after their engagement ended. Her family were relieved to have her out of the way until the gossip in their village had died down.

Veronica spoke matter-of-factly; she was clear-sighted and

a little disillusioned. Despite her sophisticated and affluent family life, she seemed as displaced as Dorothy. Her exclusion of the other boarders was plain bad manners, but it was hard to resist the sense of intimacy she created within the public social occasion. She asked Dorothy about her family.

Dorothy sighed. "Well, my mother is dead. I have three sisters. My father lives with the eldest, Kate, and her family at Long Ditton in Surrey."

Her father was unchanged, despite everything that had happened. He still clung to the appearance of power, while lacking the substance. He laid down the law in Kate's household, and depended on the charity of Kate's husband. Dorothy sent him half a crown as often as she could, and visited less and less.

There was a pause.

"Doesn't talking about anybody's family bore you?" Dorothy asked eventually.

"I hope I didn't bore—"

"Oh no," she said hastily, "I didn't mean that at all, I loved hearing about your family. It's just . . . I . . . I find it difficult to speak of mine."

When the meal came to an end, Veronica said, "I had a marvelous evening. It's been a long time since I met anyone I can talk to as easily as you. Would you like to go for a walk? Perhaps we'll find a café, and we can sit and talk some more."

Dorothy declined as politely as she could. She escaped back to her room, vaguely promising to be at dinner again quite soon.

DOROTHY'S OPPORTUNITY TO talk to Mrs. Baker presented itself at the weekend, when the landlady came to clean her room. She knocked softly and pushed open the door, hovering just inside the threshold. "Ah! I hoped I'd find you in, young lady."

"Yes, here I am."

There was a pause while Mrs. Baker came fully into the room and set down the mop and pail. She shut the door firmly behind her.

Dorothy said, "I'm glad to see you, because there's something I want to speak to you about."

"Actually, young lady, I need to speak to *you*."

Dorothy looked at her in surprise. But Mrs. Baker's tired face was expressionless, revealing nothing.

"You know I think a lot of you," Mrs. Baker told her. "You've been one of my best boarders, from the moment you arrived. To tell the truth, I've a bit of a soft spot for you."

"And I for you, Mrs. Baker."

"Well, I know you're busy. I don't want to waste your time, so I'll get straight to the point. It's about him. The Canadian doctor."

"Dr. Weber?"

"Yes. He was worried almost out of his mind about you."

"What on earth do you mean?"

Mrs. Baker flushed and drew herself up to her full height. "You may be wondering why I'm here, bringing this up . . . you see, Dr. Weber saw you in the street with that . . . that man of yours."

"Which man? Benjamin?"

"No. I wish to goodness it *had* been Mr. Benjamin."

"Who was it? Who did he see me with?"

"The other fellow. The *writer*."

Dorothy felt herself blushing deeply.

"Oh, I feel so badly about it," Mrs. Baker continued. "And the worst of it is the doctor never let slip a single word until he left."

There was silence while Dorothy tried to take everything in. Dr. Weber had gone . . . disappeared back to Canada. Some smart pretty Canadian nurse would snap him up . . . he hadn't even said good-bye.

"I feel I have to tell you," Mrs. Baker said. "You see . . . Dr. Weber had made up his mind to ask for your hand."

"Oh."

"He was one in a thousand, mark my words. It was the chance of a lifetime, and you've lost him. Lordy! I wish I'd known what you were up to with that married fellow. I would have told you to stop it at once."

Dorothy recoiled. She had lost all desire to talk to Mrs. Baker about Mr. Cundy. She only wanted her to leave—as quickly as possible. "My goodness," she said in a trembling voice. "Dr. Weber was an awfully decent man."

"Isn't it a shame?" said Mrs. Baker with real feeling. "It vexes me dreadfully to think how foolish you've been."

The room throbbed with tension. Dorothy couldn't meet Mrs. Baker's eyes. She looked instead at her small battered chest of drawers, the yellow wardrobe and the bed tucked under the slope of the attic, feeling wildly estranged from them. Mrs. Baker had violated the tranquility of her room. Dorothy wondered if her beloved things would ever seem familiar again. She willed Mrs. Baker to leave. She only wanted to be alone with her thoughts.

"Well, I felt obliged to come up and tell you," Mrs. Baker

said, at last. "I felt you ought to know what happened. I couldn't have lived with myself otherwise."

"Yes. It was the right thing to tell me. Thank you. It's like, um . . . a mountain out of a molehill."

"It's no molehill, believe me," Mrs. Baker said darkly, brushing at her skirt. "I hope you'll give the fellow up, now you know how carrying on with him is harming you."

Dorothy stared at her, a multitude of unspoken thoughts and questions rushing through her head. How many people knew? Was everyone gossiping about her and Bertie? She shuddered at the thought of the judgments, the acid commentaries that were being directed their way. Mrs. Baker thought it was a scandal.

It was the first time she'd realized her affair with Bertie might have wider repercussions. It was like throwing a stone into a pond: the ripples kept spreading. Another scandal could damage Bertie's career. Dorothy's reputation was in shreds, though she was still a virgin. A sudden thought brought her up short: *If her reputation was already wrecked, what was the point of staying a virgin?*

Her mind flew back to a conversation she'd had recently with Mr. Badcock. She had been hurrying to leave work. He'd hinted he didn't like her new hat; that it was a bit on the showy side. It made her look fast, he said. He'd seemed worried about her, in a brotherly sort of way; he seemed to feel responsible. His concern was quite touching, but she'd snapped back "Please don't worry yourself about the speed of my clothes, Mr. Badcock."

People who knew her—people she cared about—could sense she was becoming risky and disreputable. Half of her minded very much, but the other half didn't care at all.

Mrs. Baker still was going on about Dorothy associating with a married man; warning her it would ruin her. "The thing is we've all got to settle in life, at some stage."

That was all there was, for Mrs. Baker. Settling. She believed no woman was complete without it; she didn't see there was so much more to life. Though Dorothy was exasperated and ashamed, she couldn't help a secret selfish flare of pride. Mrs. Baker knew she could have settled if she had wanted to—and settled well.

Ten

DOROTHY DIDN'T KNOW WHO REACHED OUT FIRST. They hugged each other tightly, rocking back and forth, Bertie's face buried in her neck. He felt warm and solid against her body. His mouth covered hers and his hands were underneath her hair, stroking the back of her neck. They were in their rented rooms, and everything else in Dorothy's life seemed far away and unimportant. There was only Bertie and the feelings he ignited in her.

Breaking off to draw breath, Bertie took her hand, kissed the soft skin on the inside of her wrist. "You get more beautiful every time I see you. I don't know how you do it. Your whole face is glowing today."

"If that's true, it's because of you."

"I missed you. Badly."

"Don't. Missing is for people you aren't going to see again. I'm always here for you."

"Really?"

"Yes, really."

She kissed him again; she was ravenously greedy for him. It had been two long weeks since they'd seen each other, as a bout of bronchitis had kept Bertie trapped at home. As the days dragged by, Dorothy found herself wanting more from their situation. In the beginning, the luminous times in Russell Square were enough, but she was changing. When Bertie was with Jane, missing him was a physical ache that had grown stronger than the pleasure of solitude. At work, Dorothy was unexpectedly tearful. She wanted to be the one who nursed him back to health. She wanted to have his company all the time. To share mundane, intimate, domestic things, like sitting in front of the fire and reading together, or bringing his early morning cup of tea and watching him drink it in bed. The meaning of life seemed to dwell in these small, real, everyday details. She was filled with ugly, scalding jealousy toward Jane for being in possession of them.

Bertie started undoing her buttons. Easing her dress over her shoulders, he let it fall to the floor. As he unfastened her undergarments, she could feel the determination in his fingers. This time, he would not tolerate refusal, and her own fear of sex was being eroded by the desire to bind him to her as closely as possible.

When she was naked, she stood in the middle of the room, shivering slightly, more from embarrassment and nerves than cold, as he took off his own clothes.

He looked at her with longing, as though she was a confection he wanted to devour. He said softly, "You're a glorious sight." She felt she should return the compliment, but she couldn't say anything at all because she was thinking how different his body looked naked, its lines free from the interruptions of clothes. It was interesting, but not attractive. The history of his life was etched on it. The thin arms and scraggy chest were the result of years of being poor and insufficiently fed; the slight tumescence of his stomach reflected his recent prosperity. His face and forearms were bronzed by the sun, but the rest of his body was so pale, the skin had a bluish tinge. The funny hang of the pouch between his legs, his thing nestling against it, looking for all the world like a soft pink snail without its shell, were almost ridiculous.

A stab of pity shot through her, taking her by surprise. She suppressed an urge to clasp him comfortingly to her bosom. All his confidence, his ideas, seemed absurd bravado; the posturing and strutting of a vainglorious peacock. Without his clothes, he was less than himself. Insufficient and weak.

He took her by the hand and led her to the bed. They lay down and he rolled on top of her almost at once, parting her thighs with his hand. She could feel his penis nosing between her legs, hard as a weapon; an unshelled snail no longer. His urgent breathing rasped in her ear. He muttered, "Is this all right? Can't wait any longer, darling, I want you so much."

It hurt more than she could have thought possible. It took all her strength of mind not to wince or cry out. But after the first agonizing moments, she found it was possible to move through the pain and emerge beyond it, entering a no-man's-land where she floated in limbo, her mind clear and active, curiously disengaged from what was happening down below.

She couldn't believe this was all. This great event in a

woman's life; alluded to in elliptical, whispered asides by her mother and sisters. It didn't seem possible.

Bertie's eyes were closed as he moved on top of her. He had an expression of great concentration on his face; she wondered what he was thinking. He began to move with growing urgency. Suddenly, he moaned and fell on top of her, a dead weight.

Afterward, there wasn't enough room for both to lie on the bed without one of them being on the damp sticky patch, or on the daubs of her own blood on the sheet. So Bertie sat upright, his back against the wall.

He was unusually quiet and calm. The curtains were drawn; the light was muted and faint. He picked up his box of cigarettes and offered her one. She shook her head. She reached for the counterpane and pulled it over herself; she was in a daze. Bertie lit up and inhaled deeply. Dorothy wondered if he felt as deflated as she did. Blowing smoke from his nostrils, he turned to look as her.

"Are you all right?"

She nodded.

"I know it hurts the first time. It gets better."

Despite the reassuring words, there was an expression on his face she hadn't seen before. It was gentle, questioning, somewhat puzzled. He gazed deeply into her eyes, as though he was searching for something inside her very soul.

Dorothy was flooded with sadness. They knew so little of each other. How could any man and woman hope to know each other?

DOROTHY AND BERTIE made love many more times, but it was no better. It didn't hurt anymore, but always Dorothy found her mind disengaging itself. It seemed to hover in the air above them, observing, weirdly dislocated from the actions of their bodies.

She was fully conscious of her failure, for she knew how badly Bertie craved perfect physical relations with a woman whose mind was in tune with his. Her lack of sensual response must have been a bitter blow to him. But Bertie was kind and gentle, burying his disappointment deep. They never spoke of it.

She, too, was disappointed by this side of their life. It was uncomfortable in every sense. She wanted to join his transports, and her inability to do so made her feel lonely and left behind. At the same time, she disliked the way he lost himself, turning into a creature of instinctual, unconscious hunger. There was a blind, rooting quality about him that reminded her of a baby, fastened to its mother's breast.

Her disappointment was compounded by an acute sense of isolation. There was no one she could share her feelings with, nor talk to about the love affair. Her sisters, scattered all over England and living in a different universe, would be shocked and upset. They had been through enough with their mother without Dorothy causing additional grief. Her London friends were too new to trust with such a secret. Ironically, she felt the one person who would have understood was Jane.

When Jane and Bertie met, he was married to his cousin Isabel, a dark-haired girl with a grave and beautifully shaped face and a slim, graceful body. Bertie was profoundly attracted to Isabel, yet the marriage was not a success. Isabel was naive, unperceptive, frigid or shy in bed, and totally lacking in ambition. She was ill equipped to deal with Bertie's imagination, his aspirations, or his moods of searing dissatisfaction with life. Amy Catherine was a student in his science class at the University Tutorial College. Disappointment with his marriage made Bertie vulnerable to what he felt he was missing, and the attraction between them developed quickly. Amy Catherine was witty, intelligent, educated, and beautiful. She shared Bertie's intellectual curiosity, encouraged his literary ambitions, and reciprocated his growing feelings for her. It was a terrible dilemma. Bertie eventually left Isabel and went to live in lodgings with Amy. When his divorce came through, they married. Dorothy had heard only the bare outlines of the story, but she realized there were enough parallels between their situations for Jane to know exactly how Dorothy was feeling.

Dorothy's isolation was made worse because of Bertie's aversion to being seen with her in public. "It's an unstated law of public life that an open scandal kills a career," he explained. "My publisher would drop me like a hot potato. Society penalizes people who abandon duty for love. Power, influence, and authority belong mainly to men with blameless lives, men who have never tasted passion."

SOMETIMES, THE OLD magic returned.

He took her to the theater. She borrowed a midnight-blue cloak from her sister and spent an entire week's salary on an evening blouse. But it was worth not having the money for food when she saw him responding: drawing himself upright, smiling back at her, his grey-blue eyes dark with longing. "You're a lovely sight in midnight blue. You are always pretty. But tonight . . . tonight, you're dazzling."

It began as the sort of night that lived forever, arrested in time. The glancing gleaming light inside the hansom cab as they hurried down dark empty roads, not talking much, listening to the leathery rattle and jingle of the harness, the clop of horses' hooves, the slur of wheels; the smell of horse and leather mingling headily with Bertie's cologne. He was spruce in evening dress, his warm body pressed against hers, his arm securely around her, cushioning the jolts. She leaned her head against the curve of his shoulder; it was a point of perfect rest and contentment. Presently, they reached gold-lamped streets that seemed to be full of other hansoms carrying dinner and theater people in evening dress, all talking and laughing.

The cab dropped them in front of the wide light-spangled front of the theater. Bertie paid, leaving a tip that made the driver smile and say "God bless you, sir, and your pretty missus."

They found themselves caught up in the crowd of people flowing inside the building. The men looked distinguished; the women were like so many gorgeous birds in their richly colored gowns. They possessed an easy confidence that came of having enough good nourishing food and freedom from fatigue and anxiety. They seemed to float in a private atmosphere of privilege.

Bertie and Dorothy sat discreetly hidden in a box at the very top of the building. The orchestra began to play and the lights dimmed. The curtain rose with a smooth swish, revealing the lit battlements of Castle Elsinore. Soldiers on their watch were speaking in hushed tones about the ghost they had seen, and Dorothy was transported into another world.

She glanced at Bertie. His face, shadowy in the half light, looked perfectly contented. He was at ease; this evening in town was his time off. It was a break from the long, isolated hours spent at his desk, striving to achieve, compelling himself on to ever greater endeavors. It was a break, too, from Jane, who had long ago ceased to be his lover, and had transformed herself seamlessly into the custodian of his well-being.

"What are you thinking?" he whispered, taking her hand.

"*Hamlet* is wonderful. I never realized it was so full of quotations."

He laughed, but gently.

During the interval, a waiter brought a bottle of champagne to their box. Bertie picked up a dish of almonds and offered it to her. "Well, what have you been doing since I last saw you?"

"Oh, just drifting along."

He took a handful of nuts and crunched them loudly. "You know, I can't help feeling you could do more with yourself. You're highly intelligent and energetic, yet most of your capabilities are unused."

"I'm happy the way I am. Free to dip in and out of societies and lectures whenever I want; be it socialists, anarchists, Tolstoyans . . ."

"What has it taught you?"

"I've realized, in the midst of my admiration and interest, that there's something missing in all of them. Though I did go to something the other day that felt like a homecoming."

She told him about the Quaker meeting, in a tiny hall above the cramped old shops of St. Martin's Lane. She described the congregation, who were surprisingly young and modern, and the way her initial horror that men and women were seated separately had given way to excited astonishment at the alive, positive quality of their silences, from which everything fell into proportion and clear focus. It was a revitalizing atmosphere that existed in reference to a higher presence, yet was unlike anything she had ever met in church.

"You ought to be a journalist, Dora. Your lifestyle provides masses of material, and you have a real gift for creating sketches that's wasted on Harley Street. Granted it would be a risk to chuck in your job, but you have courage in heaps. Most women would have been ground under by the life you've led, but you rise above it all, quite unravaged. You've managed to retain a wonderfully open quality; there's not a trace of bitterness about you. I admire that."

"I don't want to chuck in my job. It suits me precisely because it leaves my mind untouched to explore other worlds. At the end of the day, I walk away and work simply scrolls up and vanishes. Anything with more responsibility would mold and brand me; it would take away something vital. That's one reason I can't be a journalist."

"What's the other?"

"I loathe taking sides."

"Well, you'll have to take a stand in the end. All that promise and potential must attach itself to something worthwhile, or it will fizzle out. You're wasting your life."

"How can one waste life?"

"Drifting isn't living life to the full."

"On the contrary. Most people are so busy striving to become, they have no time for reflection and solitude. They lose their essential core."

"Life, if we're to achieve *anything*, Dora, doesn't allow for in-depth explorations of each other's souls. We can't just sit around, wallowing in feelings. We're constantly moving, we've got to keep moving, or things will crumble; they'll slide away from us."

Dorothy hesitated, biting her lip. There was no way of getting him to acknowledge the individual reality that lay deep within; he was not in the least bit interested. It ran contrary to everything he stood for. She could feel all the unexpressed things surrounding her mockingly. It seemed there was always some unexpressed thing between them, some barrier to communication. So much time was spent trying to meet him on his terms, in a world shaped by his scientific way of thinking.

She sipped her champagne. She had hardly eaten anything during the day, and she could feel the alcohol leaping to her head and coursing through her bloodstream, spreading warm silky fingers.

"You've had no end of a good time in London," Bertie was saying. "It's been a terrific adventure. But if you're not careful, it'll end up grinding you down. You want a bucolic existence. A baby. Then you'd be able to settle down and write . . ."

As he talked, Dorothy found herself looking at the inward picture conjured by his words. Leafy woodlands, shimmering and rustling softly in the wind, all dappled light and shadow. Green open country, untrammelled and empty beneath soft grey skies; the fresh raw smell of mingled earth and rain; a little house with a garden . . . The perfection of the vision was marred only by Bertie's desire to try to shape her.

She found herself yielding to his spell. She began to listen to the tones of his voice, rather than his words, to its high huskiness and all the small creaks and intonations. She became caught up in it, surrendering to champagne and the undeclared promise in what he was saying. His voice was like the texture of his skin . . . at that moment, it seemed more intimate to be listening to him than touching him.

"You're very quiet," he said at last.

"Do you mind?"

He picked up her hand and kissed the soft skin on the inside of her wrist. "A fellow would always rather be listened to than talked at."

Afterward, they stood outside her boardinghouse, holding hands like a couple of young sweethearts who couldn't bear to part (she didn't care who saw them; she was shameless). He had promised Jane he would be home that evening.

"Good night, my love."

"Good night."

"Sleep well."

Their hand slid apart; only their fingertips were touching.

"I'll write to you tomorrow. No, I'll write on the train home tonight."

"Will you? I'd like that."

"I must go now," he said.

He took a few steps away from her. Dorothy could still feel the tingling warmth of his fingers on her skin.

"Goodnight," Bertie said again. He raised his hand in a half-wave; then turned and started walking toward the station, back to his home and Jane.

As Dorothy let herself into the unlit house, she realized he hadn't fixed a time for their next meeting. The thought punctured her happiness abruptly, cutting her adrift. She saw afresh how precarious their love was, how clandestine and duplicitous. It was bitter as ashes.

The hall was silent and full of shadows; the dim staircase disappeared up into darkness. She untied the midnight blue cloak, slipped it off her shoulders, and began to trudge up the stairs with it over her arm.

She noticed a rip in the delicate fabric of her new blouse. Damn! She hadn't realized it would tear so easily. What on earth had possessed her to buy it?

She had wanted to dazzle Bertie with the blouse. More than that, she'd cherished a secret fantasy (no use denying it) of toppling the fragile balance of their arrangement. It was amazing what power she'd attributed to a piece of silk. She had hoped to turn Bertie's head, to bring his barriers crashing down, to have him helplessly promising . . . promising what exactly? To leave Jane, to love Dorothy eternally, to be lost without her? She wasn't quite sure what she'd hoped for, but she did know her lack of control over their situation was galling. She hated the gaps between meetings, spent waiting for him to be free. Well, the blouse hadn't worked any magic. Faced with a week of going hungry, it seemed a stupid and ruinous extravagance.

By the time she reached her attic, she felt exhausted and convinced of her unworthiness to lay claim to any significant part of Bertie's life. He had such a profusion of interests: they seemed to float, vivid and alluring, just out of her reach. What could she possibly offer to match them? Only her unconnected dissenting self, poor in every sense of the word, peculiar and unworthy . . .

Perhaps it would be better to give him up entirely than to

have such a meager share of him. The joy of his company was virtually extinguished by the uncertainty and the dislocating wrench of parting.

THE ENCHANTED TIMES came around less and less often. Sometimes, they had dinner at a quiet restaurant in Bloomsbury where he was not likely to be recognized. But increasingly, Bertie preferred Dorothy to buy food and they would eat it in their room, not venturing outside together at all.

For the relationship to continue, she had to surrender to these limitations. She had to accept that only a fraction of his attention was hers. He was given to periods of intense work lasting for many days and nights, which were followed by moods of irritability and depression if the writing went badly. He and Dorothy were together when he could leave his work and Jane, not when it suited Dorothy. On more than one occasion, he came to London at short notice, and she had to disrupt her plans to see other people.

She faced the fact that Bertie would never leave Jane. Her feelings about Jane fluctuated wildly between remorse and bitter envy. Like one's tongue helplessly seeking out a sore place in the mouth, she couldn't stop thinking about them together. Did Bertie look at Jane with that focused gleam in his eyes; was he touching her, asking what she was thinking? She felt haunted by Jane: her old friend had become her nemesis, her living ghost.

At times, Dorothy's jealousy goaded her into making cruel remarks.

"It's unnatural to be this tolerant," she grumbled one day.

"Jane must be made of ice water, not blood and nerves and guts. I mean, she must suspect *something*; you're never at home."

Bertie's eyes were dark, the grey and blue fused by anger. "I won't listen to this," he said tightly. "Jane's the most loyal wife and friend I could hope for."

"Any woman with an ounce of spirit would challenge you. If it were me, I'd be making the most awful scene. In fact, I'd probably get revenge by taking a lover of my own."

"Will you stop this perpetual sniping? It isn't part of our pact."

Dorothy fell into a sulky silence, beneath which she was churning. Lashing out at the constant inescapable presence of Jane was like striking with your bare hands at something as fixed and enduring as a marble statue. It was utterly ineffective and it hurt Dorothy more than it hurt Jane.

She was not even sure if she wanted Bertie to leave Jane. She could never manage Jane's role. She couldn't run his house and navigate his moods and make a haven for his creative life; she had no interest in doing so. If Bertie divorced Jane and married Dorothy, they would have a terrible time. Displaced from his cozy and secure life, Bertie's feelings of guilt would destabilize him. He would not be able to carry on.

She was beginning to understand that although Jane's position must at times have felt unbearable, it was utterly secure.

A BAD ATTACK of neuralgia brought home to Dorothy how unsatisfactory it all was. For three days, she was confined to her bed in a darkened room. Every movement sent a jagged pain through her head, so piercing it felt as if her brain was going to shatter. Burning chills coursed through her body. The sounds of London traffic from outside were magnified; they grated unbearably on her ears. Despite her increasingly desperate requests, Bertie couldn't get to London to see her.

The troubled darkness, which had been banished by Bertie's nearness, returned with an intensity that almost unhinged her. As she lay in a stupor that stubbornly refused to turn into sleep, trapped and enduring, she found herself plunged back into a chaotic void, where everything in the world seemed hostile and useless. She was tortured by memories of the past and goaded to the limits of endurance by the grime and uncertainty of the present. Her life appeared in a bleak relentless light: she was poor and isolated, hovering permanently on the brink of catastrophe, without security or prospects. A combination of hard work and insufficient nourishment was destroying her strength. If she wasn't fit to earn a living, what would become of her?

For the first time, she regretted losing Dr. Weber and the shelter and security he offered. If it wasn't for Bertie, she might be married by now and living in a home of her own, unscathed by poverty and uncertainty.

She was frightened, lonely, and angry with Bertie. She hadn't been through so much, nor won her hard-earned independence to be subject to a man who offered so little of himself in return. Her pride and independence—the very traits he had fallen in love with—rebelled against the situation.

He came a few days later with armfuls of flowers, a bottle of sweet wine, and tasty delicacies to build up her strength. He was full of contrition and more loving than he'd ever been. She lay with her head in his lap, inhaling his honeyed smell, while he massaged her temples and called her his true love. His high, husky voice enfolded her, his dark-ringed blue eyes looked down on her tenderly.

Nothing was more glorious than being in the full glow of his attention.

ON HER NEXT visit to the Wellses, Dorothy found Jane in the drawing room with a guest. As she hovered at the doorway, she remembered Jane had mentioned in a letter that a friend's daughter was coming for lunch.

"Hello, Dora dear," Jane exclaimed, getting to her feet and drawing Dorothy into the room. "How lovely to see you. I hope you had an easy journey?"

Dorothy said it had passed uneventfully.

"Dorothy, I'd like you to meet Anne. Her father and Bertie have known one another since Bertie was a struggling teacher; they used to work at the same school. Anne, this is Dorothy. She's an old friend, too, you know. We were at school together."

The girl stood up and Dorothy held out her hand, fighting to keep the dismay from her face. The presence of an extra person was a hindrance; there would be less of Bertie's attention to go around. "It's a pleasure to meet you," she said.

Anne took her hand shyly. "I'm glad to meet you, too." She was very young; she could scarcely have been more than eighteen. She had a dreaming face upon which the soft contours of childhood were still imprinted, hazel eyes and thick brown hair.

"Where is Bertie?" Dorothy asked Jane.

"Just finishing work. He'll be here in a minute."

No sooner had she spoken than Bertie came bounding in, his energy lighting up the room. He greeted Dorothy affectionately and turned to Anne, looking her up and down.

"Why, the last time I saw you, you were in pigtails," he said, sounding surprised. "You've grown into a lovely young woman." The little creak in his voice meant he was anticipating pleasure. The sound of it caused Dorothy a pang; previously, it had been there for her alone.

Anne blushed deeply and thanked him.

"I'm sorry to rush you, but I think we'd better eat," Jane said, in her bright bustling way. "Lunch has been ready this past half hour; it's going to spoil."

Dorothy felt a flash of irritation with Jane for her unfailing cheeriness, for keeping everything going, as usual. Contrition followed almost immediately. She seemed to have no control over her emotions, they ricocheted all over the place, destabilizing her.

"Come and share the feast with us," Bertie said to Anne. He gave her his arm as they walked into the dining room, and pulled out a chair for her at the table. "How about a bit of chicken?"

He carved chicken and dished up salad and new potatoes from the sideboard; he insisted on serving her himself. "Have a biscuit and butter, Anne? No? Another glass of wine?" He sat down next to her and busied himself with his lunch.

"Now my dear, how's your father?" he asked. "I want to hear all the news; you must tell me everything you've been up to at home. What are your interests these days? Do you read? Which are your favorite authors? How old are you? Do you like salad?" He scarcely gave Anne time to reply, often starting the next question while she was still talking.

She spoke thoughtfully and intelligently, in a soft hesitant voice. She had just read his *Sea Lady*, she told him. She'd delighted in his tale of a man who falls in love with a woman he rescues from drowning, only to discover she is a mermaid. She found it whimsical and pertinent and marvelous.

There was nothing arch in the way Anne flattered Bertie; she was simple and heartfelt, speaking to him like a sort of jolly boy, man to man. Yet she was graceful in a way no boy could have been, and she wore silver earrings that danced in time to every movement she made.

"Mother said she always thought you had it in you to succeed," she went on, shyly, "even when you were teaching with Daddy. She said you were so focused and full of energy, yet you had a kind of faraway gleam in your eye . . . it made me think of what your Sea Lady says in the book: 'Perhaps there are better dreams . . .'"

Bertie gave Anne a swift look. "Oh, my dear! Coming from your young lips, that's awfully sweet to hear."

Dorothy and Jane ate and listened. Dorothy, cutting up food that she could hardly swallow, hated herself for being dingy and dull. She could feel herself grow paler and paler; reduced to a nonentity. The beginning of a headache was creeping up the base of her skull. She must be looking dreadfully plain. Bertie occasionally addressed a remark to her or Jane, but he was almost entirely focused on Anne.

After lunch, they played tennis. The glorious spring had given way to a disappointing summer, grey and cool. It was perfect weather for sport.

It was a relief for Dorothy to lose herself in the game. There was only the sea air flowing around her and the feeling of the ball in her hand. She tossed the ball into the air, feeling her whole body turn into a tightly drawn missile as she slammed down with her racquet. The ball skimmed low over the net and bounced just out of Bertie's reach.

"Miss Richardson serves from the treetops and my wife returns from the heavens. Together they're unbeatable!"

It was pure happiness. It took her back to her old life, before the money worries began. She felt herself young and carefree, transported to a sunlit era of tennis parties with her sisters and their friends, sandwiches and enormous jugs of lemonade afterward, and the exhilaration that came with simple physical exertion.

Bertie was in a terrifically good mood. He played with great energy and almost no style, hitting the ball hard and managing to rush all over the court and maintain his witty commentary at the same time.

When the game was over, they went for a walk around the garden. Bertie took Anne's arm and gave her a guided tour, leaving Jane and Dorothy to follow. Bizarrely, Dorothy felt closer to Jane than she had for some time. The shared experience of failing to hold Bertie drew them together.

A storm was brewing. The low-hung sky cast a greenish light upon the landscape; a hazy unearthly glare. The trees seemed obscured, yet they loomed, huge and permanent; the densely lined evergreens glowed through the mist. Clouds of midges danced in air that had turned heavy and motionless. The sea hissed and roared emptily in the background; a hard flat grey glimmer, dissolving invisibly into the sky. Gulls hovered over the water, crying hoarsely.

Dorothy found herself longing for rain, for the sudden multitudinous thudding of drops against her face and dress which would break up the afternoon. It was like being in a vacuum, without oxygen. She felt breathless, unbearably hemmed in.

Anne bent over to admire Jane's roses, now in their full glory. The sun was struggling to break through a thinning bank of cloud. The garden had turned lurid grey, incandescent with masked sunlight. The clouds parted suddenly and unveiled light fell full on Anne's face, just as she stood upright. Setting her hair aglow, it framed her in a fiery halo. Bertie was openly staring, every fiber of him fixed in motionless concentration, his eyes narrowed to practically invisible points.

He was lost to Dorothy. He had turned into a stranger.

Dorothy's entire body throbbed with tension. She told herself it meant nothing, that an appreciation of pretty girls was an integral part of Bertie's character. Besides, Anne was scarcely more than a child. He would never take her up, pursuing her as he'd pursued Dorothy. Or would he? How well did she really know him? He had broken his marriage vows once; he was capable of doing it again.

The thought was unbearable. Don't let me break down and blurt out something that will smash everything, she prayed. Jane must live with this tension, this pressure to keep things going, all the time. How does she maintain her facade of calm humor? How does she manage to prevent an explosion?

Dorothy felt something must give. Murderous feelings surged inside her. She craved pain, she wanted blood to stream from shredded skin. She could have stabbed all three of them and turned the knife on herself.

The rain started after Anne left, slowly at first, but gaining power and momentum, until large drops were plocking onto the roof and rattling against the landing skylight. Wet trees sighed and rustled in the wind. The maids lit the lamps early; the summer afternoon was all but extinguished by the downpour.

Bertie was in high spirits. "I feel like a new man!" he exclaimed. "Young girls have a marvelous quality; they seem to hold the essence of life in their hands. When Anne looked at me with that slow hazel-eyed smile . . . well, I would have turned the world upside down for her."

Jane shrugged her shoulders and smiled. She was indulgent with him, as one might be with a small child. Her smile seemed to say, "What will this extraordinary man of mine do or say next?"

Dorothy was overcome by jealous misery that sent her into a horrible torpor. She took a book from the shelf, but she was unable to absorb a single word of it. The furniture in the darkening room and the figures of Jane and Bertie seemed a great distance away. She couldn't respond to either of them, but Bertie hardly seemed to notice.

She was made still more wretched and confused by her own guilt. What right had she to feel upset by Bertie's reaction to a pretty girl? This was exactly how Jane must have felt when Dorothy first came to stay.

Eleven

MRS. BAKER'S PIANO SMELT MUSTY. THE KEYS WERE loose and discolored by age, but they were miraculously in tune. The last movement of Beethoven's Pathetique Sonata rang out into the stillness of the drawing room: urgent, stormy, and grand. The crash and vibration of the chords was satisfying; it released the pent-up emotions of the past few days and carried her out of herself. Dorothy hadn't played since her school days; she was relieved to find her hands still remembered the notes. She resolved to spend more time at the piano.

Through the music, she heard the sound of the door being softly opened. She carried on as someone glided lightly into the room; one of the boarders, or perhaps Carrie, now hidden in a chair. When she came to the end of the piece, they would get to their feet and thank her and say how much they loved the piano.

It was with a sense of inevitability that she recognized Veronica sitting on the floor beside her, with her skirt draped gracefully over her feet and her chin cupped in her hands. Again, she seemed conscious of the impact her beauty made, and also, in clear daylight, presenting it as something to be evaluated, like a painting, impersonally, for its own sake.

The sonata faltered and came to a halt.

"I am interrupting you," Veronica said, not sounding in the least bit sorry. With a rapid movement, she was on her feet, her face tilted toward the light streaming through the window, standing immobile as Dorothy looked at her.

"I used to be prettier, before Paul and I broke up." Veronica paused, a little pleat appearing between her eyebrows. "I met him in Paris. It was a *coup de foudre*; I knew the moment I saw him. Have you ever felt that way? Like you belong to the other person? I gave myself to him, body and soul. But it was doomed from the start . . . he was engaged to someone else."

Dorothy hesitated, unsure how to respond to this impossible confession that was also a demand for intimacy. She resented the demand, placed so prematurely on their friendship, while admiring the courage it must have taken to make it.

Veronica said "It wrecks the quality of the skin. It is never again quite as clear and fresh."

There was another pause.

Veronica said at last, "Does it change your opinion of me? Are you shocked?"

"No," Dorothy said slowly. "Not in the slightest."

The story of Veronica's love affair was perhaps not so different from hers with Bertie. If only Veronica knew. Dorothy fought back a desire to reveal everything.

"Are you sure?" Veronica queried. "You must be a bit shocked. The other women in the house would be. They are virtuous; it builds a brick wall between us. One can't say these things to an Englishwoman."

"You've said them to me."

A swift secret amusement shone from Veronica's face, making her lips quiver. Her expression became inward-turning, as if some private hope or suspicion was being proven.

"Yes, you are English," she remarked thoughtfully, "yet you are un-English as well. I saw that as soon as we met."

She paused, holding Dorothy with her eyes. Again, Dorothy felt a strange, alarming demand being placed on her, amounting almost to an invasion.

Veronica lowered her gaze; the thick eyelashes fluttering onto her cheek. Her eyes came up again and met Dorothy's. "I nearly forgot why I came in. I would like to invite you to a picnic."

"That sounds lovely, but isn't it a little cool for the park?"

"We'll picnic indoors. In my room, next Saturday. Just you and me. We'll be able to talk without interruption. Please say you can come."

BERTIE WAS WORRIED about his work. A novel was on the cusp of being published, and he was anxious about its reception. He felt his publisher wasn't putting enough "go" into his books.

"I can predict it all," he said gloomily. "The glimmer of interest, the faint stirring of publicity, the flop, the flop." His words were humorous, the emotion behind them was not.

He and Dorothy were lying on the bed in Russell Square. The sheets were in disarray, half coming off the mattress. Bertie lit a cigarette.

"My writing just isn't good enough," he went on, drawing smoke deeply into his lungs. "I feel like I'm always trying to catch hold of something, but I can never get it properly said."

"That isn't true. I mean, it's not you. You're better at expressing yourself than anyone I know. It's words. Nothing real can be expressed in words."

He expelled smoke forcefully through his nostrils. "That doesn't help much, Dora. Words are all we writers have."

She gave him a wry smile. "Yes, I do realize that."

There was a pause. The smell of smoke combined, not unpleasantly, with his sweat. Dorothy was mesmerized by the bulge his lips made as they pulled on the cigarette, the feral gleam of teeth below the straggly mustache. They repelled her faintly, yet they were part of the magnetism of his smile. And they were continually redeemed by the charm of the way he put things, by the powerful appeal of the intense, lightning-swift eyes.

"You know what scares me more than anything?" he asked at last, leaning over to tap a long column of ash into a saucer that lay next to the bed.

"No, what?"

"My peak is over. I've reached my peak and I've produced nothing at all that will stand the test of time . . . nothing good enough to leave a lasting imprint after I die."

"That's not true. If there's one thing I am sure of, it's that your writing will stand the test of time."

"I don't think so. I'm yesterday's news."

Dorothy tried her best to reassure him, but it made no difference. His insecurity was like a bottomless pit; however many words she threw into it, she couldn't plug it. She was dismayed to see him like this: as inadequate and helpless as any other human being. Usually, his intellect and his certainties made him seem invulnerable.

He mashed out the cigarette and put his head on her breasts. "Having you around is no end of a comfort," he murmured, his mustache tickling her skin. "Stay with me, Dora. Don't ever leave."

"I'm not going anywhere."

"You hold me up. You're the only thing standing between me and a smash." He dropped a kiss on her neck. "I need you. If I don't watch out, I'll get to the stage where I can't write without you."

"What nonsense," she murmured, secretly delighted.

"I'm glad I showed you those passages. You really pulled them together. You've got good style, a clear mind, and a lethal critical eye . . . I feel like this book's our baby."

He began idly caressing one nipple between his thumb and forefinger, creating sensations in her which were half pleasurable, half painful.

"How can it be our baby when you won't show me the whole of it?" she grumbled.

His hand paused. "I'm afraid it wouldn't come off if you saw it before it was ready . . . Call it a writer's superstition, if you like."

"Do you show Jane your work?" It was impossible to keep the jealousy from her voice.

"Yes, I do. She's quite helpful with the punctuation and grammar, but she doesn't have your grasp of language."

Dorothy was mollified. The thrill of reading the rich layers of manuscript while it was still in embryonic form, knowing he was waiting eagerly for her comments, had been no small compensation for the ups and downs of their shared life. The process of editing was a surprising joy. From a blank mind, the right words miraculously appeared and stated themselves. Instinctively, she found better ways of phrasing certain passages. She knew how to give shape to whole sections, knew where elaboration was needed, where to tighten or clarify. She had been able to express her suggestions tactfully enough that he'd accepted them with gratitude. It was a privilege to be part of the process: witness and helpmate in his achievement.

Bertie was getting hard again. He turned toward her, pressing himself against her; there was something blindly beseeching about the way he did it. The immortal author was exactly like a small boy begging for a treat, she thought, suppressing a smile.

"When are you going to write something, Dora?" His voice was growing thick. "You're lucky to have a fount of quirky and interesting experience to draw on. You should write it up. I keep telling you."

She pulled away from him and sat upright. "Actually, I detest those written-up things. You know they're going to be false through and through. 'Mr. Meakins always wore his hat at a jaunty angle.' They're so contrived, they drive me crazy. It's the same thing that makes me dislike so many novels: the endless accumulation of external detail. Where's the life in it?

Reality isn't fixed; it's continual movement and fluctuation. I'd love to find a way of writing that captures it . . ."

"You could write the first dental novel," Bertie said, "or the confessions of a modern woman. Though perhaps you'd be better suited to journalism. The trouble with women novelists is they're only really good when writing about personal experiences. Falling in love, and so on. They aren't inventive."

"Ah, invention. Don't you mean half-truths . . . ? Unreliable."

If she could engage him in talk about books, perhaps she could avoid making love again. She didn't have the energy; she knew it would make her sore. She wished, for the hundredth time, that her body didn't shut down during sex. Holding his hand created such a poignant tingling all over, yet whenever they were naked together, it was as though a shutter slammed down, cutting off her senses. Why?

He put his hand between her legs; his fingers started creeping upward. She fought back a sigh. His insatiability was exhausting; they were both slaves to it. Was it a sign of his great need for her? Or was it—as she was coming to suspect—a more general need: the scratching of an overweening physical urge that also filled in the irksome gap between finishing his work and dinner. Necessary and reinvigorating for him, but anyone could provide it. Any woman's body would do.

VERONICA HAD ONE of the large high-ceilinged rooms on the first floor. Its dilapidated grandeur—the long French windows edged with dingy lace curtains, the dusty chandelier and the wide chipped marble fireplace—was barely noticeable beside the piles of clothes, hairbrushes, and cosmetics that lay strewn about. The eiderdown was bunched untidily on the bed and photographs of Veronica's family covered every available surface. The excessive detritus of femininity made Dorothy feel like a man.

They picnicked on the floor. Veronica had laid out a feast on fine Empire china: cheese, pâté, salad, bread still warm from the oven. A pyramid of blackberries glistened with dissolving sugar.

"Come and join me at my queenly table," she said, gesturing toward the faded rug. She sank to her knees, a graceful figure in a dusky-pink kimono with a string of chunky cream-colored beads around her neck. She handed Dorothy a plate. "You're to help yourself. I want you to feel quite at home."

Veronica ate with unselfconscious appetite, tearing bread and taking food with her hands. For Dorothy, food was usually an uninspiring necessity, tolerated to keep life going. But this meal had an unaccustomed savor: she felt almost intoxicated by the rich smells and flavors that nourished her senses as well as her body. Was the transformation Veronica's gift to her?

"This is heavenly, Veronica, and such fun. Everything tastes far more delicious than it would at a table."

"I am happy you like it. But you haven't tried the cheese. Have the brie, it's divine."

Veronica cut a piece for her. Ripe and creamy, oozing between her fingers as she held it out to Dorothy.

Dorothy took the cheese. "Did you guess why I wasn't shocked when you told me about Paul?"

Veronica was licking brie from her fingers; she turned eagerly toward this promising opening.

Dorothy lifted her eyebrows a little and paused, waiting for realization to fall. Veronica was looking thoughtful, the little curve of her chin drawn in. The sweetly rounded face dimpled and flushed; she raised her eyes gleefully to Dorothy's. "Don't tell me you are also seeing a man who is taken?" she exclaimed.

Dorothy made a wry face. "Yes, he's married."

They gazed at each other, mutely delighting in the shared experience.

"What is he like?" Veronica asked, at last.

Dorothy hesitated before the impossibility of conveying a fraction of Bertie's quality in words. "He's a writer."

"What's his name? Will I recognize it?"

"I expect so. He's quite well known."

Veronica said, "You are more than I thought you were . . . I can't express how happy I am to have found you."

"Me, too."

"I want to know all about the time you spend with him. Is it heaven on earth?"

"It's heaven and it's difficult . . ." Dorothy explained how she had to share Bertie with his wife and his work, and her uneasy sense that she was less important in his life than either of them. "There's another thing . . . in the beginning, I really felt he was my partner and my mate, but as time goes on, our needs and views seem more and more mismatched . . ."

"It's not unusual to feel like that, believe me. There's always a barrier between men and women. When the first rapture of being together passes, one is aware, somehow, of an obstruction, a difference . . . one realizes direct communication is impossible; the two sexes can never meet. I was always uneasy, even when blissfully happy with Paul. I remember being entertaining and charming with him; to all appearances, being entertained and charmed in return. He thought that all my talk and flirting came naturally, and made me as happy as it made him. He had no idea of the struggle, the sheer exhausting effort of bending myself into his masculine way of thinking and staying there, even for a short while."

"That's how I feel; you sum it up exactly. It's such a relief to find someone with the same way of seeing things . . . it makes me feel that I can go on."

Veronica broke in, agreeing joyfully.

They fell silent, suddenly intensely aware of each other, but not awkward in the least. On the contrary, there was a strange powerful sense of unsaid things flowing between them.

Suddenly Dorothy exclaimed, without thinking, "This is the best day of my life," and bit her lip, feeling foolish. As Veronica hurried to throw her arms around her, Dorothy was back in the moment of being a small child standing between banks of flowers in the sunlight, feeling at one with the warm smells and the bees swaying drunkenly across the path in front of her. It was a moment of revelation, surprising and marvelous. In Veronica's company, Dorothy could feel the reality she had known for so long in solitude, coming out into life.

"What are you thinking?" Veronica asked, drawing back. "Has anyone ever told you that every single one of your thoughts shows on your face? It's really very appealing."

Dorothy told Veronica about the bee memory, and then somehow—she wasn't quite sure how it happened—the story of her pain-shadowed family life came pouring heedlessly out.

Veronica's small soft hand slid into Dorothy's while she talked. She listened in silence, her eyes welling up. The tears that trickled down her cheeks seemed to promise not only absolution, but that Dorothy would never again have to bear the bitterness of her grief and guilt alone.

BERTIE GAVE DOROTHY a proof copy of the new book. She stayed up the whole night to read it, warm in her flannelette dressing gown, her eyes strained by the insufficient gaslight.

The heroine was an intelligent girl, brought up by a limited and unimaginative father to be a "young lady" in the suburbs, which were still ruled by Victorian assumptions. Stifled, she ran away to find freedom in London, where a number of landladies mistook her for a prostitute, and she struggled to find secretarial work. The only person who offered tangible help was the one she understood least: a prosperous older man, whose protuberant eyes indicated clearly to the reader his motivation in being kind to her. Eventually, her father reluctantly allowed her to study biology at a woman's college. She fell passionately in love with her married science teacher, and didn't even wait for his divorce before living with him. Her sensuality was portrayed as natural and welcome; their triumphant attraction more important than social convention or economic consideration.

It unmistakably mirrored Bertie's early life with Jane. Dorothy, reading with a mixture of enjoyment and pain, thought there was something of herself in the heroine as well. Though Dorothy was a less enthusiastic lover, she found distinct echoes of her London life and her conversations with Bertie in the book. No wonder he hadn't wanted her to see it before it was printed. He had shamelessly taken material from his own life, modified it a little—presenting himself in the best possible light—and retold it. There was something underhanded about it; a cheap trick. His readers, not realizing he had stolen his characters from life, erroneously believed him a creative artist.

She felt exposed and raw, as though a layer of skin had been peeled away. She realized that if you shared the life of a writer, it would be naive not to expect parts of that life to appear in his work. She tried to tell herself not to feel surprised or betrayed, but being defenselessly fished up and put into a book was a shock nothing had prepared her for.

IN THE RELATIVELY small orbit of London journalism, there were already whispers about H. G. Wells and women. When the novel came out, the heroine's open admission of desire for a married man created tremors of shock. Critics pounced on it and tore it apart as immoral. An article in *The Spectator* by St. Loe Strachey, its influential editor, was especially wounding. It claimed that Bertie was a danger to society:

> *The loathing and indignation which the book inspires in us are due to the effect it is likely to have in undermining that sense of continence and self-control in the individual which is essential in a sound and healthy State. It teaches,*

in effect, that there is no such thing as woman's honour, or if there is, it is only to be a bulwark against a weak temptation . . . If an animal yearning or lust is only sufficiently absorbing, it is to be obeyed. Self-sacrifice is a dream and self-restraint a delusion. Such things have no place in the muddy world of Mr. Wells's imaginings. His is a community of scuffling stoats and ferrets, unenlightened by a ray of duty or abnegation.

Bertie, showing the article to Dorothy, admitted he didn't know whether to laugh or weep. He shrugged his shoulders hopelessly. "This outcry could wreck my career. Can't they see that my books hold important and honest principles? Must they distort everything with their false morality? It's obvious that women will produce sturdy children only if they are free to choose the mates they desire."

He got to his feet and began to pace up and down the room. "I'm going to write a defence in *The Spectator* saying as much. Sexual desire should be celebrated because it leads to the right breeding partner. It's biologically beneficial to the human race!"

BEFORE BERTIE HAD a chance to finish writing his defense, the correspondence columns of *The Spectator* exploded into assault, and condemnation of Bertie's "poisonous" book was unanimously voiced from church pulpits. Many libraries refused to keep copies.

Despite his initial defiance, Bertie fell into a depression, a sort of death of the imagination, where he found himself discouraged, misunderstood, and adrift. He looked at his life in a bleak, harsh light: it seemed a catalog of bad judgments, coarse gaffes, and dishonorable behavior.

"Despair is always close to me," he confided to Dorothy. "In my worst hours, it's as close as a black tidal wave bearing down on an unsuspecting beach walker. Right now, I'm almost swallowed up by it."

They were silent for a long time, sitting side by side on the faded sofa in Russell Square. It was a crisp, clear day. There was a subtle change in the light streaming through the large bay windows: it was losing the melted butter quality of summer and becoming whiter, harder. A melancholy unease settled over Dorothy, fine and sad as dust. She took Bertie's hand. It lay inert in hers, unresponsive to her touch.

The shabbiness of the room had at first been charming; redeemed by high ceilings, a fine carved marble mantelpiece and elegantly molded cornicing. Now, the peeling wallpaper, the dim-globed chandelier, and the faint but unmistakable smell of mildew seemed only squalid. Dorothy longed to be outside, walking the streets of her beloved London. But Bertie refused to go out. He wouldn't eat. For the first time since Dorothy had known him, he didn't want to make love.

"My life's a mess" he said, in a low voice. "My work is a failure; I'm not producing the caliber of book I want . . . I'm cruel to the people I love best."

Dorothy shivered. "That's not true."

"I'm cruel to Jane. She tries to hide her loneliness and depression, but I know perfectly well how she feels." He turned to look at Dorothy. "I'm not being fair to you either. You ought to have a husband and a houseful of apple-cheeked children. You'd have splendid children . . . I'm torn between you and Jane. I don't give either of you what you need or deserve."

For a moment, Dorothy imagined herself married to a respectable man and free of Bertie. Free of passion, free to rest . . . "I'm quite sure I shall never get married," she said softly.

She got to her feet and drifted helplessly to the large window, which was edged with grimy lace curtains. She stood silently looking at the square. The dusty leaves of the trees were beginning to turn; there was a light scattering of crispy leaves on the ground. Dorothy found herself longing for the serenity of autumn, for the softness of morning mists and leaves in varying hues of gold and brown, for damp dull grass and the smell of smoke from a bonfire . . . She yearned for the first astringent breath of cold in the air, diluting the sensuality of late summer, soothing her troubled heart.

Bertie's despair frightened her. In the stale air of the room, it felt heavy and palpable. It closed in on her, making her nauseous. She no longer had the resilience to manage; she was tired and spent. She found herself almost wishing that Jane was present. With her tart humor and admirable tact, Jane would know how to handle him.

"I disgust myself," he went on. "I'm vain and feeble; my ambitions are no more than extravagant, futile pretensions. I've lost my grip on life."

Dorothy reluctantly turned away from the window to face him. "Why don't you start writing a new book?" she suggested. "In the past, you've been able to get the better of these unhappy feelings by working."

"I'm too drained to write. I have nothing to sustain me, no

incentive to action. I am so fed up with everything, I can hardly bear it."

The room was close with gas. He stood up and began to pace around it; he was incapable of sitting still.

As the long evening wore on, his restlessness drove him into a near panic. He couldn't eat the dinner Dorothy had prepared, and he couldn't sleep. He was like a prisoner in the small space.

In the early hours, he started to talk about a trip abroad. "It's my damned fugitive impulse. I thought that meeting you had conquered it, but it seems nothing and no one can. It's an inescapable part of me, I fear."

"Perhaps you need a holiday."

"You're right, I'd like to get away from England. Time's running to waste. Life is passing me by and I'm not writing the books I should be. I'm afraid I'll never get the things I want to say properly said."

"You have an unequaled gift for expression."

"Bless you, Dora, for believing in me. But this time, it's not enough to stop me falling. I have to get away and rethink my life. I feel suffocated, trapped in a morass of dulled response. I must have the distraction of new places and experiences, or I shall wither away."

Dorothy got out of bed.

"What is it?" he asked impatiently.

She was searching for something in the cupboard. She brought out a large enamel bowl, her hands were trembling. She placed it hurriedly on the floor, knelt over it and began to retch.

Twelve

BERTIE WANTED HIS OPINIONS TO REACH AS MANY people as possible, and he was chronically short of funds: as well as maintaining his home with Jane, he supported his parents and supplied Isabel with a small income. As a result, he accepted too much newspaper and magazine work.

The strain was immense. Neither his personal life nor his work had a stable core. Both his articles and his novels were deteriorating in quality, as he began rehashing old arguments in them. This was unsurprising considering the amount of work he took on, and his unsettled lifestyle, shuttling between two women. He moved restlessly from his house to Russell Square and back again, torn between the contrary imperatives of conscience and desire. A spell of unusually cold and rainy weather brought on another chest infection, and it took him a long time to recover. He was run down and often heart-rendingly overworked and exhausted. It was destroying his writing, and it made him short-tempered with everyone around him.

One evening, he appeared at Mrs. Baker's boardinghouse with a small suitcase. Dorothy and Veronica were having tea in Dorothy's room.

"I see I'm interrupting," Bertie said peevishly. He stood by the door, passing the case from one hand to the other.

"Why didn't you warn me you were coming?" Dorothy answered ungraciously. "I could have met you somewhere else; it's too risky coming here. Mrs. Baker must have been horrified."

"I can leave now, if you'd prefer."

"No, I'm sorry, I didn't mean it that way. You had better come in. Bertie Wells, meet Veronica Leslie Jones."

Veronica held out her hand, poised and elegant; she was not in the least perturbed by the unannounced arrival of a Great Man. Bertie put the suitcase down and moved across the room to take her hand in both of his. "So this is your Veronica," he said. "I've heard a great deal about you, my dear."

Veronica answered with pleasant little phrases about how glad she was to meet him. She was at once vivacious and engaging, in the way of someone doing their best to cover up a faux pas. Or perhaps, by hoisting a discreet flag above it, she was pointing to where it stood.

While Bertie settled himself in the most comfortable chair, Dorothy went downstairs to fetch more milk for their tea. By the time she returned, she saw he was restored to buoyant sociability.

"I agree with you!" Veronica was saying. She was sitting on

a stool at his feet; she appeared to have capitulated delightedly to his charm.

Bertie's eyes, which for the moment were entirely blue, roved around the room, taking in every detail. In the soft light, it looked less threadbare than usual, and Dorothy hoped its appeal wasn't lost on him. His eyes came back to rest on Veronica's face.

"So many young women," he said reflectively, "marching in a long ardent line, bringing London to its knees. Wonderful."

So they were talking about the suffrage. Dorothy wondered how much Veronica had told him about her passion for the campaign. Had she described going to suffrage meetings, being won over to militancy by Mrs. Despard, whose refined Victorian exterior, all muslin and old lace, concealed a will of steel? Perhaps she had told him her father was so enraged by her becoming a suffragette that he had cut off her allowance. She'd been forced to work as Mrs. Baker's skivvy from six in the morning to late at night, until her doting older brother stepped in and rescued her once more. She now existed, in the faded grandeur of her room, on almost nothing but bread and tea. It was a brave step for an indulged girl, who had never wanted for anything, and the experience was improving her; she had begun to drop some of her affectations.

"They won't all be young," Dorothy broke in. "There'll be middle-aged women and even grandmothers, like Mrs. Despard, marching and singing and waving flags together."

Bertie started to say something, but Dorothy cut across him. "Tell him about Mrs. Despard, Veronica."

Veronica described Mrs. Despard with reverent admiration, making them see her smooth white hair, frail spare figure and stately bearing, and the peculiar impression she conveyed of being more spirit than body. It was this spirit that drove her, in old age, to smash through the conventions of a lifetime and fight—violently if necessary—for the right to vote.

"I suppose the essence of suffragism was in me before I met Mrs. Despard," Veronica said thoughtfully. "She only crystallized ideas and feelings I'd had for as long as I could remember."

"Such as?"

Veronica paused, turning clear eyes on Bertie before answering: "When I was young, I used to stand at my bedroom window, watching my brothers playing in the grounds of our house. I was desperately jealous of their freedom. I burned to be like them; to romp and climb trees, unfettered by the constant deadening pressure to be ladylike. They were allowed to take hold of life in a way I couldn't. 'She should have been born a lad,' my father used to say, watching me sadly.

"As I got older, I became more and more aware of how differently boys and girls are educated. My parents thought about my brothers' schooling far more seriously than mine; I remember them discussing it for hours. But my education was scarcely considered. They seemed to feel the main purpose of sending me to school at all was so I'd learn how to make a pleasant and comfortable home for the men . . . I felt choked by the unfairness of it. I adored my father and brothers, but nobody ever suggested they make the house nice for me. I couldn't understand why there was one set of rules for boys and another for girls. When I asked my mother about it, I was instantly sent to bed for insolence. I never got a satisfactory answer."

The lamplight danced in Veronica's eyes while she spoke; it accentuated the liquid sheen of her hair. She cupped the flowerlike curve of her cheek in a slender hand. Bertie encouraged her with thoughtful comments and questions, and she answered him with patient smiling veneration.

Dorothy wondered, with a pang, if Bertie was as acutely conscious of Veronica's beauty as Dorothy was. How could he fail to be moved by it? A memory of the lunch with Anne entered her mind: Anne with sunlight streaming through her hair; Bertie transfixed, staring wordlessly. She had heard no more about the girl. But would she ever feel sure of Bertie? Could she, for that matter, feel sure of Veronica?

When Veronica fell silent, Bertie turned to Dorothy. "You haven't been persuaded to join the campaign?"

Dorothy shook her head. "I can see how important it is for women to have a political voice, because they have such utterly different views and needs to men. It's outrageous we are denied the vote, but I don't want one myself. No, I want to have a vote and not use it. Taking sides simply wipes me out."

Bertie clicked his tongue gently at this continuing evidence of her inability to take a stand. "Women are good reformers," he said. "They are admirably suited to keeping the peace and making the world a decent place. And it's better for men if their mates are equal. Being yoked to an inferior is like dragging a lame leg after you."

He yawned and looked at his watch; his amiability was flagging. "You ladies may have the energy to sit around talking until all hours, but I need my rest. And it would be good for you, too, Dorothy, to sleep, whether you want to admit it or not. Are you coming with me?"

Dorothy said yes, reluctantly, for she'd discovered that the desire to stay behind and discuss him with Veronica was stronger than the desire for his company. Veronica at once rose to her feet and excused herself gracefully.

"Your Veronica is quite a beauty," Bertie said, when the door had closed behind her. "You never told me how pretty she is. I like her reforming zeal, too."

THE FOLLOWING DAY, Veronica was waiting in Dorothy's room when she got back from work. She held Dorothy's small wooden chest in both hands. Looking remorseful, she explained in a rushing torrent of words that did not allow Dorothy space to interject, that she had dropped and broken it.

Dorothy took it from her without saying anything, wondering how the accident had happened. What if Veronica had come into her room last night while she was with Bertie, or today during work? Perhaps, overwhelmed by curiosity, she had taken the chest from where it stood on top of her cupboard. But how could she have been clumsy enough to drop it? It was old and solid; it could hardly have slipped through her fingers. Dorothy had inherited it from her grandmother; she used it to keep Bertie's letters in.

Dorothy looked at the break. It was a smooth clean line. A suspicion was kindling in her mind. Since the contents were so light, a straight fall would not have caused any damage. Had it been hurled to the ground from a height? Had it been determinedly and violently smashed down?

She put the chest on her bed, trying to forget about it.

"I'm sorry," Veronica said again. "I'll buy you another one."

Dorothy shook her head. "It can be fixed," she said. "The break won't even show."

A new thought was emerging. Had Veronica read Bertie's letters? Knowing what the chest contained, had she deliberately set out to plunder it? Dorothy didn't know if Veronica's urge to demolish barriers and taboos was valiant or delinquent. But the chest itself reproached her, displaying its damage from where it sat on the bed. It had been in her family for as long as she could remember.

It wasn't the first time something like this had happened. A few weeks before, Veronica had begged to borrow Dorothy's seed pearl bracelet, luminous and delicate: Benjamin's first gift. She'd returned it with the clasp half ripped off. Veronica seemed to have an unerring instinct for destroying only treasured things. She was like a hurricane, sweeping into Dorothy's life, tearing her possessions from their places.

"Let's make some tea and forget about the casket. I'm longing to hear what you thought of Bertie," Dorothy said.

Veronica sighed. "He was exactly as I suspected. Charming and articulate, yes. But he is just like his preachy books, he tries to take you over." She mimicked: "It would be good for you to sleep, Dorothy, whether you like it or not." She captured the high husky voice perfectly. Her petulance surprised Dorothy.

THE TURBULENCE IN Dorothy's life was making it impossible for her to concentrate on a new and compelling activity. She had begun to write, and was amassing a growing pile of penciled half-sheets. She worked in the evenings, at a rickety wicker table pulled up close to the window of her room.

Her theme was herself, her early life, for she felt this was the only subject she could hope to know or express. Also, her story seemed representative. There must be countless other strong-minded women out there, born to a world that was discouraging if not flatly antagonistic to their sex, who were struggling for independence and identity, like she was. It was a struggle worth setting down on paper; she hoped it might succor all the women whose experience paralleled hers.

So far, she had produced a collection of formless jottings; experiments really, nothing that approximated a narrative. She was more engaged with the process than the result. It was like mining, tunneling down through layers of self to a region far inside, to where the unsullied precious ore lay. It was a painful and unpredictable unfolding; her ability to tap into it was intermittent. But when she was successful, her pen flew across the page as though of its own accord, propelled by some mysterious essence from within. Writing made her feel deeply and serenely alive; anchored to a profound sense of self that was definite and constant.

Once words started flowing, the rest of the world fell away and she only wanted to keep going. The paper-strewn lamplit circle became her world; even Bertie's hold loosened. The whole of life was there, inside her mind, a boundless fount of experience. She could summon any part of it and hold it up for examination. It amazed her how much space was within her. Writing brought an energy her work at the dental practice had never awakened, from the depths of her being. Hours were consumed without her noticing; she wrote through much of the night.

How should she put it down, the soft exclamation the little girl made as she carefully carried the heavy dish of fruit? Knowing she was entrusted with an important task, walking with such attention, her whole being concentrated on the hands that carried the dish.

How could she catch that moment; how to make the words come alive on paper, exactly as they were lived, directly from the center of consciousness? How to record the very process of consciousness as it experienced life at firsthand; life's minute to minute quality.

None of the writers she knew had done it to her satisfaction, not even Bertie. Especially not Bertie. There was always some narrator barging in, getting in the way, describing events from the outside and silting up the arteries of the story with an inert mass of detail. Yet leaving out something essential at the same time, so that life was distorted. One couldn't get away from the author in the background—a master puppeteer yanking strings—and either admiring, or hating, his orchestration.

She would have to smash the old way of writing and make something new. The part of her nature that flailed out and destroyed things would have no problem smashing the novel. But could she successfully remake it? Did she have the courage and the talent?

She hadn't told Bertie about her writing. He would want to see it, or at the very least have it described to him, and she was afraid that his forceful reaction would destroy it. Her work was like a frail young seed germinating deep within the earth; it would disintegrate if it was exposed to daylight too early.

She was struck by the contrast between her writing, snatched in nooks and gaps of the day, and Bertie's. He had a whole household attending to his comfort and well-being; everything in it geared toward catering to his needs and nurturing his talent. Dorothy envied and half-resented the single-minded concentration this allowed him.

The reason women didn't produce much "art" was because they were pulled in different directions; torn and scattered by the unending multiplicity of their preoccupations and tasks; unable to do any one thing properly. It was a state of being unknown to men. Art demands what present-day society won't give to women, she decided.

THERE WAS STILL a feeling of peace and freedom that came every time she was out in London. The evenings were growing shorter; it was already dark when Dorothy left work. She strolled home slowly, feeling the tedium and fatigue of her day at work coiling up and vanishing into the familiar dearly loved city atmosphere.

Could one girl's consciousness be the subject matter of an entire book, she wondered. Was it enough?

The opening words of the novel she wanted to write were fixed in her head: *Miriam left the gaslit hall and went slowly upstairs*. But what then? It was impossible to go on "telling" about her. To let reality filter through, she had to keep her own voice out of it—no explaining, summing up, depicting characters and incidents in hard immutable lines. There had to be another way of writing convincingly—what was it? She didn't want to instruct her reader what to think and feel. Reading should be a process of collaboration between reader and author, a path of discovery. It should be an adventure.

It had rained recently, and lamplight glistened on puddles and spread a bright sheen over the moist pavements. Traffic slurred through wet roads. The air still smelt of rain: washed and earthy. It was a relief to stride through benevolent streets that seemed both intimate and spacious, lined by quiet grey stone buildings. There was hardly anyone else out walking, and the few people she passed did not know what she was really like.

Presently, she became aware of an uncomfortable prickling sensation at her back, as though someone's eyes were on her. She glanced behind, but the lamp-haloed street was empty.

Her thoughts returned to her book. She didn't want some arbitrary plot imposed on it, distorting the truth. There was anyhow such a dearth of narrative endings for women in existing novels: getting married or dying, or becoming a governess, which was a sort of living death. She was starting to believe that narrative conventions were simply an expression of the vision, fantasies, and experiences of men, and as such were dependent on a whole set of dubious agreements and assumptions between reader and writer. She'd had it with all of that. If a novel managed to catch hold of the essence of lived reality, then that should be more compelling than any manufactured plot.

She carried on her way, but the uneasy prickling feeling was still with her. She looked behind again and saw a pale shriveled girl hunched deep inside her coat—she looked like an office worker hurrying home—and the respectable figure of a man in a raincoat and bowler hat.

There was no cause for concern. Yet she was not comfortable; the sense of being watched would not leave her. She told herself she was being silly and overanxious. She turned a corner and glanced furtively over her shoulder. The man in the raincoat was a short distance behind her.

She quickened her pace. There was a small lane ahead. She turned into it and leant against a wall, trying to catch her breath, feeling the chill of damp bricks through her thin coat. She forced herself to count slowly to sixty, hoping this would give the man time to pass. He looked harmless enough; perhaps her imagination was getting the better of her. But cold shocks of fear were pulsing through her body, sharpening all her senses. Her thoughts flew helplessly to garrotting and worse. This was the seedy underbelly that poisoned the deep brightness of London nights, coming inevitably to meet her.

When she emerged, he was looking into a shop window farther down the street. Dorothy could feel the small hairs rise on the back of her neck. She resumed her walk, conscious of his tapping footsteps behind her.

She reached the point where Endsleigh Gardens opened out of Gower Place, beside the shadowy bulk of St. Pancras Church. Plane trees lined the road, their rain-soaked autumn leaves bringing the fresh smell of country lanes to the midst of the city.

This could not go on. The man could not be allowed to carry on polluting her most treasured spaces. Gathering all her courage, she forced herself to come to a halt. His footsteps stopped also. The blood was roaring in her ears. The moment of turning around to face him seemed to stretch out endlessly, sickeningly . . .

He raised his hat and lamplight fell onto his face; he was smiling foolishly. He had moist brown eyes and plump crumpled features, which looked as though they were made of melting wax. His teeth were horribly blackened; one or two were nothing but rotted stumps.

Fear jolted through Dorothy again, but his attitude was self-abasing. There was something almost cringing about him; he was like a dog expecting a whipping.

"Why, you're a beauty . . . my dear girl . . ." His voice was a sibilant whisper; the words whistling and slithering together. "Shall we walk a little way together?"

Boiling anger ripped through her. How dare he? What did he take her for? What in her appearance or bearing made him think it was acceptable to behave so improperly? "Certainly not," she snapped irately.

"Oh," said the man, sounding crushed, "I thought we were going the same way."

She drew herself to her full height, fixing him with a stern glare. "I'm afraid you are mistaken."

Without another word, the man stepped into the gutter and hurried away across the road. The clear notes of St. Pancras Church pealed the half hour.

Dorothy strode furiously onward with shaking legs that refused to stabilize themselves. The man had been easy to get rid of, but he had taken the delightful sense of freedom with him, leaving something altogether more disturbing in its wake.

By the time Dorothy reached the sanctuary of her room, she only wanted to rest. The curtains were open: she could see the gentle reassuring bulk of housefronts across the road; their upper windows dark or burnished blue in the reflections of streetlamps. Most of the French windows along the balconies were lit, golden and inviting. She fetched a candle and took off her hat in front of the narrow mirror.

The glass was blurred. There was something blocking her reflection: some sort of foggy mess. Holding the candle up so that it shone directly onto the mirror, she saw writing, flamboyant and feminine, thick with loops and whorls . . . made with *lipstick.* Bemused, she wondered who on earth could have got into her room? Still more puzzling, who could possibly want to disfigure her mirror in this bizarre manner? She moved the candle across the glass so she could read what the letters spelled.

I LOVE YOU they said.

A bolt of shock jerked through Dorothy's body from deep within her belly, taking with it all she knew and all she was.

Only one person could have done this. She could see Veronica gliding swiftly upstairs to her room. Had Dorothy in her abstraction left it unlocked? Or had Veronica gone to Mrs. Baker and begged for the key, on some pretext of needing access.

Joy and horror impaled her. The familiar surroundings of her room seemed new and strangely transfigured. Veronica had driven through the last of the barriers standing between them.

With a rapid intake of breath, Dorothy wondered if Mrs. Baker had seen the writing on the mirror when she came up to clean.

Thirteen

VERONICA OPENED HER DOOR AT ONCE, AS THOUGH she had been waiting for Dorothy. Their eyes met, and Dorothy found there the searching gaze she had often seen in turning suddenly toward her during some lively exchange of words. Instead of looking away, Dorothy felt herself sinking into their warmth; or rather, plunging, as if she was falling off the edge of a cliff.

It was a long moment of wordless realization, more hidden and marvelous than love between a man and a woman, yet flowing from the same depths. But it was also a claim, so potent it tugged her to the brink . . . a soft exclamation escaped from her lips. The warning voice within her was shouting aloud now, urging her to escape . . .

With a cry of joy, Veronica drew Dorothy into the room. She shut the door and kissed her full on the lips.

Dorothy pulled away and took a few steps backward. There

was a sensation in her stomach that was like being in a suddenly dropping lift. She leant against the door, grateful for its solid indifference against her spine.

Veronica's cheeks were flushed, her eyes glittered. "You know how I feel about you," she said softly. "I want to be as close to you as it's possible for two people to get. And unless I'm badly mistaken, you want it, too."

"Yes, but—"

Veronica moved across the room and put her arms around Dorothy.

It was strange, momentarily, to hold a different person to Bertie. But almost at once, it became entirely familiar, and the way their bodies fitted together was as close to perfect as anything Dorothy had known. Veronica's body felt hot through the fabric of her kimono; her heart was beating recklessly against Dorothy's breasts.

Smoothing Dorothy's hair away from her face, Veronica kissed her again, tenderly at first, but with growing urgency. The inside of Veronica's mouth tasted of apples. Dorothy slipped her hands around Veronica's waist, feeling her eloquent curves beneath the smooth satiny fabric of her kimono . . .

Dorothy was lost; she was drowning in sweetness. There was no going back.

She had no idea how long they stood like this, glued together, exploring each other. Veronica's hands were stroking her face, pulling the pins from her hair. Dorothy felt it cascade down her back in a heavy wave. She could not peel herself away. She had become a different creature, her body no longer defined by weakness and fatigue, but burning and shuddering from head to foot, consumed by uncontrollable physical hunger.

With deliberate daring, Veronica slipped one hand between Dorothy's legs; she started rubbing in exactly the right place. For an alarmed instant, Dorothy thought *she has done this before.*

She opened her eyes. Veronica's eyes were open, too; she was watching Dorothy intently. Dorothy wondered what she must look like: wanton, lost in sensation. Then she stopped thinking anything at all, as her body filled with pleasure.

They began moving toward the bed. Dorothy stepped out of her shoes and kicked them aside. She heard the rustle of Veronica's kimono as it slithered to the floor. Hardly daring to look at her, Dorothy started tugging at the hooks of her own dress, and then her petticoat and underclothes. When she was quite naked, she got into bed beside Veronica and pulled the covers up to her chin, feeling suddenly shy and awkward. Veronica drew them away, gently but insistently. "I want to see you," she murmured. Her voice was strange and thick, as though she had something caught in her throat. "I've wanted to for so long."

After she had gazed her fill, she knelt between Dorothy's legs and kissed her stomach, lingering over the soft mound of Dorothy's belly. Her mouth moved downward, with deliberate slowness that threatened to draw the soul out of Dorothy's body. Dorothy groaned as Veronica's tongue found what it was seeking.

It was as different as anything could be from Bertie's full-on assault. Waves of unbearably exquisite sensation poured over her, each more powerful than the one before. She was tingling, soaring, plunging; she was full of shimmering light, wet and slippery as an eel. She hadn't known her body was capable of such pleasure. She bucked and grasped hold of Veronica's thick hair; she cried out in abandon. She was unrecognizable to herself.

Afterward, they lay in each other's arms. Nothing could have been sweeter than the velvety sensation of Veronica's skin on hers; the way her head fitted perfectly into the soft curve between Dorothy's neck and shoulder.

Ecstasy was passing too swiftly into an awareness of what she had done. Yet joy refused to be quenched. The cool night air poured in at the open window, silently stirring the long lace curtains . . . The generous room was bathed by the dusky orange glow of the streetlamp on the corner. The clear chimes of St. Pancras clock rang out; the rumble of traffic was an unchanging song, a lullaby.

All Dorothy's perceptions were heightened. She felt exalted and luminous. They exchanged tender caresses and murmurs of endearment; words spoken from the heart's wisdom. Unsought sleep descended on them both at almost the same moment.

DOROTHY WOKE UP the next morning, her body feeling deeply refreshed. Veronica was still sleeping beside her: one arm flung over Dorothy, her cheeks lit by a soft flush. Dorothy stretched limbs that were full of cool strength, so utterly different from the fevered weariness of the day before. She watched the sunlight streaming through the curtains, falling in liquid strips on the eiderdown. It was just like the wakings of childhood.

But as she looked the facts of the night full in the face,

contentment gave way to shame and agitation. For as long as she could remember, she had been dimly aware of her double-sided nature. Certain sights—the swell of a breast beneath a tight blouse, or a delicate pulse beating in the soft hollow of a throat—caused a quickening of her breath, an inward stirring that was half pleasure, half pain. Until last night, this side of her had been submerged in the depths of consciousness; scarcely acknowledged. Having succumbed to her feelings, she must confront them.

Why was she made like this? What was she, standing midway between the sexes? Did she have a corrupt spirit, a diseased mind . . . was it some kind of congenital abnormality? And yet there was nothing strange or profane about her feelings for Veronica; they were fine and pure. There seemed something inescapable about them; they were as much a part of life as breathing.

The response of her own body shocked and amazed her. Carried along on an uncontrollable tide of desire, she had acted without shame or inhibition; she had lost herself. The memory of it made her burn with mortification, yet there was pleasure in the feeling, too. Impossible to deny that the night with Veronica had given her the most intense gratification she had known.

What was she going to do? Her feelings for Bertie were waning. This new, more powerful attraction was weakening his hold, sweeping him aside. She was bound to him, nonetheless, by strong ties of loyalty and affection. Her dual allegiances would pull her this way and that, tearing her apart.

Worse still, she was betraying those she loved the most. She had taken her oldest friend's husband as a lover, and now she had committed a blissful yet unholy act with Veronica, which betrayed Bertie as well. She was doubly, trebly corrupt; she was the vilest creature that ever crept over the face of the planet. Were there no limits to what she was capable of? It was horrifying to acknowledge the many layers of her own treachery.

Could this be the same person who had looked in wonder at the flower beds and the bees, innocent and unchanged? It was herself and not quite herself. She had grown duplicitous, capable of deceptions in the pursuit of her own selfish pleasure. Yet her pleasure was bought at a shameful price.

She shifted restlessly in Veronica's bed. She felt heavy and sick; clogged up with iniquity. She was hurtling out of control, toward she knew not what. Her deceit had as yet brought no punishment. Retribution lay somewhere in the future, coiled like a motionless serpent; waiting. She didn't know when or where it would rear its head and strike, but strike it must.

Veronica opened her eyes and smiled when she saw Dorothy.

"Did I dream you up?" she murmured huskily, stretching out her arms for a hug. Her body was warm and lithe; her fingers played lightly over the back of Dorothy's neck, underneath her hair. Dorothy breathed in her musky scent, feeling herself quicken and grow warm with desire.

She pulled away. "Don't, Veronica. I must get up this instant. It's half past eight and I'm going to be late for work."

She got out of bed and dressed hurriedly, trying not to be distracted by Veronica's adoring gaze. "I'll miss you today," Veronica said simply.

Dorothy battled a labyrinth of feelings. She could feel the

coming day at work begin to devour her, but it was also a relief to get away from Veronica.

She paused at the door and turned to face Veronica. "You know what happened last night?"

"Wasn't it wonderful?"

For a moment, Dorothy hesitated. She said slowly, "It was the most heavenly thing that's ever happened to me. But it was all wrong, and it mustn't happen again."

She walked out and closed the door behind her, not daring to look back.

DOROTHY SPENT THE next few nights on her own in the Russell Square rooms. She felt it was best for both of them if she avoided Veronica for a while. She knew that in Veronica's presence, she would only cave in to the attraction that was stronger than she was. She needed time to put what had happened in a box and close the lid; she had to regain control of herself.

If it was not for what had happened with Bertie, she might have surrendered to her feelings. But bitter experience had taught her what lay ahead. Life with Veronica would be as full of subterfuge and pretense, of half-truths and evasions, as the one she led with Bertie. In both cases, the world said their love was wrong. If it was discovered, they would be condemned: ostracized and cast out. She knew that in time, the unsatisfactory nature of their position would erode the joy of being with Veronica. The price was too high.

Dorothy wished she could change her nature. She was tired of falsehood and duplicity; she had lost her will to fight. She wanted to hold her head up, to look the world in the eye without flinching. Why was she so awkward and queer; what attracted her so unerringly to the illicit and the inverted? She longed to be at peace. In bed, battling to sleep, she wondered if her feelings for Veronica would give her the strength to break free of Bertie. She forced herself to smother all thoughts of loving Veronica.

But there was no peace in separation. The slightest thing called up the touch of Veronica's lips on hers, the texture and smell of her skin. Small shocks of excitement detonated in her belly when she thought of Veronica's hands on her body; she couldn't get her out of her mind.

Dorothy felt wrung out and exhausted. She was plagued by a sense of being indefinably ill and getting a little worse all the time. She put it down to a combination of turmoil, overwork, and poor diet. It was no doubt aggravated by her writing. She was scribbling feverishly, far into the night. She still hadn't found a way of writing that satisfied her, but the attempt allowed her to forget herself; like a strong narcotic, it tugged her into a different world. Yet while it shored up her sanity, it tapped reserves of strength she did not possess.

One night, she woke in the still hours, feeling so utterly alone and bereft, it was as though someone had driven an axe into her breastbone, to the hilt.

She had no idea how long she lay sleepless, impaled and stunned by longing. Presently, a cool and lucid thought filtered through the tumult, making her sit upright in bed. The heroine of her novel, the girl she had called Miriam, who was so closely modeled on her, was alone, too. She was just as solitary and isolated in her world as Dorothy was. *No one else was there to describe her.*

Miriam must speak for herself; she must meet experience head on.

Dorothy was galvanized: it was a revelation, changing everything. Flinging off the bedclothes, she got up, switched on the lamp, and pulled her dressing gown around her, for the room was chilly. She picked up a pencil and sat down at the table.

At last, she had it: the method of her novel. She would banish her narrator entirely. The inner world of her heroine—her maturing developing consciousness—would be all there was.

As narrator melded into character in her mind, words began to fall from her pencil:

> *Miriam left the gaslit hall and went slowly upstairs. The March twilight lay upon the landings, but the staircase was almost dark. The top landing was quite dark and silent. There was no one about. It would be quiet in her room. She could sit by the fire and be quiet and think things over until Eve and Harriett came back with the parcels. She would have time to think about the journey and decide what she was going to say to the Fräulein.*
>
> *Her new Saratoga trunk stood solid and gleaming in the firelight. Tomorrow it would be taken away and she would be gone. The room would be altogether Harriett's. It would never have its old look again. She evaded the thought and moved clumsily to the nearest window. The outline of the round bed and the shapes of the may-trees on either side of the bend of the drive were just visible.*
>
> *There was no escape for her thoughts in this direction.*

The sense of all she was leaving stirred uncontrollably as she stood looking down into the well-known garden.

Out in the road beyond the invisible lime trees came the rumble of wheels. The gate creaked and the wheels crunched up the drive, slurring and stopping under the dining-room window.

It was the Thursday afternoon piano organ, the one that was always in tune. It was early today.

She paused and reread what she had written. It felt utterly right; finally, it was beginning to live and breathe in her hands.

This way of writing might be the most real thing in life, coming closer than anything else, offering her another world to step into; an absolutely satisfying world that she could order and control as she wanted. Not diminishing her longing for Veronica, but enabling her to turn pain into something seen from the outside, abstract and interesting. Offering deliverance, if only for brief periods.

WHEN SHE WASN'T writing, a nauseous weakness sucked at her greyly, persistently. It imbued her waking hours with a quality experienced in nightmares, where invisible forces fastened her legs to the ground and every step was like pulling through treacle.

Getting through the day at work required a gigantic effort. She didn't have the energy to run up and down stairs with heavy ledgers, or answer the dentists' bell, or for the endless standing, or the paperwork. The task of cleaning used instruments seemed more repulsive than ever: she could hardly bring herself to handle the bloodstained serviettes, the extracted teeth looking like monstrous fangs in their bottles of spirit, or the forceps that made her feel queasy and faint.

Mr. Badcock hadn't said anything, but once or twice he'd looked at her with an unspoken question in his gentle grey eyes. He would be shocked and disgusted if he had the slightest inkling of what was happening in Dorothy's life outside work.

One afternoon, she left the surgery to find Bertie standing a little way down the street, waiting for her. He looked older; his skin was lined and seemed to sag on its bones, his face was bleached of color. His mustache sprouted untidily.

"Are you mad taking such a risk?" she asked crossly, as she reached him.

He looked deflated. "I thought you'd be happy to see me."

"You'll be recognized. People will talk."

"They're talking already," he replied sourly.

Out of the corner of her eye, Dorothy saw Mr. Badcock leave the practice: tall and dignified and preoccupied. He glanced around him, before putting on his hat and setting off in the other direction. Had he seen her locked in argument with her seedy and instantly recognizable lover?

Without a word, Dorothy began to walk away from Bertie, toward home. He caught up with her and took her arm. She tried to ignore him, concentrating instead on the solid feeling of the pavement under her feet and the clipped sound her shoes made on it.

They walked past a boy selling newspapers, an old woman with a crooked back, crouched beside an enormous basket of roses. Crowded hansoms and horse omnibuses rumbled past; the smell of horse assailed her nostrils pungently. The sky was a cold, even grey; the crisscross of telephone wires above her head seemed like the roof of a prison.

"Let's find a café," Bertie entreated. "Don't be angry. I'm hungry and tired, and I badly want the warm glow of being close to you."

"It's always about what you want!" The words burst out of Dorothy, almost before she knew what she was saying. She realized they'd been pent up inside her for a long while. It was time to let everything out.

She stopped walking and turned to face him; she was a little short of breath. "You're utterly selfish," she told him, her voice shaking with suppressed fury. "And you're the most fickle man I've ever met. You're incapable of lasting selfless love. You don't love Jane fully, and you don't love me . . . you don't even love your writing, to which we all take second place. You don't have enough love in your heart. That's why you have these fluctuations and depressions—"

"But does perfect love exist?" he interrupted. His eyes were flashing dangerously. "Do *you* love me perfectly, Dora, with your unbecoming jealousy, your unrelenting carping?"

Dorothy couldn't answer. Waves of nausea were beginning to sweep over her. She clamped one hand across her mouth. Not here, not in public. She'd be mortified and shamed beyond anything.

Bertie was looking at her with concern. "You're not with child, are you?" he asked in a softened tone.

For a long moment, they stared at each other, as the true reason for her tiredness and sickness began to dawn on Dorothy.

Fourteen

INITIALLY, BERTIE WAS EUPHORIC. THE NEWS GAVE him exactly the lift he had been in need of.

"When I think about that tiny creature nestled inside you, within earshot of your heartbeat, I feel so blessed we've created it," he told her, putting his arms around her.

He was as mellow and tender as he had been in the beginning. His attitude to Dorothy had shifted—it was respectful, bordering on reverential. She was his Madonna with Child. Their physical relations had tailed off. Dorothy was relieved; she felt sick all the time, and her breasts were tender. She did not want to be touched by Bertie.

But Bertie's sweetness could not obliterate her growing fear and dismay. Was it not for the child she carried, she might have broken free of him once and for all. Now, they were irrevocably bound together.

Every day brought a worse feeling of illness; her body was

weak and nauseous and heavy. Every night, she tossed and turned in the breathless stuffy room. It was tormenting to be plagued by this terrible tiredness, but to find that sleep eluded her. Toward dawn, she would drop into an uneasy, nightmare-haunted doze.

She had a recurring dream that she was watching a body drifting upstream. Bloated and waterlogged, its grey face gazed blindly upward toward a flat dull sky. It was cut off from the rest of humanity, endlessly journeying, beyond comfort or help. Dorothy knew the figure was herself, but she could not reach it, nor do anything to ease its plight.

When she awoke, the moment of hope that her pregnancy had been a bad dream vanished in an instant, and chasms opened at her feet. Every secure item in her existence was under threat. Presently the unbearable day would begin again, the exhaustion of dragging herself through streets that were noisy and packed with unbreathable odors, the endless hours at work. There was nothing to turn to. Just this horrible sense of apprehension.

Part of Dorothy's misery was because Bertie didn't appear to grasp the reality of their situation. She couldn't rely on his blithe assurances that he would take care of everything. How was she going to carry on working and supporting herself? Even if she was well enough to work, her condition would soon begin to show. And what would Mrs. Baker say? There would be no more indulgent motherly clucking. She would probably turn Dorothy out of the house at once.

The unthinkable happens in life: her mother's death had taught her that. Dorothy faced ruin. She would bring financial and social disgrace on herself and on the rest of her family, just as her father had done. She couldn't escape her family's tainted legacy.

Giving birth to a first child is more dangerous than following the most hazardous trade: anything could go wrong. She'd heard enough stories about women who had died in childbirth.

She felt submerged by the storm that was gathering for her.

Through her misery and sickness, Dorothy had the strange feeling that her pregnancy fulfilled one of Bertie's principles. She had become his breeding partner. "Attractive and healthy people should come together and have fine, sturdy children," he declared. "They should have children and, meanwhile, prepare a world for them to live in."

In Bertie's view, her "proper" status, the proper status of all women, was to breed. It was the supreme justification for her existence.

He was engrossed in what she might become for him: the mother of his child. She was booked for maternity and following the formula he had prescribed: bucolic existence, baby, novel.

"I'm so terribly tired, and I loathe feeling ill all the time," she confessed one evening.

Bertie was at once tender and solicitous. He insisted she put her feet up on the couch; he tucked a blanket around her legs, sat beside her and stroked her belly and told her she should rest more.

"I'm frightened."

"Dora darling, you're a healthy young woman, you're perfectly constructed to give birth; it's the most natural and joyous thing in the world. And just think what a splendid baby he or she will be, with our combined natures and characteristics . . . I can't tell you how happy you've made me. I feel exalted, fulfilled . . . I could dance a jig!"

As he pulled her to her feet and whirled her clumsily about the room, Dorothy realized that he saw only a biological specimen. Of the intrinsic individual, he knew nothing, and he didn't want to know.

She still found him the most compelling and charming man she had ever met. But she began to sense a terrible emptiness behind his spellbinding words. Science and literature were the only things in the world that could get his full attention. There was nothing for Dorothy individually, nor for anyone else.

More than ever, Dorothy longed for silent communion, understanding and peace—qualities that were lost with Bertie.

DOROTHY KNOCKED ON Veronica's door. There was no answer. Dorothy patted her hair and passed her handkerchief once more over her burning face. Perhaps Veronica had gone out? Dorothy was about to walk away, when the door opened slowly and here was Veronica. Here was the shock of her loveliness as she stood, slender and pale, in a creased ice-blue kimono. She stared at Dorothy silently.

"Aren't you going to ask me in?"

Veronica pulled the door wide and Dorothy stepped into the room. It was untidier than ever. The bed was unmade, and a faint smell hung in the air, slightly sour.

Veronica's eyes were puzzled. Stricken. Dorothy felt a pang: Veronica, more precious than anyone in the world, was suffering because of her.

"It's good to see you . . ." she began.

"Why have you been avoiding me?" Veronica burst out. "Why are you like this, so strange and distant?"

Speech refused to come because words were beyond reach. Veronica's nearness was heady and confusing; it brought back everything Dorothy had been trying to suppress.

"I don't understand why you left," Veronica went on. "Is it Bertie; do you suffer from some false sense of loyalty to him? Do you think he doesn't make love to his wife, whatever he may tell you otherwise?"

There was silence.

"Haven't you thought about what it would be like, you and me together?" Dorothy asked, eventually. "Think about it; about what being lovers would really mean. We'd be forced into a life of continual secrecy; hiding how we feel about each other, being careful about every single thing we say in public. It would mean lying by omission, if not by actual words. We'd have to endure strange glances, knowing people were wondering about us, whispering behind our backs . . ."

"I don't care what anyone else thinks! I just want to be with you. I love you; can't you see that? How can it be wrong?"

Dorothy shook her head. "I don't want to live in fear and subterfuge. If we were found out, we'd be shunned, persecuted, called unnatural and perverted—"

"I never thought you were a coward."

Dorothy flushed deeply and bit her lip. "I'm simply realistic enough to know that I can't take on the whole world," she said.

She fell silent again, wondering what confusion of emotions Veronica must be reading in her face. For while everything she said was true, it was also true that nothing could compare with what Veronica had given her. Nothing could be more profound or marvelous than the time they spent together, intensely aware of each other, moved by every thought and every response of their bodies. But it was too late. If there had ever been a time for them as lovers, it had passed. The child she was carrying made it impossible.

"I want to be your friend." Dorothy spoke as though she was in a trance. "Anything more is . . . out of the question."

"I don't see why."

Tell her. Tell her you are pregnant. Still, the words refused to come. "What have you been doing since I last saw you?" she found herself asking.

Veronica sighed. "I've been working hard on the suffrage campaign," she said tonelessly. "To tell you the truth, it's a relief to have something to think about other than you. This week, I've handed out thousands of flyers, chalked announcements about meetings on pavements, and knocked on more doors than I can remember. We've been especially busy because in a few days the militants will be marching on the House of Commons."

"I'd forgotten about your march. Must you really take part? It's going to get out of hand; you might get hurt."

"Don't you *know* that the militant route is the only route to getting what we want? Peaceful means are absolutely useless. The mild suffragists have been asking for votes and having civilized processions for sixty years and more. They are refused time and again, and nothing changes."

Dorothy sighed. "Promise me, at least, that you'll be careful."

"What do you care what happens to me?"

"That's unfair. You know I care."

"Show me."

Slowly and deliberately, Veronica laid a hand on Dorothy's breast. Her spine arched as pleasure rippled from her breast, down through her belly and between her legs; there seemed to be an invisible thread connecting these places. She saw Veronica watching her helpless reaction, and she closed her eyes.

"Let's be sensible," she pleaded, trying to ignore the way her blood was leaping, so hot and sweet and keen.

Veronica replied with a kiss that unleashed a fiery torrent of longing. They sank to the floor. The way her body asserted its autonomy over her mind and drew her irresistibly toward Veronica suggested overwhelmingly that this was her true nature. She vowed to crush it to the death. Then all thought was blotted out by the deep delight coursing through her, and she gave herself over to it.

DOROTHY MOVED HELPLESSLY between Veronica and Bertie, trapped by confused feelings and the unborn baby. She was adrift: her life had lost direction, there was no order. She was being tested and found flawed and weak-willed. The messiness of her situation made her writhe. She saw it clearly, but she could not find a way out.

Through her own agitation, Dorothy tried to impress on Bertie that he could not vacillate any longer. He needed to think about what he really wanted. Some sort of decision had to be reached.

His first impulse was to run away with Dorothy. Together, they discussed the details of their escape. They would go to the South of France or Italy, and take a house on a sunlit hill by the sea, surrounded by olive groves and vineyards and weathered marble ruins. Dorothy would grow ripe and bronzed; in time, she would bear a sturdy, bronzed baby. Bertie would write the novel of his life. It was pleasurable to talk about, yet the conversation had the quality of children playing make-believe. They knew perfectly well he would never leave Jane. He couldn't do without her.

They knew also that if the relationship with Dorothy came into the open, he would be shunned by society and would face losing everything.

Certain measures would have to be taken to escape publicity. Dorothy's family and Jane must be told, and their acquiescence secured. They talked of finding suitable lodgings for Dorothy by the sea, not too close to London, but near enough for Bertie to visit from his home.

Dorothy imagined herself in a desolate house on a wintry and bleak coast. Utterly solitary, except for a sulky impertinent servant, who'd be only too well aware of the irregularity of Dorothy's situation, and would take it out on her accordingly. Dorothy would be totally dependent on Bertie's visits for company. Dependent on him for everything.

She felt imprisoned. Stifled, petrified, trapped.

"HAVE YOU TOLD Jane?"

Bertie nodded.

"Well?"

He sighed and raked his hands through his hair, making it stand on end. "She listened to me without saying anything, but I watched her get paler and paler. When I'd finished, she told me she wanted to think it over, and she went into her study and shut the door. She was in there for what seemed like eternity . . . When she came back, her eyes were swollen and red with crying. She sat beside me and gripped the sleeve of my jacket, holding on so tightly that when she let go, there were deep creases in the fabric."

"Oh no." This was the reaction Dorothy had dreaded.

"Yet her smile held a trace of its old warmth, as she said softly, 'If it had to be anyone, I'd rather it was Dora.' "

"She really said that?"

"She did, she's a remarkable woman . . . I forced myself to look her squarely in the eye. I said, 'I'm so sorry. I can't imagine the pain this must give you, and I'm the cause of it.'

"Jane shrugged. 'If it wasn't Dora, it would be someone else. It's the way you're made, dear. I realized that a long time ago.'

"But despite her reasonable words, her lips quivered, and I thought she was going to break down again. A few moments passed; I watched her force herself into composure. She asked me, in a voice that was hardly more than a whisper, if I meant to go and live with you."

He paused, looking at the carpet.

"What did you say?"

"I said no, that I would visit you, but everything would go on as before."

Dorothy inhaled sharply. "What happened then?"

"A few tears fell from her eyes. They trickled down her

cheeks and she made no effort to wipe them away. Presently, she admitted that she couldn't bear to see you again."

Dorothy swallowed. The bonds of her oldest friendship were severed; bonds with the past. She felt herself cut adrift . . . falling . . . Briefly, she wondered if Bertie was worth it. Was any man worth it?

"Jane wanted to know if you're having a difficult time," he said, "and she told me to look after you . . ."

They fell silent. Dorothy was imagining the supreme effort it must have taken Jane to maintain her control during this conversation. She was an accomplished ice queen, but at what cost to herself?

At last, Bertie asked: "Have you told your father or sisters?"

Dorothy gazed at the oil lamp standing in the little fireplace, its single flame glaring nakedly against the black grate. "No. They've suffered so much already, I don't want to add to their pain."

"You can't avoid them forever," he said gently.

Fifteen

A LETTER FROM BENJAMIN ARRIVED. THE SIGHT of his familiar handwriting filled Dorothy with trepidation. It was almost certainly another demand or plea for help, and she felt incapable of giving the succor he needed. But his opening lines assured her he was not in trouble. He simply missed talking to her and wanted to call on her. "I come as friend. No requests, no complications. On my honor."

The letter transported her back to a more carefree past. She wrote a hurried reply, saying she was available the following evening after work, and was looking forward to seeing him again.

On her way back from the postbox, she decided to play the piano, if the drawing room was free. Reaching the house, she paused outside the drawing room door. All sounded quiet within; she turned the handle cautiously and went in. The gas was out and the room was dim, but there was enough light to see two figures talking quietly and earnestly on the sofa. There would be no solitary music making tonight.

It was Mrs. Baker and Mr. Cundy. Her concerns about them had been knocked from her mind by her own troubles. As she moved toward them, a tide of shock and disbelief roared in her ears and made her eyes film over, dimming the forms in front of her. *They were holding hands!*

Briefly, she wondered if her vision was playing tricks. Mrs. Baker tried to withdraw her hand when she saw Dorothy, but Mr. Cundy kept firm hold of it.

"I think you've realized by now," he said to Dorothy, "what we mean to each other."

Dorothy was lost for words. Mrs. Baker managed to free her hand from Mr. Cundy's; she took Dorothy's and pressed it ardently. Dorothy bent down to kiss the haggard cheek, and was rewarded with a motherly hug. Straightening up, she offered her hand to Mr. Cundy, who grasped it and pumped it up and down. Looking into his eyes, Dorothy read a confusion of tenderness and half-abashed pride. So his feelings were real. Outside the house, St. Pancras clock chimed the quarter hour into the night.

How in the world had Mrs. Baker allowed such an astonishing thing to happen? But it was also touching and marvelous. Marvelous that Mr. Cundy was discerning enough to see the pure-hearted woman beneath the harassed exterior. He had arrived at the struggling house, just as Mrs. Baker's vanishing youth was making her failure with it absolutely heartrending to watch. Yet he had fallen in love with her glorious smile and the courage behind it; undaunted by the difference in their ages. He knew she was innocent and rare and beautiful.

When the flurry of congratulations subsided, Mr. Cundy excused himself saying, "I'll leave you two ladies alone to talk."

"I feel for him," breathed Mrs. Baker, as the door closed behind him, "getting tied down to me."

"Why on earth? He's the luckiest man alive," said Dorothy stoutly, sitting down beside her.

"Really? I'm glad you think so; I've fretted something awful over him. I've been saying no to him this past year and a half."

There was a brief pause, while Dorothy digested this extraordinary fact. She had been too self-absorbed to see the drama taking place under her nose.

"I worry because he's ten years younger than me," Mrs. Baker confessed, blushing. "He'd be better suited to Carrie."

"But he looks and acts far older."

"He does, it's true. His mother passed away when he was young; his father remarried and his stepmother was shockingly hard on him. He says this is the first place he's felt at home and wanted; he's happier than he's ever been in his life."

The whole time, Mr. Cundy had been hanging around the house, apparently at a loose end, making annoyingly flippant comments and seeming to prey on Mrs. Baker. When in fact, he had been feeling at home and cherished and joyful; his joy growing as their love grew and blossomed . . . Was he worthy of Mrs. Baker? Dorothy still wasn't sure if she liked him, or approved of the match.

"It's wonderful news," Dorothy said. "Mr. Cundy is a lucky man."

"Yes, it's all fine and good for now, but there's plenty of obstacles in the future. He wants me to sell this house and get a place just for us. But there's my girls to think of. I can't give up the boarders till they're settled. I keep telling him, I must do the right thing for my girls."

"Of course you must, and you will. He's a lovely man, I'm sure he understands." But how noble and bounteous the failing household suddenly seemed, when the alternative was sharing some poky dwelling with Mr. Cundy. Dorothy could see him coming home in the evening, and Mrs. Baker waiting to greet him with the house spotless and dinner on the table, growing more rundown and exhausted every day. She would be an old woman before he turned forty.

While Mrs. Baker talked on, Dorothy found herself torn between pity and wistful admiration. Mrs. Baker had achieved something that Dorothy had failed at. Mrs. Baker was going to be a wife; it was, supposedly, the highest destiny of woman. She had settled triumphantly, justifying her everlasting confident smile.

As Dorothy left the room, there entered her mind an image of herself introducing Benjamin to Veronica. It stood there, vivid and complete, as though it had taken root while she was talking to Mrs. Baker. It seemed to offer a future miraculously cleared of encumbrances. Ridiculous. The whole idea was ridiculous, yet it was compellingly attractive and persuasive, too.

What was left of her conscience checked her, insisting on an examination of her motives. In her current unstable state, she had to be absolutely sure the introduction would not have hurtful or damaging consequences for any of them. As she looked within, trying to analyze her true intentions, she found herself confronted by her own reflection . . . something deep inside, unattached to any specific motive, had chosen this course of action, was refusing to heed any conflict attached to it, and was already viewing the decision as made. This unequivocal unconscious response, whose purpose was impenetrable, might be harmful or benign, but it was impossible to ignore.

IT WAS A side to Veronica she had never seen before. Veronica playing hostess to a man she had never met. Veronica, in one of her kimonos with the pale chunky beads around her neck, opening the French doors and leading Benjamin outside; showing him, with a graceful sweep of her arm, the view of the square, and her scented geraniums in their grey-stone basins that brought the small balcony to life. "I feel like a queen up here, watching the world go by," she said.

As she poured tea from the Empire set, Benjamin stopped her putting milk in his cup. "To a Russian, that is not tea," he said. "It's a weak greasy mixture, quite undrinkable."

"Sorry, I didn't realize. Sugar?"

"Yes, please." He took a lump and placed it between his lips. Dorothy braced herself for the inevitable sucking of tea through it, while Veronica handed around a plate of small, golden, sugar-dusted biscuits.

"Why don't you sit over there, Benjamin?" Veronica said, gesturing toward the armchair. She took her place on a little carved wooden stool beside him.

Veronica listened to Benjamin's stories and gazed with

calm gravity at his glowing opulent beauty: the thick black hair and neatly pointed beard, the melancholy eyes, the wide forehead and strong gentle features. He drank his tea through the sugar lump with audible sips, talking all the while in a voice grown thick and slurred, yet she gave no sign of finding the ritual unusual or abhorrent. He was telling a story about his married sister that Dorothy had heard before.

"My brother-in-law was determined she should not go to the Sabbath service at our synagogue. She had a heavy cold; she had been up half the night with the baby, who was also sick, and she absolutely needed to rest. But my sister is headstrong, she will not listen to reason, so he tried to stop her in the only way he knew. He locked her hat cupboard—a married woman is forbidden, you know, to enter the temple bareheaded. But can you guess what he saw when he looked out of the window half an hour later?" Benjamin drained his cup and looked at Veronica, who encouraged him to go on with a gracious smile. "He saw his wife, my sister, walking down the road in *his* big black hat with a blue lace scarf twisted most stylishly around it!"

The laughter with which Veronica met this suggested that she found his idea of how to entertain a lady in a social situation just as funny the story itself. But there was also warmth in her voice, as though she was humoring a particularly winsome child. "I like your sister's unquenchable spirit," she told him, when her laughter subsided.

"A strong woman will always find a way to do what she wants . . . we men are no match for a strong woman."

Dorothy flinched inwardly; she'd heard too many of Benjamin's neat generalizations. Charming as his stories were, his vision of life seemed to miss some vital element: it was too clear, too one-dimensional to embrace the rich paradoxes and constant fluctuations that made up life.

She wondered what Veronica really thought of him, beneath the amiable mask that was her social manner. Dorothy had told her their history. Did she appreciate his mellow dignity and simplicity, or did she find the stream of anecdotes merely tedious? There was something in his bearing that many people would not like; something heavy and stolid: an absence of mirth.

The occasion was given a poignant duality by the consciousness of what Dorothy and Veronica were to each other. While Veronica flirted with Benjamin and gave every appearance of being charmed and charming, she belonged to Dorothy. While Veronica offered more tea, promising to remember not to put milk in it this time, Benjamin sat within touching distance of the bed on which they lost themselves to passion, night after night. There was undeniably a charge in the air. Veronica placed a cup of tea on Dorothy's lap, her fingers brushing Dorothy's thigh, and Dorothy felt her cheeks flush and her underclothes grow warm and damp. She glanced at Benjamin, who was saying "This is delicious. It's rare to find an Englishwoman who knows how to make tea"; so innocent and oblivious that she was ashamed. She had the strange sense that while the scene was playing out, it had already happened in some distant universe, and was proceeding upon preordained lines to its inevitable conclusion.

After about half an hour, Dorothy could see Benjamin caving in to the fatigue that swept over him during any conversation failing to engage his full interest. His eyelids were growing heavy and his face looked paler than ever. Slumped in his armchair, he gave a sigh that turned involuntarily to a yawn. The white lids were almost closed. "You can probably tell how the story ended," he said opening his eyes wide, and Dorothy saw in them the desire for escape. "And I think I have talked enough about myself. I'm afraid I have started to tire you."

He looked at his gold pocket watch and got to his feet, saying gently—and Dorothy thought a little guiltily—"We had better go to dinner now, Dorothy. We are already running late." Turning to Veronica, he thanked her for the tea, and took his leave formally, bowing over her hand as he raised it to his lips.

Dorothy sent him downstairs to wait for her, shutting the door behind him, so that Veronica could freely vent her opinion of him and of the occasion.

But Veronica was not paying any attention to her. She stood gazing out of the window, showing her clear profile and the curve of her cheek, very upright and slender, lost in thought. Dorothy walked over and stood beside her, looking down at the blazing colors of the autumn trees in the square. A group of young men and women was approaching along the wide pavement, laughing and talking; a blare of lively voices reached them. Veronica's continuing silence held Benjamin's presence in the room; it came between them, breaking them up. Dorothy waited, with increasing impatience, for her to speak, conscious of Benjamin standing captive in the hall.

"Dorothy!"

"Yes, what? What did you think of him?"

Veronica fell silent again, as though gathering her thoughts, while Dorothy's pulse quickened with apprehension. Perhaps she had sacrificed Veronica, forcing her to undergo an unpleasant meeting so that Dorothy might have the gratification of managing a social event.

"Was it an ordeal?" Dorothy asked. "I'm sorry if you hated it. Let's put it behind us, shall we? We'll pretend it never happened."

"It wasn't an ordeal at all. I was just thinking . . ." Veronica paused dramatically, drawing herself to her full height. "If you want respectability so badly, why don't you marry Benjamin? If you should be with any man alive, it's him. He'll let you breathe and be yourself. It isn't too late; I can tell by the way he looks at you."

Everything wavered and went silent; Dorothy could not feel her feet. She could not believe she was being abandoned by Veronica, who seemed to have crossed sides and was standing in league with Benjamin. But Veronica was right. Veronica saw both Dorothy's lack of backbone, and the cruelty of pushing Benjamin away to fend for himself in the world. These things were so blindingly evident to her that she was ready to renounce their joined life, at the drop of a hat.

The room stopped heaving and shuddering, but Dorothy was left utterly chilled and depleted. Betrayed. She thought she knew Veronica, but how could she suggest relinquishing their life together so easily? A gulf was opening between them, leaving Dorothy desolate. For the first time, she realized that Veronica was fickle; running through personal relationships, wanting to clear the ground for fresh conquests and excitements. Beside this discovery, Veronica's failure to understand the impossibility of marrying Benjamin was trivial.

"I've never met a man so transparently good," Veronica was saying, "and so beautiful."

Her words brought a faint improbable hope, nudging Dorothy out of dejection. As she pondered a future which did not hold any place for her, she found a reply forming in her mind, and she let the words fall hurriedly, without pausing to think about what she was saying: "If you feel like that, why don't you marry him yourself?"

"I would! In an instant!" exclaimed Veronica. "I'd adore to have children with him. Just think what beautiful children we'd make."

"Beautiful," Dorothy repeated. "Yes, they would be beautiful," and she looked, excited and cut to the quick, at this image from which she was shut out. Veronica, Benjamin, and their children: a family. They gazed back at her with dark inscrutable eyes, lovely and secure.

She said a hasty farewell to Veronica, freshly seen and irrevocably lost. Who would have thought that Veronica, of all people, might rescue Benjamin? Their good-bye was unlike all those that had gone before: it was matter of fact, almost perfunctory. Veronica was too preoccupied to reach out to her for their usual loving and protracted parting.

THE CAFÉ WAS hot, noisy, and crowded. Dorothy felt overwhelmed by the fug of tobacco fumes and frying meat, the clamor of voices, the clatter of cutlery and dishes being set down on marble-topped tables. They found an empty table at the back, near the kitchen, and she sank onto the red velvet sofa seat gratefully.

Benjamin had difficulty summoning a waiter. Eventually, a tall stooped man in a stained white uniform ambled over.

"We must have service!" Benjamin bellowed, while Dorothy sat shrinking by his side. "Bring me two glasses of red wine at once! And please wipe the table, it is revolting!" He gestured, with the hand that bore the jeweled ring, to the blots of beer and cigarette stubs left by the previous clients.

Dorothy waited until their drinks had arrived before she asked Benjamin what he thought of Veronica.

"She laughs for no reason; it is most annoying."

"She is still young."

"That is no excuse. She is not ten years old. But let's not talk about Veronica. Tell me, rather, what you are thinking. I can see a thought on your face now that is most troubled. It has wiped away your dimples, and brought a pale and worried countenance."

"I was just thinking . . . oh, nothing, really."

"Ah, you must tell me"

His solicitude made her want to confide in him. Glancing at him, she was touched by the concern in the steady dark eyes, as he sat waiting for her to speak.

She told him she was pregnant; the words falling numbly from her lips. She felt as though she was talking about another person entirely; one distantly known, but not particularly relevant to either of them.

For a few moments, he was silent; every fiber of him motionless, brooding on what she had said. His face was a blank mask. Through the hum of conversation and the bustle of meals being served, he began to question her, softly and doggedly. She told him everything about her and Bertie, sparing neither of them. She did not mention Veronica.

When she had finished, he fell back into silence. His usual pallor was heightened. Though his expression was composed, his hands shook as they rested on the table, and his mouth was a hard line. He would not look at her. She could not see his eyes.

What had she done? She wished she could cancel the blundering words. She had lost his good opinion, so dearly valued. She was beyond his help; she had only succeeded in shocking and alienating him.

"Let's not talk about me anymore," she said at last, desperate to break the awful silence. "What have you been doing?"

"After your news," he said, trying to control the unsteadiness of his voice, "what is happening in my life is trivial." He paused. "Oh Dorothy, now will you marry me? As a friend? Let's do it quickly." His voice broke on the last word. He took her hand, still not looking at her. "The child will have father and name."

For a few moments, she could not speak; touched to the heart by his unexpected proposal. When words came, she thanked him from the depths of her being, and refused as gently as she could. "Dear Benjamin, if marriage to you was impossible before, it's now doubly so." He let go of her hand and turned to face her. The hurt and disappointment in his eyes gave her the usual pang.

As though in sympathy with the pain of her guilt, a sudden sharp spasm in her lower stomach took her breath away. It was like an iron claw, crushing tender organs and tissue in a vice. She curled over involuntarily, shutting her eyes; her hands clutching her belly.

"What is it? What's the matter?"

She couldn't answer. The contraction was beginning to ease; the sensation of being clenched in an inhuman grip was dwindling. Now, it felt like the baby was dancing in metal-capped boots; as though the tiny being, whose existence she wanted to blot out, insisted on making its presence known.

She straightened up and opened her eyes; her face was beaded with sweat. Benjamin was looking at her, pale and frightened. What had they been talking about?

"We must go now and find a doctor," he said.

She shook her head, and drained the contents of her wine-glass. "No, I'm fine. It has already passed."

Sixteen

THE LONG PROCESSION OF WOMEN MARCHED IN orderly ranks, four abreast. They were festive with flags in the militant tricolor, purple, green, and white, and banners bearing various mottoes: "Votes for Women," "Deeds, not words," "Where There's a Bill There's a Way." They sang "The Women's Marseillaise"; their voices rising into the clear air.

March on, march on
Face to the dawn
The dawn of liberty.

Enormous crowds lined the pavements. Every class was present and every degree of opinion on the suffrage question, from sympathy through incomprehension to furious animosity. Some watchers were simply curious: there for the spectacle, but lacking interest in its purpose. Cheers and catcalls mingled with the suffragettes' singing.

Dorothy, standing among the spectators, only had eyes for Veronica, who was walking near the front, dressed from head to toe in white. She looked enchanting; fully composed before her immense audience, marching lightly, gracefully down the sunlit streets, apparently unhampered by the enormous banner she carried. Dorothy's eyes were suddenly cloudy with tears. Veronica seemed a fitting symbol for the entire army of women: serious yet exhilarated, demure yet radiating pride.

Dorothy tried to follow her, pushing her way through the thronging pavements. This was the first time Veronica had asked for her support in the campaign; she wondered, with a sudden pang of jealousy, why Veronica had wanted to keep this part of her life separate. Either she regarded Dorothy as unfitted for any kind of tough political cause, or (and this seemed likelier), there were people in the organization she wanted to keep to herself.

Ahead of her, the crowd was growing restive and unruly, and was being pushed back by the police. A group of young men in drab work-stained clothes, their foreheads bisected by flattened cloth caps in a way that accentuated their puniness, shouted at the suffragettes: "Go 'ome and do your washing!" One of them shook his fist and spat just in front of Dorothy's shoes. "Go 'ome and mind the baby!"

"Hooray for the women!" cried a soldier, with enthusiasm. "Never give up! Votes for women, I say! Votes for women!" The youths cast angry glances in his direction and seemed to consider challenging him, but thought the better of it. Dorothy passed a man in a soft felt Homburg, who hissed: "Damn the suffragettes! Brazen unwomanly bitches!" A spray of saliva spouted from his lips; Dorothy felt flecks of it fall onto her wrist, and she drew back in disgust. She met the man's gaze. "What the suffragettes need are husbands, but they're too busy fucking each other," he said distinctly. His eyes, peering mistrustfully at her through rimless pince-nez, were the color of liver sausage.

Dorothy hurried away from him without a word, her cheeks flaming and her heart pounding against her rib cage.

Near Westminster Abbey, the marchers found their route blocked by a row of police standing shoulder to shoulder, with mounted officers close behind. In their conical helmets and stiff black tunics, the policemen looked solid and menacing; they towered over the suffragettes. At a curt order from their chief, they began to break through the line of protesters, trying to turn them back. Bravely, the women ignored them and pressed on toward the Houses of Parliament, but the constables seized them around the ribs with both hands, lifted them clean into the air, and threw them back. The policemen's faces were impassive; they were simply following orders. Suffragettes flung into the thick of the crowd had their fall broken by the wedge of bodies, but others were not so lucky, landing hard on the pavement. Again and again the women picked themselves up and returned, and each time they were hurled back with greater force. The banners were ripped from their hands, torn to pieces and trampled underfoot.

When the onlookers realized what was happening, there were angry murmurs of "Shame!" "Shame!" The murmurs soon turned into irate cries and the crowd became a mob: shoving, howling, and brawling. The tumult grated unbearably on Dorothy's ears. Supporters of the suffragettes cheered them as they tried to force their way, crying "Go on! We'll push you through"; calling to the police "Let her proceed! She has a right."

Dorothy saw a woman with blood streaming from a gash above her eyebrow go up to the man with liver sausage eyes; she seemed to be asking for help. He raised his arm and struck her hard across the face. As she stumbled backward, he grasped one of her breasts in a meaty hand and twisted it cruelly. Dorothy saw her face crumple in pain and outrage.

A brawny policeman wrenched a flag from an elderly suffragette, giving her a shove in the chest that nearly pitched her backward. The frail woman cried, "We will go on! You cannot treat women like this." In response, he punched her in the face; Dorothy heard the sickening crunch of his fist meeting tissue and bone. The suffragette screamed and the man grabbed her by the throat until she began to choke. She struggled uselessly in his grip and was swiftly arrested. Next to them, a woman lay unconscious on the ground.

In rising fear and distress, Dorothy found herself trapped by the crowd that hustled and surged chaotically around her. She had lost sight of Veronica and was trying to find her in the sea of people, but it was almost impossible to push her way through. She felt smothered by the press of strange bodies, and the heat and unbreathable smells they generated: the comingled rankness of many unwashed skins; the reek of sweat cutting through, sharply rancid; a pungent cologne that was almost worse than sweat. The fetid cocktail made her nauseous.

Suddenly, brilliant flashes of light and soft explosions tore through the air, startling her. She looked about, frantic and disoriented; the noise and lights intensified her sense that normal life was melting into surreal nightmare. Eventually, she realized they came from flashlights belonging to a nearby group of newspaper photographers.

The rules holding society together seemed to be collapsing before her eyes; she could scarcely believe that upholders of the law were treating defenseless woman with such brutality. She had never seen women being manhandled by constables before, except, once or twice, drunken women in the street. The disproportionate show of force directed at obviously respectable women, many of them far from young, was deeply shocking. The government seemed determined not only to crush the suffragettes' demonstration, but to annihilate the hunger for emancipation lying behind it. The very earth seemed to be shifting under Dorothy's feet, giving a glimpse of dark forces beneath.

At last, Dorothy caught sight of Veronica, locked in combat with a policeman who was grasping her hard by both forearms. Dorothy made her way toward them. Veronica's cheeks were flushed; her broad white hat was askew and her hair escaped wildly from its pins. Momentarily, she managed to break free. Taking a stone from her pocket, she flung it as hard as she could at the windows of the House of Commons. The stone missed, landing harmlessly on the ground, but a second policeman seized Veronica roughly from behind, pinning her arms against her sides so she couldn't move. Lifting her off her feet as easily as if she had been a doll, he carried her away.

Veronica's head lolled back at an awkward angle; her skin was grey and waxy with shock, seeming too tightly drawn over the bones of her face. Her eyes were closed; she looked like she was struggling for breath in the implacable grip of her captor. Her feet flailed helplessly, a few inches from the ground.

Dorothy could no longer quell her growing nausea. Crouching over, she vomited copiously into the gutter; her skin clammy, her breath coming in shallow gasps. When she was able to straighten up and look around, Veronica was nowhere to be seen.

Too ill and weak to attempt a search of the local police stations, Dorothy made her way slowly home. Her legs trembled and she could not feel her feet. A brisk wind had come up; the weather was changing rapidly, growing overcast. As she let herself into Mrs. Baker's house, a bank of heavy cloud obscured the sun, shrouding the surrounding buildings in gloom.

The rain started when she reached her room. A brilliant flash of lightning illuminated the sky. The crack of thunder that followed made her jump. She was still nauseous; unsure if it was pregnancy or fear for Veronica. Waves of fear were rolling off her body like a smell; her skin was damp with it. She could not sit still.

Outside, a young woman laughed. Dorothy hurried to the window, but it was not Veronica. She watched the woman walk past; she had pale hair, as fine and soft as a child's. She was holding the arm of a young man; both of them sheltered beneath a large red umbrella.

Dorothy began to pace up and down the small room. The intervals between lightning and thunder were gradually growing longer; the storm was dying away. But the rain was relentless, fat drops plocking onto the roof and windows.

Hardly knowing what she was doing, Dorothy crept downstairs to Veronica's room and opened the door. The bed was smooth and undisturbed; Veronica's nightgown had been carelessly tossed onto her pillow. Dorothy lay full length on the bed and put her head on the gown's soft material. It smelled of Veronica, and Dorothy was instantly undone by longing.

She was trapped in a nightmare; unable to stop reliving the violent scenes she had witnessed. What was happening to Veronica now? Dorothy kept hoping for the familiar sound of Veronica's footsteps in the passage, her hand on the doorknob. She prayed for Veronica to come through the door, wet and disheveled, laughingly recounting what had happened, as if it was simply another one of her escapades.

But she did not come. Dorothy listened to the rain beating against the windowpanes, wet trees rustling and sighing in the wind. Veronica could be anywhere in the vast darkness outside this house. Most likely, she was being held in some dismal police station. What was going on in her head right now? Dorothy hoped she wasn't cold and frightened; that she had been given something to eat, and was being treated with reasonable kindness. But the scenes she'd just lived through had stripped away her belief in the fundamental goodness of men.

She let the tears come.

DOROTHY MUST HAVE fallen asleep. Veronica got into bed beside her, fully clothed. The room was dark; the house silent. Veronica's dress was sodden and she shivered with cold. She touched Dorothy's damp face with icy fingertips. "Why are you crying?"

"I thought something terrible had happened to you."

Veronica didn't reply. Dorothy reached over and lit the gas. A soft exclamation escaped from her lips. "Good God; just look at you! What happened?"

Veronica's cheek was badly gashed. Her white dress was bedraggled and grimy. One sleeve had been half ripped off; it drooped against her body at a grotesque angle, like a broken limb.

"I was held in a stinking overcrowded cell for hours, then sent before the magistrate."

"You're hurt."

"The march turned into quite a scuffle."

"Yes, I saw. Let's get these wet things off you. I'll see to your cheek."

Veronica got out of bed and stripped down to her underwear. Dorothy hung the damaged dress over the back of a chair. "What a pity, you looked so splendid in it," she said sadly. "But I'm sure it can be mended."

"After today, I hate the very sight of it. I'd like to burn it."

"You've had an awful time."

"The trial was a complete farce!" Veronica said angrily. "The prosecution put forward the most barefaced lies. I could hardly believe what I was hearing!"

"What did they say?"

"That we set off on our march with loud yells and songs; that we behaved in the most disruptive and violent way. They accused us of knocking off policemen's helmets and biting and scratching them as we passed, even using our hatpins as weapons!"

"I can't believe it."

"Our testimony, and that of the defense witnesses, was ignored completely. When I tried to speak out for myself, I was cut short in the rudest way possible."

"It's a disgrace. This is supposed to be a civilized country.

"Justice exists for men in England, not for women."

Dorothy sighed. "Let me at least clean up your poor cheek. Have you eaten? Shall I get you something?"

"Thank you, but I couldn't face food."

As she submitted to Dorothy's ministrations, Veronica said she had been sentenced to a month's imprisonment in Holloway, beginning tomorrow. "I've been released on bail for the night. The magistrate said I was a little firebrand; he told me prison would cool me down. Ouch, you're hurting me." Veronica pulled away.

"Sorry, I'll try and be gentler. What was the charge?"

"Assaulting the police." Veronica's mouth was a grim line. "Nothing could be further from the truth. The police were assaulting me! And the worst of it is that I won't be imprisoned in the first division."

"What's that?"

"It's the section for political prisoners, where you're treated less harshly and given a few privileges. They're putting me in the second division with the common criminals, the thieves and drunkards. I'll be strip searched when I arrive, put in solitary confinement, and forced to submit to all the other lousy rules imposed on female offenders."

"How can they get away with that?"

"If you have no political status and no civil rights, the law says you don't qualify as a political prisoner . . . Dorothy?"

"Yes, what?"

"I'm frightened . . . don't go." Her voice had sunk to a thready whisper. "Stay with me. I really need you tonight."

"Yes," Dorothy said. "I'd like that more than anything."

It was their first night not spent making love. Veronica, shorn of her vivacity and her conviction, seemed much younger; weak and vulnerable. Dorothy ached with a new feeling: a tenderness that was so overwhelming, her whole being reverberated with it. She put her own illness and anxiety on one side, wanting only to comfort Veronica. They hardly spoke, though neither of them slept. Dorothy kept her arms around Veronica the whole night, trying to steady her limbs, which would not stop trembling.

AS DOROTHY APPROACHED the forbidding central tower of Holloway, dread began to seep through her. The high prison walls, coated with pigeon droppings, cast a deep ominous shadow. The rows and rows of narrow constricted windows seemed designed to let in the minimum of air or light. Veronica had not been allowed visitors for the first fortnight of her sentence, and Dorothy had spent the time in an agony of impatience and uncertainty. She was shown to the visiting room by a cold-eyed young wardress with a neat figure and carefully tended chestnut hair. She wore a dark blue uniform in the style of a hospital nurse, and her posture was very upright; there was something in her manner that reminded Dorothy, incongruously, of a chaperone at a dance.

They walked past a large hall that was surrounded by cells opening onto narrow galleries, fenced in by iron railings. The different floors were connected by a small iron staircase in the center. All the balconies and stairs were draped with wire netting. Dorothy supposed this was to prevent prisoners committing suicide, but it gave the impression they were trapped inside a gigantic and hellish cage.

The wardress began to lead her through a series of passages. Their footsteps resounded dully on the stone floor, which felt chilly and damp beneath Dorothy's cheap thin-soled shoes. (She needed a new pair, but where would the money come from?) The atmosphere became danker and colder by the minute, and Dorothy was gripped by claustrophobia and horror. From somewhere above came the clanging of metal gates; Dorothy thought she could hear a woman sobbing wildly.

This part of Holloway was like being inside a tomb. And yet it was not the dead who were shut up in here, it was the living. The passages were stuffy and draughty. A thick smell of filth and damp hung in the air, like the stink of drains, rank and rotten. It crept around Dorothy, permeating her clothes. Trying to breathe shallowly, so as to absorb as little as possible of the noxious air, she felt her face grow tense and small feverish spots of exhaustion begin to burn on her cheekbones. She hoped she wouldn't vomit or pass out.

At last, the wardress ushered Dorothy into a room. "You're to wait here. The prisoner will be brought to you shortly." She did not look at Dorothy as she spoke; she seemed to talk past her into the air, in a voice that was completely empty of expression. It sounded odd and unnatural, as though she was speaking from behind a mask, through which no glimmer of personality was allowed to escape. Dorothy stared at her averted face, trying to imagine the indignity and anguish the prisoners must feel being spoken to like this every day. They would be thrown back on themselves, alone and unsupported, continually thwarted in their longing to be recognized as human, too.

When the wardress had gone, Dorothy looked around her. It was an ugly stark room. The walls and ceiling were dirty, and there was one small high window, whose glass panes were so grimy and smeared, the weak daylight could scarcely penetrate. The only furniture was a table, running almost the length of the room, with a hard chair at either end. It would be nearly impossible to talk across it.

Dorothy sat down to wait. After about five minutes, she saw another wardress walking down the corridor, trailed by the slight figure of a woman in a shapeless prison dress made of coarse brown calico. The dress was too short at the sleeves and waist, which made her look like a grotesquely overgrown child. Her hair was hidden under a lumpy white cap and she had a white apron tied around her waist. These garments were none too clean; they had evidently been soiled by many previous wearers. As the pair entered the room, Dorothy realized the prisoner was Veronica.

They stared at one another in dismay. The hideousness of the uniform and the subservient humility it so powerfully suggested had changed Veronica beyond recognition.

In the same expressionless tone as the first wardress, and without looking at either woman, the guard told them to sit at opposite ends of the table, and not to touch one another, nor pass anything between them. The door was left open and she stationed herself outside, to monitor their conversation.

"I thought you weren't going to come," Veronica said.

"Of course I'm here; nothing would have stopped me. How could you even doubt it?"

Veronica sighed. "I think it's the effect of being shut up in here. I feel as helpless as a child, prey to terrible fluctuating feelings. I was convinced you'd forgotten or discarded me."

"I'll never do either."

"Thank God."

"You look so different," Dorothy said angrily.

"Yes," Veronica said flatly, with an apprehensive glance toward the wardress.

Dorothy lowered her voice. "I hate seeing you like this. Are you all right?"

Veronica gave the wardress another look. "I'm fine. They treat me well enough." But the struggle for serenity, evident in the lift of her eyebrows and the way she pressed her full lips together to stop them trembling, contradicted her reasonable words.

"What's it like?"

"The worst thing is the drinking water." Veronica was almost whispering. "It's only changed once a day and it's kept in tins, which are cleaned with soap and brick dust, but not washed out. I can't tell you how horrible it tastes." She shuddered. "I also hate not knowing if you're being watched or not while you're in your cell. There's a peephole in the door; you're never quite sure if there's an eye staring through it or not. Then at any time and without warning, keys jangle, locks grind, and the door is flung open. It feels so hurried and noisy you think something out of the ordinary has happened, like a fire or a breakout. But it's invariably routine: time to exercise, or bathe, or have an inspection. It's just so startling and invasive every time; you never get used to it." She paused, scratching her head under her cap. "Other than that, the days aren't too bad. But my God, Dorothy, the nights!"

"Tell me."

"For one thing, I can't sleep, because the plank bed is hard and there's no pillow and the cell is freezing. I can't explain how utterly chilling the atmosphere of prison in the dead of night is . . . there's something about it that paralyzes your will and tightens your nerves to snapping point. You feel so cut off from love and warmth and hope. It's like being cast out from the rest of humanity."

Through the sickness that was threatening to engulf Dorothy, she longed to reach over and pull Veronica against her and show her how untrue this was.

"The silence is dreadful," Veronica continued, "like a thick cold shroud wrapping round you. But the sudden screams and cries that break it, tearing through the darkness, are worse . . . There are so many sounds and each one fills you with dread; you can't interpret them and they are never explained afterward. Last night, there was a woman groaning and shrieking somewhere on the floor above me. It was a frightful noise, like an injured beast, scarcely human. I've never heard such fury and despair in all my life." Veronica shook her head, as though trying to dispel the cries that still haunted her. "She was rattling the gate and hurling herself against it, until it trembled on its hinges. The poor creature seemed to be possessed by an awful strength and wildness; she carried on for half the night.

I'll never know if she was drunk, crazy, or just plain terrified. Nobody will answer your questions; you're kept in total ignorance of what's happening outside your cell." She broke off; she was shivering.

"It sounds terrible, but at least time's passing. You're more than halfway through your sentence now."

"That's true, but the last part is going to be the hardest of all."

"What makes you think so?"

Veronica paused dramatically and lowered her voice, so Dorothy had to strain to hear her. "I've decided to go on a hunger strike."

"No!"

"Some of the other suffragettes have already started. We won't submit to being treated like ordinary lawbreakers. We're asserting our right to be treated as political prisoners, with the same privileges male political offenders have. We won't touch food until the government yields our point."

"And what if the government doesn't yield? They haven't given in to any of your other demands. What will it achieve? You've brought enough suffering on your—"

Dorothy broke off. The lacerating stomachache was back, in its full force. She bent over, hands on her belly, clamping her lip between her teeth to stop moaning. She was drowning in pain, alone. What was happening to her body? How long could she carry on ignoring it?

"What's wrong?" Veronica asked.

"Nothing . . . just cramps." Dorothy's breath came unsteadily and her voice shook.

"You're deathly pale."

It was some moments before Dorothy could answer. At last, the spasm began to ease. She straightened up and tried to smile.

"Feeling better?"

"Yes, I think so."

"You don't look well at all."

"I'm fine. Really."

"Tell me what you've been doing since I last saw you," Veronica pleaded, almost desperately. "What's happening at the house? Are you missing me? What are you thinking right now?"

They began to talk about the latest comings and goings of boarders, clinging to the ordinary everyday details of the life of Mrs. Baker's house, which seemed, at that moment, infinitely precious.

Another prisoner was making her way down the corridor; she walked listlessly, with a wardress beside her. The inmate's skin was yellow, as though she had jaundice, and her eyes, set in deep hollows, were vacant. She looked like she had lost her way, given up, retreated to a place deep inside herself. Seeing Dorothy distracted, Veronica followed her gaze. The prisoners exchanged the slightest of nods.

"We sat next to each other in the Black Maria on the way here," Veronica explained. "Her husband's an invalid, and she isn't in good health herself. She earns a pittance taking in washing. It's nowhere near enough to feed her children so, in desperation, she stole a couple of loaves of bread for them. When she was caught, she received neither understanding nor mercy; she was simply thrown in here. Listening to her story, I realized all the things I've heard and read about are true. Now at least I know who I'm fighting for. There are countless others in equally bad situations. Women who are in dire need of a political voice, and are so ground under and broken, they don't even know they need one. It's because of them that we can't afford to wait. Having the vote isn't just a right; it's a burning necessity."

The wardress had come into the room while Veronica was speaking. "Time's up," she said flatly, adding to Dorothy, "You're to wait here till you're fetched."

Veronica's lips trembled; the next moment, tears were spilling silently down her cheeks. Without a word, the wardress put her hands on Veronica's shoulders and yanked her roughly to her feet, leading her out of the room as though she was an animal. Veronica submitted meekly to this unnecessary treatment, but Dorothy found it unbearably degrading; she burned with helpless anger and revolt.

"I'll see you soon," she said uselessly, to Veronica's departing back.

DOROTHY MADE HER way home, ill and anguished. The grim central tower of Holloway receded with every step, but the prison smell still hung about her clothes, persistent and sickening. The thought of Veronica on hunger strike was torment; Dorothy had heard that other suffragettes were forcibly fed when they refused to eat, and she feared for Veronica's safety. As she walked, their conversation played and replayed in her head.

I want to know what you've been doing since I last saw you . . . Are you missing me? What are you thinking? I want the thought that crossed your face a moment ago—that one.

Dorothy felt tired and slightly dizzy; she could hear the breath rasping in her throat. Momentarily, she was disoriented. Did the voices in her head belong to her and Veronica, or were they hers and Bertie's? She shook her head to dispel them, and they disintegrated, leaving a thousand echoes. *What was that thought? . . . I want that one . . . that thought . . .* Sweat was trickling under her armpits and between her breasts.

She willed the voices to leave her. She was dead tired, feeble with fatigue. She only wanted to be left alone, to recover in peace.

The sky was aflame with pink, spread out behind gilded clouds that hid the wilting sun. London was transformed into a glittering celestial city; the buildings were rose-colored, their grey roofs glowing gold. The light seemed almost viscous as it deepened and spread over the buildings.

It was hard to reconcile the magnificence before her with the horror of Holloway. London was a place of terror and beauty, squalor and splendor. But the contrasts were more than she could bear; they jarred on her, almost painfully.

Bertie was right when he said it was London that got you in the end.

She reached the boardinghouse with relief. As she climbed the flight of winding stairs that led to the top floor, the forgotten wealth of her solitary attic began to steal round her once more. Her time with Veronica, so joyous and so full of pain, began to feel strangely far away.

Her door opened with its usual rising squeak. She walked over to the window and looked at the tree-filled square and the housefronts opposite; their windows dark, or suffused with mellow golden light. She lit her lamp and the room came alive with a thousand flickering shadows. It was aloof and mysterious, just as if she was seeing it anew.

She sat down on her narrow single bed. She seemed to have used up every drop of feeling and, for the first time since Veronica made her astonishing declaration of love on the mirror, Dorothy was at peace.

The relief she was experiencing at Veronica's absence was a shock, both guilty and pleasurable. Stretching her arms over her head, she soaked up the stillness and the feeling of enclosure. An evening of freedom unfolded before her . . .

Her deepest, most intimate self, which had been choked off by everything that had happened, was beginning to revive and expand. The realization that it had not died, that it was still buoyant and untouched, brought a warm moment of joy. Able once more to simply be, she sat quite still, listening to the familiar rumble of traffic from Euston Road, relishing the feeling that came from being alone and at ease. She was filled with her old sense of the marvelousness of life; how extraordinary it was that anything at all existed.

St. Pancras clock chimed the half hour, and she wondered if she was strong enough to write. But she felt bilious; there was still a slight dragging ache in the pit of her stomach. She lay down on the bed and drew her knees up, waiting for it to pass.

Seventeen

DOROTHY WOKE FROM A DREAM FILLED WITH ANguish and tears.

She lay in the dark, unable to escape the feeling that something was dreadfully wrong. A mild pain was beginning in the pit of her stomach; a dull throbbing, similar to the sensation which accompanied her monthlies.

There was a trickle between her legs, sticky and warm. She got out of bed hurriedly, which made her so dizzy that she had to lean against the wall to steady herself.

Deep inside her, she felt something falling away.

When she'd recovered sufficiently to light the gas, she saw bright red blood, mixed with darker pieces of gelatinous tissue. Her mouth opened in a soundless cry. Blood was pouring out of her body, and the clots that came with it were huge—one or two the size of a crab apple. Its metallic smell hit her, her knees gave way, and she sank to the floor in shock.

After some minutes, she had the presence of mind to go to the small lavatory. She sat on the toilet bowl, waiting fearfully as her body expelled the tiny speck of life that had failed to adhere to it. And it seemed to her that the blood was tears shed by her womb, deeper than heart's blood.

The pain grew stronger; powerful contractions that arrived closer and closer together. The iron claw was back, crushing her womb; she was doubled up and crying out in agony. When she was sufficiently lucid for thought, she was grateful for the thick walls of the house, sheltering the other boarders from the noise she was making.

Her pain had its own rhythm. Behind her closed eyelids, it assumed colors as well: fiery red, burnt orange, dull brown and black. It was the screech of a metal point being scraped down a blackboard, a toothed saw on stone. It was a pressure so relentless, it crushed her into a ball tinier than a pebble. She could tell when it was at its height because she heard a little trickle of blood falling into the lavatory at the peak of each contraction. Then the wave would recede, and a new crescendo would begin its buildup again. Everything had disintegrated, past and future and present; she was nothing but this terrible pain that inhabited and possessed her.

The heavy stillness of the house pressed down on her; she was shaking violently. There was no one she could call at this hour. Probably she needed medical attention; what if she bled to death? She heard her breath rasping in her throat; she began to feel hot, sweaty, and faint. She tried to put her head between her legs, though it was not enough. Black spots danced before her eyes and the walls of her skull caved in. As she fell to the ground, she was sucked into black nothingness.

When she awoke, she had no idea how long she'd been out. It was still dark outside. There was a sharp pain in her hip; she must have bruised it falling. She was lying on the floor with her face pressed against the cool boards. The contractions were beginning to ease, the bleeding was slowing down.

After a while, she was able to get up. She washed her face and hands at the shabby open sink cupboard, and drank some water from a battered enamel cup. She fetched a sanitary towel from its packet and crawled back to her bloodstained bed.

The room was cold and stuffy. She was deathly cold and clammy; she couldn't stop shivering. She heaped all the covers over herself but it was no use; her body felt like it had been submerged in icy water.

She started to cry. She cried until her throat ached, an abandoned animal-like wailing that shocked her, for it sounded like it was coming from someone else. She cried for her pain and her fear; she cried for the thing that had died inside her without ever properly existing; she cried for the loss of magic and mystery between her and Bertie. She cried for Veronica and for Jane; she cried for her mother. She cried because she wanted to.

When she had cried herself out completely, cold calm descended on her, and something bordering on relief. She closed her eyes and an image came into her mind of floating amongst the clouds with her baby, looking down at treetops and houses far below. It comforted her. She had a sense of belonging to an order that was much larger than herself, and a feeling of restored faith in its mysterious workings.

A new thought arrived. She was free. She didn't have to be a hostage in Bertie's demented world any longer.

Eighteen

AS TIME PASSED, DOROTHY'S BODY HEALED SLOWLY, but a strange cold numbness crept into her soul. It stole around her like a shroud, inviolate and impenetrable, unlike anything she had ever experienced before. She moved through her days feeling cut off from other people, isolated in chilly bleakness. Yet as she stood with Bertie in the Russell Square rooms, her lack of feeling seemed like armor, protecting her, and she was almost glad of it.

"I can't believe you're doing this. Is it really what you want?" Bertie's voice was little more than a whisper.

Dorothy nodded wordlessly. Each sound and movement came to her as if from far away, failing to penetrate the force field of isolation. She wondered if she would always feel this alone. If so, she must learn to bear it.

"Don't break us up, Dora. I'm begging you."

"I have to."

The numbness lifted without warning, and she found herself hardly able to speak for the pain that flooded through her. She cleared her throat and tried again. "We had our chance at happiness, and we've made a damned mess of it . . . a terrible waste and mess. Jane's betrayed and hurt, we're all damaged . . . we can't carry on as though nothing happened."

Bertie swallowed audibly. He tried to take her hand, but she moved away.

He put his head in his hands. "I was shattered, you know, when we lost the baby. Your pregnancy lifted me into a state of tremendous elation, and when it ended, I came crashing down from a great height. But I never, for one moment, thought I'd lose you as well . . ." His voice was trembling. "We'll be miserable apart. It will tear a great hole in my heart. I'm sure it won't leave much in yours . . . I'm finished without you."

Dorothy was experiencing the old pull toward him . . . there was nobody quite like him. Her throat hurt with the effort of holding back tears; with the effort of not putting her arms around him. She'd give anything to lean into his solid warmth one last time. The strength of the desire was like a physical force, stronger than she was. She wanted to dissolve into him, to give herself over to being shaped by him . . . One hand reached toward him, halted before it touched him. She knew that if she succumbed, she would never summon the strength to break free. Sternly, she reminded herself that being with him had nearly destroyed her. It was wrong; it couldn't lead to happiness. She forced her hand to drop. Though the room was warm, she felt shivery and sick in her stomach.

Bertie stood up and walked toward her, both hands outstretched. "My darling Dora, you aren't yourself. You've been through a horrible ordeal, and you're weaker than you realize.

Don't break us up now, you might feel differently when you're better."

Dorothy shook her head. "I've made up my mind. There's nothing more to say."

Despite the certainty with which she spoke, she couldn't extinguish the wild hope that he would suddenly turn into the person she was searching for . . . that he would say or do some marvelous thing to redeem himself and save them both.

There was silence.

"I've handed in my notice at work," she said at last.

Bertie made a sound that expressed amazement and derision. "Why chuck everything over at once? What a fearfully silly thing to do."

"It's hard to explain . . . I need a complete break, to be totally free, to start over . . ."

"How will you survive? What are you going to *do*?"

Involuntarily, his hand reached toward the inside pocket of his jacket, where he kept his wallet.

Dorothy shook her head. "I shall manage."

He sighed. "I can't help feeling that you've taken leave of your senses."

She bristled. "On the contrary; I've never felt so sane and clearheaded in my life."

There was another pause. Eventually, Bertie said "You'll still support me, take an interest in my work?"

She nodded, unable to meet his eyes.

He said sadly, "You know where to find me if you need me."

VERONICA STOOD IN the middle of her room. A wild disorder of garments and belongings were strewn over the floor, and over every surface. She looked frail and sickly; her color was bad and her eyes seemed too large for her thin face. Making her way to the bed, she began to fold a heap of blouses; her movements were slow and careful. Her old speed and supple grace, her way of throwing herself into everything she did, had gone.

She was packing to go home, in disgrace. Her brother's goodwill and indulgence, stretched to its utmost limit on so many occasions, had finally snapped under the indelible dishonor of prison.

Veronica paused in the middle of what she was doing, and sat down heavily on the bed.

"Are you all right?" Dorothy asked. "Should you be seen by a doctor, in case? The things they did to you could have caused an internal injury."

"Oh, I'm not too bad. I do get tired more easily these days, but I expect that a combination of taking it easy and Mother's cooking will put me right."

"I can't imagine how ghastly it must have been."

"I haven't told you about the forcible feeding."

Dorothy pressed her lips together. "I didn't ask, because I don't want to make you relive it."

"I'll tell you . . ." Veronica paused, half closing her eyes. She began to speak in a flat expressionless voice, very matter of fact, as though she was talking about someone else.

"It took five of them to do it. Two wardresses pinned my arms down, one wrenched back my head, and one had both feet, stretching my limbs to their limit, so that my body took on the shape of a cross. The doctor bent over my chest to get at my mouth; he had to lean on my knees to do it. I'd closed my mouth tightly, but he managed to prise it open by digging the sharp edge of his thumbnail into my lips. He forced my jaws wide, as far as they would stretch, and a gag was tied so my teeth couldn't close. A rubber tube was pushed down my throat—it seemed enormous, far too thick to do the job—and it made me choke, from the second it touched the back of my throat till it was thrust into my stomach. It seemed to take them forever to get it into me; I can't describe the agony of it. The choking, the lack of air got worse and worse; I was struggling desperately for breath, convinced I was going to suffocate. I'm sure they passed the tube too far down, because it caused an excruciating pain in my side.

"Then liquid food was poured very quickly into my stomach, through a funnel. My eardrums felt like they were exploding; there was a terrible burning in my chest, which I could feel to the end of my breastbone. It was too much food, too fast, and I was immediately sick over the doctor and wardresses. The act of vomiting made me double up involuntarily, but the wardresses pressed my head back and the doctor leant on my knees to keep me straight. God, it was humiliating! Vomit gushed everywhere, over my face and hair. It soaked through my dress and splashed onto their clothes and shoes. There was so much of it, and it simply stank; it was a revolting mess. It seemed an age before they took the tube out, and when it came up, it felt like it was tearing out the whole of my insides with it.

"By that stage, I could hardly remember who I was, let alone why I was there. I forgot equal rights; I forgot the other suffragettes. I was aware of nothing but my own misery. Before the doctor walked out, he slapped me across the face. It wasn't a forceful blow, but it seemed to express how much he despised me and my behavior . . . I was left almost fainting in a pool of sick. I was gripped by a fit of shivering and I couldn't move; they said it was too late at night to fetch a change of clothes for me."

"But that's inhuman! You wouldn't treat an animal like that!"

"Exactly. Yet this torture is happening to suffragettes in gaols all over the country, and it's sanctioned by His Majesty's Government . . . I was fed like that four or five times, and each time was worse than the one that went before, partly, I think, because knowing what was in store made the anticipation of it an utter torment."

Dorothy was silent, battling for composure.

"To tell the truth, I feel rather broken by it all," Veronica went on. "Damaged in health, and weakened in spirit. I keep asking myself what it was for. All our protests failed, and I'm not sure they were worth the price . . . the vote seems further away than ever. I'm thinking of giving up on the suffrage, actually."

It was almost more than Dorothy could bear to hear Veronica talk like this. "Your march failed, but one day the suffragettes will succeed," she said stoutly.

"Do you think so? Right now, having the vote seems as unlikely as you and I being allowed to love each other openly."

Dorothy paused for a moment, before saying softly "I'm sure a time will come for both. It just isn't now."

"Hmm." Veronica was examining the ragged skin around her fingernails. "At any rate, I've realized you were right. We can't stand up against the whole world."

"Don't. It kills me to hear you sound so defeated."

Shrugging her shoulders, Veronica hauled herself to her feet and turned back to her packing; for a time, they were silent.

"Are you looking forward to going home?" Dorothy asked, at last.

"Yes, I am, although being with them is only a different kind of prison—a more luxurious one, with an unstinting clothes allowance." She gave Dorothy the ghost of a smile. "It's odd, but I feel I scarcely want to be free; I've lost the will. I never realized how habit forming obedience is. You never use reason or judgment in prison; you're told what to do, and you follow orders without query or hesitation. The idea of thinking for myself, or taking any kind of initiative is quite frightening."

There was another pause.

"I'm glad Benjamin came to visit you," Dorothy said.

"I've never been so surprised in my life as I was to see him. I suppose you told him I was in prison?"

"Yes." Dorothy clamped her mouth shut to stop herself confessing that his call had been made entirely at her suggestion.

Dorothy could picture Benjamin in the horrible visiting room: the unabashedly soulful look on his face as he took in the grime and the smell, and steeled himself for a difficult meeting, not wanting to disappoint Dorothy. He would have seemed like a visitor from another world in the frock coat and silk hat of his hard-won city status, waiting for Veronica with barely suppressed impatience, his case of legal documents under his arm. These details would not have been lost on the fearsome wardresses. Dorothy hoped his visit had resulted in more careful treatment for Veronica.

Dorothy could see Veronica emerging, at last, from the bowels of the building, her beauty dimmed but not extinguished by the graceless uniform. She would have been nonplussed and speechless at the unexpected sight of Benjamin, gathering all her self-possession to manage the occasion. There would have been no sign of the laughter he had found so irrelevant and annoying at their first meeting. Benjamin had probably gazed at her in silence, the muscles in his face contracting and his eyebrows raised with effort as he sought phrases to alleviate his discomfiture, saying something like, "Hello. You will most certainly not have been expecting me." How could he fail to be moved by the radiantly accepting, grateful smile that would have greeted his words?

Dorothy wondered what they had talked about. Had it dawned on him gradually, or all at once, that Veronica was intelligent and brave as well as beautiful; that she had principles and was prepared to endure real suffering for the sake of them?

"He said he would come and see me at home," Veronica was saying. Dorothy couldn't, for a few moments, work out what the unfamiliar tone in her voice meant . . . she realized, with a shock, that it expressed successful rivalry! Veronica was competing with her for Benjamin; worse still, she believed herself victorious.

Dorothy was silent, struggling to come to terms with the fact that the train of events she'd set in motion had assumed an unstoppable life of its own, and was sliding rapidly away from her. She looked at Veronica standing in front of the French windows. Cold sunlight streamed in through the glass, falling sharply over her pale face and shoulders. There was no depth in the light. Dorothy wondered if this was how a novelist might feel who, having breathed life into his characters, unexpectedly found they had assumed independent wills, and were refusing to be controlled.

"I don't know what Mother will make of Benjamin . . ." Veronica sounded less confident. "He won't exactly fit in with her idea of an acceptable suitor."

There was another hesitation.

"Why can't we stay the way we were?" Veronica asked suddenly, with a flash of her old impulsiveness. Dorothy breathed her relief: the essence of their relationship was unchanged.

"Yes."

"Let's go away somewhere. To France or Italy; anywhere nobody knows us or cares what we are to each other. Let's pack up and leave, just the two of us."

"I wish we could."

"God, we've been happy together. I can hardly bear to leave all this. I've never been so happy in my life as I am with you."

Veronica walked over and slipped an arm around her waist; her lips brushed the side of Dorothy's mouth. Gentle and sweet, almost chaste, her touch brought their old world all about them: peerless, inextinguishable. They fell silent, reveling in the completeness of it. The whole of life flowed between them, within them, in a way no man and woman, however well matched, could hope to attain.

In a few hours, Veronica would be isolated with her family's chilly disapproval.

VERONICA WAS READY. Dorothy's hands felt large and shaky, and her feet were cold. The room looked barren and desolate without the clutter Veronica attracted. It was funny how quickly a room died without an inhabitant. Veronica turned off the gas and stood for a moment in the doorway, taking one last look. She closed the door softly and they walked downstairs together. Her luggage was waiting in the hall.

They both began to talk at once; then fell silent at the same moment, waiting for the other to speak.

"What did you want to say?" Dorothy asked.

"Oh no, you go first."

"I expect the cab is here. You'd better hurry."

Suddenly, a rain of tears was coming down Dorothy's cheeks. They fell softly and copiously, stoically, as though without her realizing, they had been getting ready for this preordained moment.

"Darling! Don't!" Veronica put her arms around her and kissed her tenderly, murmuring sweet endearments. "It's just a temporary good-bye, I promise you. I promise I'll come back. I'll find a way, somehow."

Dorothy, struggling for breath through tears, wondered if the words were prompted only by Veronica's wish to retain her hold over Dorothy. Perhaps they stemmed from her innate warmth, or were simply crumbs of comfort tossed out to a mortally hurt soul.

Veronica went, leaving the house stricken.

Dorothy was engulfed by sadness. It was like being buried alive; a kind of panic. She curled up on the floor of her room, beyond tears.

Her life was ripped up at the roots. She had lost everything: the baby, Bertie, Veronica. Nothing would ever be as good, or as vivid, as having them. And now, there was no one who would be sorry if she disappeared off the face of the earth. The thought made her flinch. It was the truth; there was no use denying it. The pretense of living would continue. She had destroyed all her ties with people, but for what?

Grinding poverty loomed. She would go on, dragging herself though her colorless existence, alone. She was worthless, an encumbrance, excluded from happiness forever. To die now and put an end to her suffering would be a relief.

She hauled herself away from this thought, searching her mind wearily for something meaningful . . . Amidst the rubble of her life, something shone . . . alive. It was the pile of closely written pages on her small table. But their value was uncertain—her writing might turn out to be shallow and empty after all. She forced herself to sit up and look at the growing paper stack. The sight was reassuring; it was all that anchored her to the world.

Something at the core of life steadied and clarified. She wrote because she had to; it was salvation, as essential as breathing. For the sake of her writing, she needed to free herself from those who would shape and possess her. It was for this she had smashed her way to a clear horizon.

Nineteen

DOROTHY SAT ON THE BEACH AT PORTHCOTHAN Bay, a strip of white sand enclosed by soaring brown cliffs. She leaned against a rock, enjoying the sun on her face and the briny smell of salt air mingling with the scent of her sun-warmed skin. London seemed far away.

The air felt like silk. Taking a warm handful of sand, she let it trickle through her fingers; it glinted in the sunshine, as finely textured as caster sugar. The tide was out. Splinters of sunlight danced on the ripples and sparkled over the bodies of seagulls hovering and dipping above the lacy shallows, emitting hoarse cries. A belt of mist hugged the horizon; sea dissolved invisibly into sky. Dorothy balanced her writing pad on her knees, intending to record it all. But finding herself strangely disinclined to set down a word, she simply sat, soaking up her surroundings like a sponge.

Why did being free make her feel guilty? Knowing she

could move on and start afresh whenever she wanted; looking at people who were tied down with pitying disdain. But her freedom was tinged with a loneliness and despair that they would never experience. It was only by the pain of cutting loose that one could have the whole of life around one, continuously.

FROM THE WINDOW of her room in the guesthouse, she could see the pearl-blue sky, with patches of pink fleecy cloud scudding across it. The small garden, backed by feathery trees, was bright coppery gold in the light of the sinking sun.

She had come to Cornwall to finish her second novel. The first had been published to glowing reviews. "Miss Dorothy Richardson's work is like nothing else in modern literature," the novelist Frank Swinnerton enthused. "It has a precision and a brilliant, inexorable veracity, which no other writer attains. It is bound to influence novelists of the future . . . Of its importance there is no question." "No one could read this book and disregard her," trumpeted *The Spectator*. "For the thing which Miss Richardson creates is as actual as the paper, ink, and boards by whose medium it is conveyed to the reader . . . the perusal of the book amounts to a sort of vicarious living."

A single shadow dimmed her satisfaction: a grudging article by Virginia Woolf, Sir Leslie Stephen's daughter. Virginia's own first novel was about to be published by Gerald Duckworth, who was also Dorothy's publisher. "I suppose the danger of her method is the damned egoistical self, which ruins Richardson to my mind," Virginia had written. "Is one pliant and rich enough to provide a wall for the book without its becoming . . . narrowing and restricting?"

Despite the critical, disaffected presence of Virginia in the background, recognition finally seemed to be within Dorothy's reach. She could not pronounce the word *fame*, even to herself.

There seemed to be an invisible balance in life, making sure that whenever something was lost, a new thing arrived to take its place . . . you were never left totally bereft . . . somebody or something making sure that life did not become absolutely unendurable.

She bent over the unsteady table, rereading the pages spread in front of her. The manuscript seemed somehow more alive than a book trussed up in its tidy binding.

The bond between herself and her work was closer than any other in her life. It was the source of the most profound joy she knew. The recording of impressions had become a necessity; without it, she was not fully alive. All roads in her life had brought her to it.

Some days, on reading her work, she felt it was good. Segments were more than good. The great joy and great suffering she had known gave her writing richness and depth, while her curious position on the edge of society sharpened her insights. But on bad days, it still seemed that she was not a writer at all: she was just a freak with a facility for words. Her task was quite simply to capture the essence of a woman's life as it was lived; its minute to minute quality. To bridge the gulf between life and the expression of it. Yet she always fell just short; she feared her writing would never match the perfectly expressive novel she carried inside her head.

A low ray of sunlight coming through the window distracted her, bringing back everything she had loved in Veronica and taken from her and ecstatically given in return: a life lived by someone who was not quite Dorothy, in a past that seemed as distant as her former self.

Veronica's presence was everywhere, catching Dorothy unawares. It was in the light pouring over the breakfast table; it lingered over the fine white sand and spilled out across the glistening billows of the sea. It spread across the deserted sandy pathway that ran down to the beach, hummocky and rambling and scented with gorse. At night, it sang in the roar of the darkened sea.

Sometimes the memory of their time together was a golden glow, and sometimes, especially during the dead hours of the night, it was a terrible unhealed wound. Dorothy would roll onto her stomach in bed, feeling her pulse hammering against the mattress. The mattress was hard against her breasts and thighs, yet it gave back no echo of a heartbeat, and she was filled with longing for it to be Veronica's pliant body beneath her. At these times, the deprivation was almost unbearable.

Often, it seemed as though a part of her still existed continuously in the past. Lived with Veronica; the two of them lying eternally in each other's arms, belonging together, as in the early days of their association. And this bit of her—a pure essence, a brightly burning flame—was somehow fused with the part of her that wrote. It was also one with the child who had stood in a garden in bright sunlight long ago, and watched in wonder as bees swayed from one blazing flower bank to another.

It was far more vivid than the grey present. She thought she would probably die with these feelings.

AS FAR AS she knew, Veronica had remained with her parents the whole time, but she was a fitful correspondent, and long silences elapsed between letters.

When Dorothy returned to London, there was a note from her waiting on the hall stand. Dorothy tore open the envelope at once. It was a hurried scrawl, a mere couple of lines, saying she was back in London and longing to see Dorothy.

THE DOMINO ROOM at the Café Royal was a carnival of color and noise. The tobacco fumes and hum of voices, the jingle of coins and the clatter of dominoes being shuffled on marble tables hit Dorothy and broke over her head like a wave. Briefly, she took in the gilded walls, crimson velvet benches, and huge ornamental pillars; the crowd of cheerful drinkers reflected in several large mirrors arranged about the room. But these sights were uninteresting compared to Veronica, who was waiting for her just inside the door.

In real life, Veronica was smaller than the space she occupied in Dorothy's imagination. She looked radiant in a clinging violet gown, which clearly showed the shape of her body beneath it. Hugging Dorothy, she exclaimed, "I can't quite believe it's you, after all this time! I think I must have dreamed you up."

"I think I'm dreaming, too." Dorothy's voice shook slightly. The feel of Veronica's body against hers was overwhelming; it brought a heady rush of memory and rendered her almost tongue-tied.

"What do you think of the place?" Veronica asked.

Dorothy took a deep breath. "It's so alive!"

Veronica nodded, her eyes glinting.

She led her past the clusters of patrons to an empty table at the rear, near the back door, which bordered on the white-clothed tables laid for dinner. They sat down facing the room, and Veronica ordered a bottle of champagne from a waiter. "This is a celebration. We're going to toast the success of your book!" she declared.

Snatches of a song, rendered in an off-key but penetrating voice to the tune of "Greensleeves," floated over to them:

Jove be with us as we sit
On the crimson soft settees;
Drinking beer and liking it,
Most peculiarly at ease.

Dorothy craned her neck to try and identify the singer, but he was hidden by the crowd.

That for life, and this for love,
"B" for Bliss and "P" for Pain
Not till midnight will we move—
Waiter, fill 'em up again!

When their champagne arrived, the waiter made a great show of opening the bottle and pouring the pale gold liquid into two tall glasses.

"To you!" Veronica said, raising her glass and clinking it against Dorothy's.

The champagne was very dry, with a delicately nutty taste. Dorothy savored the sensation of bubbles exploding at the back of her nose. "My word, this feels decadent," she said. "Champagne at the Café Royal!"

"But you deserve it! Everyone is talking about your novel; it's a sensation." Veronica began to quote: " 'A completely new and original voice, unlike any before heard in literature'; 'Feminine impressionism carried to new limits'; 'A finely tuned method of registering perception and experience.' People are comparing you to Proust."

Dorothy held out her hand, laughing. "Stop, please. This is too much for me!"

"It's the truth," Veronica protested. "And I admire your courage. It isn't easy smashing convention and creating a new way of writing. You're like an explorer in a new world—a true pioneer."

"Am I a pioneer or an oddity? Whichever, it feels like pushing boulders up a mountain. I seem incapable of taking the easy path in my writing or my life."

"You're a brave woman. And funnily enough, you've struck a more successful blow for our sex than I ever did trying to get a vote. I always knew you could do it."

Veronica's admiration, her near warm presence and achingly familiar scent were causing a hot sweet stirring at the base of Dorothy's stomach. It was intoxicating; she was like a bud, helplessly opening out beneath the warm sun. She gazed at Veronica, waiting for her words; mesmerized by the fall of the long lashes onto the softly rounded cheeks, the sweet full lips flowering for speech.

"See the bearded man in the corner, with golden earrings and a black hat and cloak?" Veronica asked. "I think it's Augustus John."

Dorothy cleared her throat. "Yes, you're absolutely right. He probably comes here all the time. And look at that beautiful girl dressed as a nun, sipping her absinthe like a professional."

"The nun is nothing compared to some of the eccentrics I've seen here."

"Have you been here before? I know so little about your life these days."

"Yes, once or twice," Veronica said, vaguely. "The first time, two beautiful Indian women in jewel-colored saris floated in wearing live snakes around their necks, like necklaces. They sat down and ordered dinner as though there was nothing unusual about it . . . There was also a South American diplomat, who ate his meal with his hands—until a screen was put up around him."

A good-looking man in officer's uniform sat down at an empty table next to them. He had a fine head of wavy, light brown hair. He was decidedly drunk, Dorothy noticed, but he managed to keep himself under control.

"Tell me about *your* life, Dorothy."

"Oh, there isn't much to tell."

"Surely that's not true. I imagine you being feted from one end of London to the other."

"Actually, I live very quietly. I don't see many people. Most of my friends and family are dispersed, or busy with their own separate lives. I've taken a room in a house in St. John's Wood. It's something of a leafy backwater, but at least it gives me privacy and peace for my writing."

"How is Bertie? Do you ever see him?

"No, it would be too difficult. Though I did hear he's in love again, in his way."

"His poor wife! What a lot she has to bear." There was an edge in Veronica's voice. "Who's the lucky girl?"

"Her name is Amber Reeves. I don't know much about her, other than she graduated from Cambridge with a starred first, and she's beautiful as well as brilliant. Bertie is greatly taken with her."

Dorothy wasn't surprised he had replaced her with such ease. Knowing him as she did, it seemed inevitable. Yet the thought of them together—Bertie looking at Amber with that focused gleam in his grey-blue eyes, saying the things he had said to Dorothy—caused an unexpected pang of jealousy.

At times, she missed Bertie. Perhaps, one never quite let go of past loves. She still had moments of wondering if it could have worked. Could they have reached a compromise, a way of existing side by side with his marriage, more or less satisfactorily?

The officer's meal was being served. With slow, precise movements, he picked up his table napkin, rose to his feet, and came across to spread it on the cloth in front of Dorothy, over the blots of red wine and cigarette stubs left by the previous clients.

"Why, thank you," Dorothy said. She could feel hot color spreading from her neck to her hairline.

The officer bowed stiffly, and returned to his table without a word.

"An act of chivalry, don't you think?" she said uneasily to Veronica.

"You've lost none of your allure, my dear."

Veronica's eyes looked huge, like lamps or mirrors. In their clear surfaces, a myriad of tiny Dorothys danced. Dorothy felt herself flush again; she looked away, trembling with hope and trepidation.

Her gaze fell on the officer, who sat ignoring his food, staring back at Dorothy with a dogged tenacity that soon became embarrassing.

To her astonishment, Dorothy noticed Benjamin making his way through the crowded room toward them, looking uncomfortable and out of place. He was a little heavier, his beard was longer and bushier, but the determined plunging walk, the thickly waving black hair and brilliant deprecating eyes were the same.

"You didn't tell me he was coming," she said in a low tone to Veronica.

"I wanted to surprise you."

They rose to their feet to greet him. His habitual expression of soulful melancholy sat oddly with the eagerness of his manner; he was like a small boy joining a party. Grasping both of Dorothy's hands, his well-remembered rich deep voice rang out: "Ah, I am glad to see you, after all this time. How well you look. I must tell you, I enjoyed reading your wonderful book immensely."

Dorothy smiled at him warmly. "My reading sessions with you were the foundation stones for my writing. What a wealth of literature you introduced me to: Turgenev, Tolstoy, Dostoevsky . . ."

Out of the corner of her eye, Dorothy saw Veronica shoot them a jealous look. "Let's sit down," she said brightly. "Dorothy, why don't you go there, in the middle of us."

When Benjamin had a drink in front of him, Veronica raised her glass again. "Tonight is a double celebration," she announced. "We have some wonderful news. Benjamin asked me to marry him, and I said yes."

A broiling wave of jealousy tore through Dorothy; the room swayed around her. It was so hot and crowded, she could not breathe. She gulped down her champagne, scarcely aware of what she was doing.

Mustering all her strength, she forced herself to composure. And found herself rewarded by a tiny glimmer of relief. At least she knew where she stood now. She no longer hung in limbo, twisting. She had been cut free, once and for all.

Benjamin's mouth smiled, but his eyes looked uneasy and would not meet Dorothy's. Veronica kept the conversation going; she seemed to feel no pain at parting from Dorothy. She was plunging ahead into her new life with only the slightest of backward glances. "Respectability, security, all the things I thumbed my nose at before," she said. "Well, they don't seem so unattractive anymore. Ben is wonderful, and not like other men . . . in a way, he is my gift from you."

There was one shadow, she admitted. Her family refused to countenance her marrying a man who was not only a foreigner, but a Jew. The wedding would take place at a small registry office. Only one of Veronica's brothers, the youngest, had relented far enough to agree to be present. Veronica was refusing to allow her joy to be dampened by her family's disapproval. She described the dress she was designing: pale grey crepe, with little ruffles of cream lace at the neck and sleeves. Dorothy could picture her in it; her glowing face framed by smooth tumbling ringlets.

"Are you still involved with the suffrage?" Dorothy asked, when Veronica had finished.

Veronica shook her head. "Actually, planning my wedding has driven all thoughts of it from my mind."

Dorothy, feeling quite disproportionately indignant for the suffragettes, bit back the retort that the suffrage movement was full of married women. She was not the only casualty of Veronica's capriciousness, she realized.

Prudently, she changed the subject: "Have you set a wedding date?"

"Yes; the twenty-eighth of October."

"Why, that's a few days before Mrs. Baker's marriage to Mr. Cundy!"

"Mrs. Baker! I haven't thought about her for ages. Do you ever see her?"

"I went to visit them a few days ago. For a couple who seem so mismatched, they are incredibly happ—"

Dorothy broke off, noticing Benjamin gazing with horrified astonishment toward a point above her left shoulder. Turning, she saw the officer standing just behind them. In his right hand, he brandished a fish knife.

"Leave her alone!" he said to Benjamin in an impeccable, but slurred accent. "I don't like your face."

Without thinking about what she was doing, Dorothy leapt up and seized him by the arm that bore the knife, holding on as hard as she could.

Benjamin half rose to his feet. Waiters hurried up to them.

Protectively, the officer swayed toward Dorothy. "Let me save you from that foreigner," he implored.

She begged him to go back to his table.

To her surprise, he relinquished the knife and shuffled off quite meekly, murmuring "I'll do anything for you. *Anything*."

Dorothy sat down and reached for her glass. Her hand was trembling.

For a while, they sat in shocked silence.

"What a drunken fool," Benjamin said, at last.

"He was harmless, poor lamb," Dorothy protested. "Drunk enough to see me as girlish and interesting, that's all."

She gazed at Benjamin lounging in his chair. He was wearing a harsh shiny suit and a black-banded grey felt hat: he looked like a waiter in a seedy cafe. Examining him with the eyes of the drunken officer, she saw only a shabby foreigner. He looked simply disreputable.

Veronica excused herself to go to the powder room. As soon as they were alone, Benjamin turned to Dorothy, reaching for her hand. "Dorothy, is it too late for us, even now?" he asked hoarsely. "Half an hour in your company means more to me than a whole lifetime with your enchanting friend . . ."

Blood surged into Dorothy's cheeks; she shook her head wordlessly, pulling her hand from his grasp. Benjamin's face was pale and ravaged. The heavy white eyelids came down; when he raised them, his eyes burned with weariness and conflict.

Knowing him so well, Dorothy understood exactly what divided him. Part of him—call it the Russian part—believed she was essential and irreplaceable, and suffered acutely in losing her. Yet the Jew in him desired to fulfill what he saw as the wider aspect: the continuation of his race. "The race is greater than its single parts," he'd said, a long time ago, and his view of life as an endless uniform pattern of humanity was one of the things that had put her off him. He was also lonely; he wanted to share his life with someone. Veronica delightfully assuaged several needs.

What a terrible mistake they were making! They were completely mismatched; they should never get married. In order to gain her freedom, Dorothy had not only introduced them, she had half-willed their union, sentencing them both to a lifetime of unhappiness.

She tried to bury the dark thoughts that crowded into her mind. *You are guilty. Guilty!* shrieked her conscience.

She told herself her friends were adults; they were quite capable of making their own decisions. In order to survive, she must drive the knowledge of her own complicity from her mind.

The officer was back at their table, fists raised against Benjamin. "I told you . . . I don't like your fa—aace."

Two waiters appeared, seized him by the arms, and bundled him without ceremony out the back door. A guard was placed next to it. When the officer tried to walk in again a few minutes later, the police were called.

"It's my fault," Dorothy said sadly, when the little drama was over. "If I had a grain of sense, I should have joined him for a short time, coaxed some food into him, and made an appointment to meet him again, which he would have forgotten by the next day. Then none of this would have happened."

"Don't blame yourself," Benjamin told her. "The man was a lunatic."

Dorothy felt tears scalding her eyes. She bit her lip to stop them falling. What an upside-down world it was; everybody wanting the wrong person. "I won't forget my thoughtlessness that caused a gentleman to be locked up," she said tartly.

WHEN SHE REACHED home, an avalanche of grief knocked her off her feet, leaving her wretched. She lay down on her bed and started to cry. Hard, painful sobs that tore her chest.

She was devoured by intolerable longing. She wanted to be in Veronica's arms, making ravenous abandoned love, their clothes a tangled heap on the floor. She gave herself up to memories. She thought about the sensation of Veronica's body moving beneath hers, the texture and taste of her. What was she going to do with the torrents of unfulfilled longing? How to quell them, when they were as much a part of her as breathing?

She cried and cried until there were no tears left, and the feeling of desolation began to lose its searing edge. She realized she was grieving for something that had died a long time ago.

New thoughts arrived; cooler thoughts. The officer at the Café Royal thought she was still desirable. Perhaps it wasn't too late to find love again? The fortune-teller she visited so long ago had accurately predicted she would become a writer. She might be right about Dorothy marrying late, too.

Perhaps she would find someone she could be with, someone who didn't want to dominate and possess her. Someone who had his or her own fertile and independent inner life, which would allow a certain distance in their relationship and give her the space to be herself. Dorothy also wanted a love she could be open and proud about. Surely it was not too much to hope for?

She was moving toward something . . . a lessening of yearning. Dare she call it peace? There were glimmers of brightness ahead. She only had to reach them.

Afterword: A Note on Sources

I stumbled on Dorothy Richardson by accident in the library of London University. I was searching for an angle on Virginia Woolf for my Ph.D. thesis that hadn't been written before—without much success. Opening a book at random, I found a review that Virginia had written about a writer whose name I did not recognize:

> *Dorothy Richardson has invented . . . a sentence which we might call the psychological sentence of the feminine gender. It is of a more elastic fibre than the old, capable of stretching to the extreme, of suspending the frailest particles, of enveloping the vaguest shapes . . .* (Review of *Revolving Lights*, Dorothy Richardson, from *The Nation and the Athenaeum*, May 19, 1923)

I was riveted. Who was Dorothy Richardson? How had she come to reinvent the English language in order to record the experience of being uniquely female? Interestingly, Virginia was elsewhere grudging in her praise of Dorothy's work, as she was about other female contemporaries, notably Katherine Mansfield. I suspect she perceived them as rivals and threats.

Further investigation led me to Dorothy's life work: the twelve-volume autobiographical novel-sequence, *Pilgrimage*. I began to read with mounting excitement, for it seemed that here was someone of undoubted importance, now largely consigned to oblivion. An enduring fascination with Dorothy was thus ignited, and a conviction that her remarkable story needed to be unearthed and retold. Many years and a Ph.D. thesis later, *The Lodger* was born.

My novel is a melding of fact and fiction, broadly following the known biographical outline of Dorothy's life. Where it suited my purposes, I took certain liberties with the facts and the time scheme. For instance, in life, the first volume of *Pilgrimage* was published after the marriage of Veronica and Benjamin. In my novel, the book comes out before they get engaged. In reality, Dorothy's friendship with Bertie Wells developed into a love affair over a ten-year period, but for the sake of narrative impetus, I fast-forwarded and had him seduce her during the course of one spring.

I also omitted some aspects of their lives, such as their mutual interest in Fabian Socialism, feeling it did not sufficiently enhance the interest of my account. I chose not to write about the Wells's two young sons. By Bertie's own admission, his children's early care was largely entrusted to nurses and governesses (*H. G. Wells in Love*, p. 29); moreover, Dorothy didn't appear to have had a relationship with either of the boys. There are other departures from fact; time and space do not permit me to list them individually.

My main source for writing *The Lodger* was *Pilgrimage*, and I am greatly indebted to it. Inevitably, there are similarities of character and incident between the two works. On occasion, I followed Dorothy's narrative quite closely, particularly in the romance between Mrs. Baker and Mr. Cundy, in the early scenes with Veronica, and in the extraordinary way Dorothy engineered the relationship between Veronica and Benjamin. More often, though, my interpretation of events differs from hers. The shape and tone of the love affairs with Bertie and Veronica are my creation, as are Veronica's prison experiences.

There are several episodes in *Pilgrimage* that are treated in a strangely oblique—almost perfunctory—manner, as though too painful, or shaming, to be voiced. Most striking among these is Dorothy's mother's suicide. Dorothy conveys this dramatic and tragic event by a blank space on the page. Evidently it was so unbearable, she literally lacked the words to describe it; she does not provide a single detail, and the reader scarcely knows what has happened without the supplementary biographical facts. Dorothy's account of her miscarriage is nearly as evasive: she presents it as a phantom pregnancy. Similarly, the sexual nature of the relationship with Veronica Leslie Jones is never explicit—Dorothy simply refers to nights spent together. These omissions—or repressions—form a significant part of my account; indeed, imagining and coloring them in was the most engrossing part of writing about Dorothy's life.

The following works were also immensely useful in my research, and my novel bears traces of all of them:

Bryher. *The Heart to Artemis: A Writer's Memoirs*. London: Collins, 1963.

Colmore, Gertrude. *Suffragette Sally*. London: Stanley Paul, 1911.

Dehgy, Guy, and Keith Waterhouse. *Café Royal: Ninety Years of Bohemia*. London: Hutchinson, 1955.

Dickson, Lovat. *H. G. Wells*. London: Readers Union Macmillan, 1971.

Foot, Michael. *The History of Mr. Wells*. New York: Doubleday, 1995.

Fromm, Gloria G. *Dorothy Richardson: A Biography*. Athens: University of Georgia Press, 1994.

———, ed. *Windows on Modernism: Selected Letters of Dorothy Richardson*. Athens: University of Georgia Press, 1995.

Hall, Radclyffe. *The Well of Loneliness*. London: Virago, 1982.

Hammond, J. R. *H. G. Wells and Rebecca West*. New York: St. Martin's Press, 1991.

Lytton, Constance. *Prisons and Prisoners: Some Personal Experiences*. London: William Heinemann, 1914.

MacKenzie, Norman and Jeanne. *The Time Traveller*. London: Weidenfeld and Nicholson, 1973.

Maud, Constance. *No Surrender*. London: Duckworth, 1911.

McAlmon, Robert. *Being Geniuses Together*. London: Secker and Warburg, 1938.

Murray, Brian. *H. G. Wells*. New York: Continuum, 1990.
Pankhurst, Emmeline. *My Own Story*. London: Eveleigh Nash, 1914.
Radford, Jean. *Dorothy Richardson*. New York, London: Harvester Wheatsheaf, 1991.
Ray, Gordon N. *H. G. Wells and Rebecca West*. New Haven, CT: Yale University Press, 1974.
Richardson, Dorothy. *Journey to Paradise*. London: Virago, 1989.
Rosenberg, John. *Dorothy Richardson, The Genius They Forgot*. London: Duckworth, 1973.
Skinner, Cornelia Otis, and Emily Kimborough. *Our Hearts Were Young and Gay*. London: Constable, 1944.
Smith, David C. *H. G. Wells: Desperately Mortal*. New Haven, CT: Yale University Press, 1986.
Swinnerton, Frank. *Swinnerton: An Autobiography*. London: Hutchinson, 1937.
Wells, H. G. *H. G. Wells in Love*. London: Faber and Faber, 1984.
———. *Mr. Britling Sees It Through*. London: Cassell, 1916.
———. *The New Machiavelli*. London: Penguin Classics, 2005.
———. *The Passionate Friends*. London: Macmillan, 1914.
———. *The Research Magnificent*. London: William Clowes & Sons, 1916.
West, Anthony. *H. G. Wells: Aspects of a Life*. London: Hutchinson, 1984.

The following passages are quoted directly from other works:

H. G. Wells quoted article in Chapter 6 (passage beginning "We are going to write about it all"): from "The Contemporary Novel," *Fortnightly Review*, November 1911. Reprinted in *An Englishman Looks at the World*. London: Cassell, 1914.

Letter from Jane to Wells in Chapter 8: from Jane Wells to H. G. Wells, February 26, 1906, quoted in Smith, *H. G. Wells: Desperately Mortal* and also in MacKenzie, *The Time Traveller*.

The Spectator article quoted in Chapter 11: from *The Spectator*, October 10, 1907.

Passage in Chapter 13 (beginning "Miriam left the gaslit hall and went slowly upstairs."): from opening of *Pointed Roofs*, the first volume of *Pilgrimage*.

Reviews of *Pilgrimage* in Chapter 19: from *The Spectator*, 1921; Frank Swinnerton, foreword to *Pilgrimage*; Virginia Woolf, *A Writer's Diary*, quoted in Rosenberg's *Dorothy Richardson: The Genius They Forgot*.